"Mehl launches her newest Christian thriller series, THE ERIN DELANEY MYSTERIES, with a gripping novel about stepping out of fear and stepping into faith."

Booklist on *Shattered Sanctuary*

"With *Shattered Sanctuary*, Nancy Mehl once again proves herself a master of suspense at the top of her game. Fans of edge-of-your-seat thrillers will find themselves eagerly awaiting the next installment—like I am!"

Lynette Eason, award-winning, bestselling author of the LAKE CITY HEROES series, on *Shattered Sanctuary*

"*Shattered Sanctuary* is a masterpiece! This suspenseful mystery gripped me from the first sentence and kept me turning pages. Readers will be riveted by this non-stop, twisty thriller set deep in the Smoky Mountains. Highly recommended!"

Elizabeth Goddard, bestselling author of *Storm Warning,* on *Shattered Sanctuary*

"Kaely Quinn is back! Nancy Mehl's new book—the first in this exciting new series featuring Quinn and Erin Delaney—will have readers flipping the pages as the two race to discover the killer before one of them becomes his next victim."

Patricia Bradley, award-winning author of the PEARL RIVER series, on *Shattered Sanctuary*

DARK
DESIGN

BOOKS BY NANCY MEHL

ROAD TO KINGDOM

Inescapable

Unbreakable

Unforeseeable

THE QUANTICO FILES

Night Fall

Dead Fall

Free Fall

FINDING SANCTUARY

Gathering Shadows

Deadly Echoes

Rising Darkness

RYLAND & ST. CLAIR

Cold Pursuit

Cold Threat

Cold Vengeance

DEFENDERS OF JUSTICE

Fatal Frost

Dark Deception

Blind Betrayal

THE ERIN DELANEY MYSTERIES

Shattered Sanctuary

Dark Design

KAELY QUINN PROFILER

Mind Games

Fire Storm

Dead End

THE ERIN DELANEY MYSTERIES

DARK DESIGN

NANCY MEHL

BETHANYHOUSE
a division of Baker Publishing Group
Minneapolis, Minnesota

© 2025 by Nancy Mehl

Published by Bethany House Publishers
Minneapolis, Minnesota
BethanyHouse.com

Bethany House Publishers is a division of
Baker Publishing Group, Grand Rapids, Michigan

Printed in the United States of America

All rights reserved. No part of this publication may be reproduced, stored in a retrieval system, or transmitted in any form or by any means—for example, electronic, photocopy, recording—without the prior written permission of the publisher. The only exception is brief quotations in printed reviews.

Library of Congress Cataloging-in-Publication Data
Names: Mehl, Nancy author
Title: Dark design / Nancy Mehl.
Description: Minneapolis, Minnesota : Bethany House, a division of Baker Publishing Group, 2025. | Series: The Erin Delaney mysteries ; 2
Identifiers: LCCN 2025004881 | ISBN 9780764243370 paperback | ISBN 9780764245671 casebound | ISBN 9781493451289 ebook
Subjects: LCGFT: Detective and mystery fiction | Christian fiction | Novels
Classification: LCC PS3613.E4254 D38 2025 | DDC 813/.6—dc23/eng/20250410
LC record available at https://lccn.loc.gov/2025004881

This book is a work of fiction. Names, characters, places, and incidents are the product of the author's imagination or are used fictitiously. Any resemblance to actual events, locales, or persons, living or dead, is coincidental.

Unless otherwise noted, all Scripture is taken from the New King James Version®. Copyright © 1982 by Thomas Nelson. Used by permission. All rights reserved.

Scriptures marked NIV are taken from the Holy Bible, New International Version®, NIV®. Copyright © 1973, 1978, 1984, 2011 by Biblica, Inc.® Used by permission of Zondervan. All rights reserved worldwide. www.zondervan.com. The "NIV" and "New International Version" are trademarks registered in the United States Patent and Trademark Office by Biblica, Inc.®

Cover design by Christopher Gilbert, Studio Gearbox

Baker Publishing Group publications use paper produced from sustainable forestry practices and postconsumer waste whenever possible.

25 26 27 28 29 30 31   7 6 5 4 3 2 1

For Clari Dees, who left us too soon.

When You Left

We looked for you, but you had gone.
Your voice we could not hear.
You'd slipped into the world beyond,
We could not pull you near.
We know you dance before the King,
But we still miss you so.
The love and joy you used to bring,
Was more than you could know.
For now, we'll keep you in our hearts,
'Till we walk through heaven's door.
And then we'll never be apart,
For death will be no more.

Nancy Mehl

ONE

I was only nine years old when I knew I was destined to be a serial killer. My best friend and I watched a show on TV that talked about them. I'd never felt more excited about anything in my entire life. When I was ten, I almost changed my mind. I went to my friend's church, and the pastor talked about Jesus. I wondered if there was another way for me to go, but when the pastor told us that Jesus wanted us to love everyone, I knew I could never live that way. Hate filled my heart and my mind so strongly that there wasn't room for anything else. The only thing I truly loved was my hate, and I had no desire to let it go. Not even my parents could steer me away from the path I knew was mine.

Now that I'm older, I'm ready to fulfill my destiny.

And I know just where to start.

At the beginning.

MONDAY MORNING IN APRIL

It was a cold and rainy night. Alex Caine stared at himself in the mirror. He looked as tired as he felt. His hazel eyes narrowed as he gazed at his chiseled features. His dark hair was beginning to gray and needed to be cut.

Erin Delaney stared at the words on her first page and laughed quietly. "Never open with weather," she said under her breath. "Never describe a character by having him look in a mirror." She sighed loudly. "How many other writerly taboos can I break?" She deleted what she'd written out of frustration. She'd finished the book but left the opening in just for fun. She was ready to edit now—something she hated a lot more than writing. But it had to be done. It was amazing how many times she could repeat scenes without realizing it. Or change someone's name. Or use the same name for different characters. She had a feeling that she had two women called Laura in the story. It was probably because she loved the old movie with the same name.

She got up from the couch and headed into the kitchen for another cup of coffee. Chester, her border collie, jumped down from his place next to her and followed behind her, his nails clicking on the wooden floor. Wherever she went, he was right beside her. Since she'd moved from St. Louis, she'd noticed that he'd become a little clingy. He'd been with her almost five months now, but he still had trust issues. Just like she did. They really were a perfect match. In St. Louis, he'd watched her carefully whenever she had to leave him in the apartment, his large brown eyes echoing the fear that someone else had caused by abandoning him. Eventually, he'd begun to relax a bit, but they obviously had a ways to go until the shadows of the past no longer held him in their grasp. Now that they'd left St. Louis for good and arrived back in Sanctuary, Erin hoped he would finally believe he was loved and that he would never be left behind again. She wasn't certain what she would have done without him over the past several months. He was her best friend and her constant companion. Together, they were facing the ghosts of their former lives.

"It's okay, boy," she said, looking down at the anxious face staring up at her. "You're family, and you're home for good. You don't have to ever worry about that again." She walked over to his treat jar and took out a dried banana chip, which he eagerly accepted.

Finishing this new book had really stressed her out. She'd waited almost two months after signing the contract to start writing, which almost caused her agent a stroke. "I've had to double my heart medication since I signed you," she'd said. "Working with you isn't worth my health." Finally, she'd passed Erin off to a different agent. "Brandon will take good care of you." Brandon West was a well-known agent and a lot more patient with her. Erin was much happier with him. He really seemed to understand her.

Her phone rang, and she picked it up. How odd. She was just thinking about Brandon and here he was, calling her.

She answered the phone and heard his deep, soothing voice respond to her greeting.

"How are things going with the new place?" he asked. "You completely settled now?"

"Getting there," she said. "But I doubt you called to ask me about that. What's going on?"

When he paused, she felt her stomach tighten. What now? Another podcast? Was he going to ask her if she was going to make her deadline?

"Look, I don't want you to worry about this, but I felt I needed to tell you that someone has claimed that she's the real author of *Dark Matters*. That you stole it from her."

Erin was so shocked she couldn't seem to find her voice. "Wh . . . what?" she said, finally.

"Don't panic. This happens more than you'd believe," he said. "Either an author supposedly copied passages from another book, or as in this case, someone accuses a writer of stealing an entire book from them."

"How could they prove something like that if it isn't true?" Erin asked.

"They can't. Unfortunately, sometimes publishers will pay out money just to keep people like this quiet. Scammers have learned this and will throw out threats in hopes of getting free money. Believe it or not, it will happen again. Probably several times."

"That's ridiculous," Erin said. "I certainly wouldn't want my publisher to give anyone money toward a scam like that. It will just encourage others to do the same thing because they think they can get away with it."

Brandon chuckled. "I truly don't believe you have anything to worry about. You just write good books. I'll take care of the rest."

"What did you tell this woman?"

"I asked her for proof. Haven't heard back. Probably won't. Like I said, don't concern yourself with it. Everything will be fine. I expect this will just disappear. If for any reason it doesn't, I'll call you. I just thought you should know."

Erin thanked him and hung up. Although he was reassuring and encouraging, unlike her previous agent, she still wasn't certain just how far she could push him. The proposed plot for this new book had been her idea, but as she wrote, she ended up going in another direction. She was afraid to tell him. Seems agents and publishers weren't fans of unannounced changes in a book under contract. She sighed. It wasn't that she didn't want to write, she did. But she was aggravated. When she wrote *Dark Matters,* she was in charge. Now she had Brandon as well as editors she had to please. Add threats from some nut who claimed she had stolen their work? What next? She was also reluctant to face other things that came with being a writer. The biggest thorn in her side was the promotion aspect that went with every release. Erin was a private person, and she had no intention of running around the country on a book tour or sitting down with interviewers on podcasts. She'd reluctantly done a few of those and actually enjoyed a couple of them—but only because she liked the interviewers. The rest were awful to get through. During one interminable interview in particular, she'd toyed with the idea of pretending her laptop was acting up and logging off.

She got up and went to the pantry where she grabbed a new box of Mallomars. She'd hoped keeping them out of sight would stop her from eating too many. They were an obsession. She tried to limit herself to one a day before bed, but when she was stressed, like now, she found herself drawn to them. Graham cracker crust, marshmallow center, and chocolate on the outside. What was there not to love? She was embarrassed by the number of boxes in her pantry, but they were only available from March through September. She wasn't sure why, but it seemed rather cruel to those who were addicted to them.

She took out a package, went back into the kitchen, opened it, and took out one of the delicious treats. She pulled the cellophane wrapping apart and was soon savoring the sweet indulgence. She felt herself becoming calmer. Every time she ate one, she thought about the mother she'd lost when she was young. She used to come home from the store, put her bags on the kitchen counter, and take out a box of Mallomars for Erin and a package of Oreos for her sister. The memories of her family seemed harder and harder to recall. Her parents had died long ago, and her sister . . . who knew where she was? Erin pushed thoughts of the past away and leaned against the counter while she swallowed the last delicious bite. Chester whined, wanting a piece, but she never gave him anything with chocolate in it.

"Sorry, dude," she said. "But these aren't good for doggies."

She brushed off the crumbs that had fallen on her sweatshirt and grabbed another banana chip. He took it willingly but gave her a sideways glance to let her know he wasn't the least bit fooled by her attempted subterfuge. Was he getting tired of the chips? She used them when training him. So far, he'd learned to sit and lie down on command. He was a work in progress, but he was smart and loved to learn almost as much as he enjoyed cuddling with her on the couch or at night in bed.

"How about a walk?" she asked him. She knew she should head back to her laptop, but it was even harder to work since spring had come to Sanctuary. Although winter was still her favorite season, she had to admit that watching nature spring back to life in the Smoky Mountains was enchanting. She and Chester had started taking daily treks through the woods near the cabin. She'd been warned that wild animals, especially bears, roamed the woods, but she hadn't seen any. People in town had assured her that unless mother bears feared for their young, they pretty much left people alone. Most of them were used to human beings living in the area.

All in all, the move from St. Louis hadn't been too difficult. Erin had gotten rid of all her furniture and most of her personal belongings, not wanting any reminders of her life there. The former owner of the cabin where she lived now, Steve Tremont, had sold her all the furniture, appliances, and decor. Some of it she liked, some of it wasn't her taste, but little by little she'd update it. Right now, she was just enjoying her new surroundings, grateful for the chance to start over. A year ago, she wasn't certain she even wanted to go on. She'd been afraid to even touch her gun, fearful that if she picked it up . . . She shook her head. She didn't want to think about that. Thankfully, things had changed. After meeting Kaely, she finally had hope. And then, of course, there was Chester. Every morning when she woke up, she'd reach over and pet him. She didn't feel alone anymore. It didn't matter that he was a dog. He loved her, and he needed her. And she needed to be needed. Life was slowly getting better. Hopefully, she would continue to get stronger. For the first time in years, she was actually looking forward to the future.

TWO

Erin was just about to retrieve Chester's leash when someone knocked on her door. She grabbed her phone so she could check the doorbell camera she'd had installed. After dealing with a ruthless killer several months ago, she felt much safer being able to tell who was outside. She clicked on the camera's icon. *Adrian.* She got up and hurried to the door, self-consciously straightening her hair and pulling it down on one side to hide the scar on the side of her face. Adrian knew about the wound she'd received from a vicious gang member's knife in St. Louis when she was a cop, but she was still sensitive about it. Thankfully, she'd put on her makeup this morning. She used a concealer that worked pretty well. It was difficult to see her scar unless you were looking for it. She wished there were some kind of concealer that worked on the wounds inside people.

"Hey," she said when she swung the door open.

"Hi. Just checking on you." He smiled, his hazel eyes crinkling at the corners. "Are you all moved in?"

"Yeah, finally," she said. "I've got some coffee on. Would you like a cup?"

"Sounds good. Jake's in the car. Okay if he comes in?"

Erin laughed. "If I don't say yes, Chester will pout the rest of the day. Please get him. I have some of those special treats he likes."

"Okay, but I can't guarantee his manners. He gets pretty excited when he's around his new friend."

"I know," Erin said. "It's fine. I love his enthusiasm. You know, I planned to take Chester for a walk this morning. After our coffee, are you up for it?"

They'd actually gone on several walks. It was becoming a habit that Erin really enjoyed.

"Sure," he said with a smile. "It's a beautiful morning."

"Great," she said. "I'll get your coffee while you get Jake."

"Sounds good."

Erin went into the kitchen and got a cup out of the cupboard. One thing she hadn't gotten rid of was her coffee cup collection. She had way too many, but she enjoyed collecting them. She grabbed one that had *Cup of Happy* written on its side and poured some coffee into it. She didn't add anything to it. Adrian liked his coffee black, just the way she did.

Adrian came into the kitchen, but Jake, his golden retriever, had stayed in the living room with Chester. Since the kitchen and living room weren't divided by walls, Erin could see the dogs smile at each other as their wagging tails signaled their pleasure at being together again. Erin handed Adrian his cup.

"Thanks," he said. "I'm used to drinking my coffee as quickly as possible. It's a skill I've had to learn as a police chief. I'm usually just trying to get a fast jolt of caffeine. Seems like there's always something that needs to be done immediately. I think I've lost the ability to linger over a hot cup of coffee." He looked at his watch. "Hopefully, we'll have plenty of time for our walk. I keep waiting for my phone to ring."

"And you can't turn it off since you're the chief and have to be reachable at all times, right?"

Adrian nodded. "Yep. Thankfully, most emergencies in Sanctuary are usually lost pets or tracking down guests who've stolen towels from the resort."

Erin laughed and glanced over at their dogs. They both knew what the word *walk* meant. Their impatient expressions were truly comical.

"We'll go in just a minute," she said soothingly to them. She looked at Adrian. "Do you think they understand me?"

"I'm pretty sure they get the idea. I have to ask Jake to wait quite a bit. He's used to it, but he certainly doesn't like it."

Adrian sat down at the counter that separated the kitchen from the living room. Erin loved the way the rooms were constructed. It made it easy to talk to guests while preparing food or drinks for them. She almost laughed out loud as she admitted to herself that she didn't actually have many guests. Kaely Quinn-Hunter, her friend and research partner for her books, and Adrian. That was it so far. She still wasn't ready to reach out to the people who lived in Sanctuary. She liked some of them, especially the cops who worked with Adrian. Maybe someday she'd make more friends, but for now, she was content just spending time with Chester . . . and Adrian. She really did miss Kaely and wished she were closer. The drive was a little over seven hours from Sanctuary to Fredericksburg, Virginia, where Kaely and her husband, Noah, lived. Faster by air, but Erin wasn't keen on flying. Ever since the night that changed her life, she'd been plagued by claustrophobia. Spending time in a metal cylinder, unable to escape, frightened her beyond words. At least the agoraphobia that had crippled her for so long had lessened some. She was now able to go into town for groceries and other things. There'd been one episode when she'd had a panic attack, but she'd been able to pay for her groceries and leave before it got too bad. Not being able to breathe was the worst part. She was actually terrified she might pass out in front of people. She'd kept an image of the cabin in her mind, assuring herself that she had a safe place to go. A place where she could lock the door and be secure. It had helped immensely.

Chester was also a big help. Except for places where dogs weren't allowed, he stayed by her side whenever she left the cabin. She was convinced that somehow, he understood how she felt and was determined to protect her. Anytime she began to feel panicked, he'd move closer to her, even leaning up against her to let her know he was there. Kaely was the one who'd initially given her the courage to face her fears, but Chester had taken up the mantle when Kaely went home. Erin was a little worried about what she'd do when it got hot. She wouldn't be able to leave Chester in her car. At one time, she'd reasoned that if she left the air-conditioning running, he would be okay. But then she read an article about a police dog in St. Louis that was left in a car while the officer went inside somewhere. He'd left the air on, but without his knowledge, it had turned off. The dog had died. Erin could never take a chance like that with Chester. Of course, she was usually only gone from her car no more than ten minutes, wherever they went. Still, she was concerned. The few times she'd left him alone in the cabin for a short time had caused them both distress. Now, she tried to avoid it.

"How's your coffee?" Erin asked.

"Perfect," Adrian said, taking a sip. "Your coffee is so much better than mine. What brand is it?"

"I special order it," Erin said, telling him the brand name. "I know it's probably silly, but my coffee is important to me. I can skimp on almost anything but that."

Adrian laughed. "The generic stuff I get from the store doesn't hold a candle to this." He took another sip and sighed. "You really do get what you pay for." He grinned at her. "I may have to stop by more often. For coffee, I mean."

Erin shrugged. Her heart beat a little faster as she said, "Any time. I never go anywhere—except when I walk Chester or go to the market."

Adrian appeared to study her for a moment before saying, "Maybe I'll take you up on that offer."

Erin picked up her cup of cold coffee so she'd have something to hold onto. She'd promised herself that after losing Scott, she would never get involved with another man. She had no desire to ever be that vulnerable again. But police chief Adrian Nightengale was making that vow a little tough to hold onto.

THREE

"So, you're sure about this?" Kaely asked Noah as they finished breakfast.

"As certain as I can be." He sighed and shook his head. "We looked at the first killing as if he'd shown us his MO as well as his signature. We thought that if he killed again, his MO would be the same. Then the second murder threw off our investigation, because everything had changed. It was then that we had a pretty good idea what the UNSUB was up to. By the third murder, we knew what to expect, but we had no idea what his next choice might be. None of us have seen anything like this before."

"It's not fair," Kaely said. "Erin is still trying to heal. She's working on a new book. How can I tell her about this?"

Noah stared into his wife's dark brown eyes and saw her concern. Her curly auburn hair framed her lovely face, making his heart beat a little faster. She looked exactly the same as the day he'd met her. No matter how old she got, he'd still believe she was the most beautiful woman he'd ever seen. Every day they were together was a gift he would never take for granted.

"I know it's hard, but we believe she needs to come in. Not only for her own protection, but because she might be able to help us. We have three bodies, and we'd like to write a profile that will help catch this guy." He leaned back in his chair. "I had to get permission for you to be the one to tell her what's happening. If you don't do it, the FBI will. I know it will be easier coming from you."

"What about the first two murders? Have you reached out to the others?"

"Yes. Todd assigned a case agent to the task force. He's sent information to the field offices that cover the area where the authors live. They sent an agent out to interview them."

Todd Hunter was the Special Agent in Charge of their Behavioral Analysis Unit. They were blessed to have him. Noah had great respect for Todd. Not all BAU units were represented as well as they were.

"Any feedback yet?" Kaely asked.

"It's early, but I heard after the initial interviews that Dan Harper doesn't seem too concerned. He's promised to tighten his security and let us know if he notices anything suspicious. Toni Sue Smith is pretty spooked. She's staying with a friend in another city. Since we just realized the connection, agents will need to talk to them more. If the BAU wants to speak with them, we'll do what needs to be done online."

Kaely frowned. "Don't you think someone should be watching out for them?"

"That's up to law enforcement in their area. Our advice would be to provide protection, but ultimately that will be their decision."

"But you want Erin here?"

Noah nodded. "She's so isolated in Sanctuary, Kaely. I'd feel better if she were here so we could keep her safe. Besides, according to you, she's got this incredible mind. I'm hoping she can see something we might be missing. We have approval from the state police to bring her to Fredericksburg. They'll interview her in person." He smiled. "I would never admit this to Todd, but her natural instincts are only second to yours."

Kaely fought back a smile. "You're only saying that because you don't want to hurt my feelings."

He got up from the kitchen table, went over to his wife, and kissed her on the head. "No, I'm not. You're still the most naturally talented profiler I've ever met."

She picked up her napkin and good-naturedly swiped it at him. Then she lifted her coffee cup and stared out the window.

She had grown quieter lately. Noah knew she was discouraged about the treatments they'd been going through, trying to get pregnant. So far, nothing had been successful. They both wanted kids so badly. He felt it was time for them to consider adoption. There were so many children who needed homes. He knew they'd love any child they brought into their lives as if they'd been born into their family. Why was Kaely resisting the idea? He'd asked her once, and she'd explained that she wanted a baby that looked like him. But he suspected there was more to it than that. Her childhood hadn't been good, and he wondered if somehow her reluctance to adopt was tied to that somehow. Her grandparents had adopted her father, who turned out to be a notorious serial killer. Was she was afraid the same thing might happen to them? It was an unreasonable fear, but he wasn't certain how to help her when she wouldn't talk to him about it.

"I told Todd that you would contact Erin today and ask her to come." He stood near the kitchen door and stared at Kaely. "Will you call me after you talk to her? Let me know what she says? If she says no, we'll have to turn it over to law enforcement out there. Adrian probably won't be involved. The state police will take over."

Kaely nodded. "Wish I knew exactly what to tell her. It's not going to be easy."

"I know, but I have faith that you'll figure out just what to say." He blew her a kiss. "Love you. I'll call you later."

She smiled at him. "Love you too. Bye."

As he grabbed his jacket and his keys, he whispered a prayer for Erin's safety and peace of mind, as well as help for Kaely as she struggled with her desire to get pregnant. He glanced back at her one more time. She clutched her coffee cup and gazed out the window as if the view outside had answers to the questions and concerns that overwhelmed her. He wished he could make things better, but until she came to terms with the failed treatments and her issues with adoption, there wasn't much he could do but just love her with all his heart. That part was easy.

Erin enjoyed her walk with Adrian. He was more talkative than she was, and that helped her to relax. They had so much in common. He'd been on the police force in Chicago, but the out-of-control crime and the lack of support from city officials had left him discouraged and wishing he were still in Sanctuary, where his grandparents had raised him. When the chief of police retired a few years ago, he'd jumped at the job.

"This place really is a sanctuary for me," he told her as they made their way down a trail that led to a large lake. "I feel so at peace here. Since my grandparents died, the people who live here have become my family. I'm especially close to my officers. Besides being great people, they excel in their jobs. I'd put them up against any police officer in any city. Sometimes I can't understand why they stay here. They could work anywhere. Like I said, things are usually pretty quiet—at least until you came to town, and we had to confront a serial killer."

"I hope you don't think my being here had anything to do with that," she said, laughing.

"No, not at all," he responded with a grin. "But I certainly was glad you were here. You and Kaely were a great help."

Erin loved the peace and quiet that had settled on the town after the killer had been caught. She hoped the only murders she'd have to deal with from now on would stay on the pages of her new book.

She'd just gotten back to the cabin and said good-bye to Adrian and Jake when her phone rang. She plopped down on the couch, and Chester jumped up next to her. He lay down and let out a sigh. Their walk had worn him out, and he fell into a deep, doggy nap.

She looked at her phone. Kaely. It had been a while. She answered it.

"Hey," she said. "Glad to hear from you."

She expected Kaely's greeting to be equally cheery, but her response seemed guarded, careful.

"Everything okay?" Erin asked.

Kaely was quiet for a moment, and Erin felt herself tense up.

"No, it isn't," she said finally. "We need you to come here. There's . . . a situation."

"What kind of situation?"

Kaely cleared her throat before saying, "The BAU is working on a really serious case. Someone is killing women, and they're using the MOs they took from certain mystery and suspense novels."

"I don't understand," Erin said, although in the back of her mind, she did.

"The third murder copies the killings in your book, Erin. Investigators need to question you, and Noah and I are concerned for your safety. Please trust me and come here as soon as you can."

FOUR

"I hope you're kidding," Erin said slowly. "I saw that episode of *Castle* too. I don't think my editor would ever allow me to write about someone copying fictional serial killers. Too derivative."

Kaely's lack of response made Erin's heart sink. *This was real? Seriously?* She heard Kaely take a deep breath.

"Actually, you'd be surprised how many times a killer uses a method he read in a novel," Kaely said. "Most psychopaths are too narcissistic to copy someone else exactly, but there have certainly been cases where the UNSUB used elements from a novel. They usually add their own twist because it makes them feel superior. But then of course, there are the killers who aren't very imaginative and closely follow an MO they read about in a book. Law enforcement tries hard to keep this knowledge quiet and away from the media. They feel like it might give potential killers ideas."

"I think authors would want to know," Erin mumbled. She sighed. "I'm sorry. I just can't quite wrap my head around this."

"I know. I'm sorry."

"I understand why investigators want me to come there," Erin said, "but why do you think I might need protection?"

"We don't know for certain that you're in danger," Kaely said, "but when a serial killer makes it clear that he's read your book and that he is patterning himself after you . . . Well, you're so alone out there. I mean, since you have to talk to the task force anyway, why not stay with us? Besides, I really miss you, and I would love to spend time with you."

"What about Chester? I can't leave him with anyone. He's too insecure."

"Of course, you can bring him. I wouldn't have it any other way. Mr. Hoover likes dogs. Have you seen Chester around any cats?"

"Actually, there's a gal who lives down the road from me who has a cat. It keeps getting out and coming here. Chester loves her. Still, I wish her owner would keep her indoors. It's too dangerous for her to be running around loose." Erin realized she was blithering. Kaely didn't need to know about her neighbor's cat roaming around outside. She was shaken by what she'd just heard and was having a tough time concentrating.

"So, you'll pack up and head here?" Kaely asked.

Erin looked around the cabin she'd grown to love. She hated to leave, even for a little while, but if she could help the FBI find this killer, she had to try. She really did miss Kaely, and she looked forward to meeting Noah. Actually, working with the Behavioral Analysis Unit excited her. Writing about it was one thing, but seeing it up close? She wished it were under different circumstances, but maybe something good could come out of this bizarre situation. Leaving home would be a challenge, but Chester would be with her, and she felt safe with Kaely. She was convinced she could do it.

"Give me today to pack," she said. "I'll head out tomorrow morning. I should get there in the late afternoon. Does that work for you? You're sure you have room for me? I can find a hotel if it would be better."

"Don't be silly. We have a lovely guest room. Besides, I'd feel better keeping an eye on you, and Chester will be happier here rather than getting stuck in some crate at a hotel."

"Okay, if you're sure. Thanks, Kaely. I appreciate it. I'd like to hear more about the murders. The MOs. Should we do that now or . . ."

"Tomorrow," Kaely said. "Let's talk about it when you get here. I can't wait to see you."

"Me too. I'll keep you updated on my progress."

"Good." Kaely hesitated. "Erin, please watch your six? As you leave Sanctuary and while you're on the road? If you get any idea that you're being followed, drive to the nearest police station, and let us know."

Erin knew Kaely well enough to understand that she really was worried. She took a deep breath, trying to calm her nerves. "Have any of the other authors been threatened?"

"No, they haven't. They're understandably upset, but so far, there's been no threat."

"So, I'm the only author who has to go into hiding?" Although she really wanted to stay with Kaely, she was suddenly concerned about looking like a wimp.

"Erin . . ."

"Okay, okay. I'll be there tomorrow. Frankly, I think this is just an elaborate ruse so you can spend some time with me."

Kaely snorted. "Yeah, that's me. I make up serial killers so my friend will come for a visit. I'm that desperate."

Erin chuckled. "All right. I'd better get off the phone. I need to pack and let Adrian know I'm going to be gone."

"How are things going with Sanctuary's handsome police chief?"

"Things aren't *going* anywhere," Erin said. "We're friends. Correction. We're acquaintances. Nothing more."

"You really are delusional, aren't you?" Kaely said. "The way you two look at each other is almost embarrassing."

"I think *you're* delusional. Adrian Nightengale sees me as one of the people he's sworn to protect. Nothing more. And Jake likes to play with Chester. That's it. Seriously." Even as she disputed Kaely's assumption, she suspected she wasn't being completely honest.

"Go pack, my friend," Kaely said. Her previous playful tone now had a more serious edge. "I'll see you tomorrow."

"See you tomorrow."

Erin started to hang up but stopped when Kaely added, "By the way, we have Mallomars in Virginia so you don't need to bring a case. I'll have some. I can't sit by and watch you go through Mallomar withdrawal. Just too brutal."

"You're very, very funny. Good-bye."

Erin disconnected the call and then looked over at Chester. "We have to travel again, boy. But you'll like this trip a lot more than our expeditions to St. Louis. You'll get to see Kaely."

Chester's ears perked up at Kaely's name. He was very attached to her. Erin hoped he'd do okay with another car trip. At least this time she was going somewhere she really wanted to go. She sighed and got to her feet. "Let's start packing, boy."

Erin started toward the stairs but then stopped and went back to get her phone. She stared at it a moment before clicking on Adrian's name. She might as well let him know she was leaving for a while. Even though she wasn't ready to admit it to anyone else, even Kaely, she was surprised to realize just how much she was going to miss him.

FIVE

TUESDAY

The trip to Fredericksburg was fairly uneventful. However, getting Chester into the car was somewhat of a struggle. He was usually very compliant, but it was clear he wasn't excited about another long car ride. She finally had to pick him up and force him inside. He was a rather large border collie, so she hoped this wouldn't become a habit. He loved short jaunts into town, but she was pretty sure seeing her suitcases brought back memories of their trips to St. Louis. She decided to fold up his crate and put it in the trunk, hoping he'd be more relaxed if he was allowed some freedom in the car. It did seem to help. After several miles of rapid panting, he finally settled down and curled up on the passenger seat. Within a few minutes he was asleep.

They stopped several times so Erin could take him out. She bought hamburgers at a fast-food restaurant and shared a plain one with Chester. She finally got a doggy smile and a tail wag.

Kaely's admonitions caused her to watch the traffic behind

her as well as the cars that pulled into the same places where she stopped. But there weren't any vehicles that kept showing up. Nothing that made her suspicious. She was confident she wasn't being followed.

When she reached Fredericksburg, she followed her GPS to a large, two-story, brick house with black shutters, a black front door, and a two-car garage. It was a lovely home. Just the kind of place she could see Kaely living. Although there were other houses in the same neighborhood, they were spaced far enough apart so that there was a sense of privacy. Good. That was one thing she loved about the cabin and had hated about her apartment in St. Louis. People all around her. It hadn't helped her struggle with agoraphobia.

She'd just pulled into the driveway when the front door was flung open, and Kaely came bounding down the stairs to greet them, her arms spread wide. The sight made Erin smile and get a little misty-eyed. Kaely was such a good friend. She'd helped Erin in so many ways. There was something about her commitment to their friendship that actually made Erin feel better about herself. It was odd, seeing herself through other people's eyes rather than believing the negative thoughts that tried to capture her mind and invade her dreams.

"You're here!" Kaely said as she wrapped her arms around Erin after she stepped out of the car. "We're so happy to have you stay with us."

"Again, are you sure you want to put me up?" Erin asked when Kaely let her go. "I saw a nice hotel not far from here."

Kaely shook her head. "They don't allow dogs. We do." She peered into the car and smiled at Chester, who was awake and clearly excited to see her.

"He was afraid I was going to cart him back to St. Louis," Erin said. "I don't know why he hated going there so much. My only guess is that somehow it reminded him of the people who left him behind. Maybe they lived in an apartment, I don't know. I'll be relieved when he finally trusts that he'll never be abandoned again."

"Well, he'll love staying with us. I put Mr. Hoover up for now. We'll introduce them later. Let's get you both inside."

"Is Noah here?" Erin asked.

"No, he's at work. They're not only working the Novel Killer's case, they also have several others. The command center is almost completely set up. Noah and a few others from his unit will work there starting tomorrow and focus only on that case. Other special agents will stay in Quantico and work the other cases. That will make it much easier for Noah."

Erin put her suitcase down. "Excuse me? The Novel Killer?"

Kaely smiled. "Some people at the Bureau are calling him that. I guess I picked it up from Noah."

"The press have this yet?"

"No, thankfully," Kaely said, "but Noah says it will leak soon. Too many people and agencies are getting involved. It seems there's always someone who is willing to sell information. For now, everything's quiet, but I wouldn't count on it staying that way for long."

It was true, unfortunately. There were those in the media who would pay quite a bit for scoops that would bring them attention. It could make a case harder to close. Not only did it give the UNSUB information that he could use to hide from law enforcement, but there were also too many citizens who were certain that their boyfriend, husband, neighbor, relative, boss, or the pizza delivery guy was a serial killer. The police wasted a lot of time chasing down leads that went nowhere while scaring the heck out of innocent people who didn't want their family, friends, and neighbors thinking they might be busy planning their demise.

"You want to bring Chester in last?" Kaely asked.

"Might be a good idea, but I'm not so sure what he thinks about that."

Chester was pulling against the restraint that kept him in his seat. It was loose enough so he could lie down but still prevented him from jumping into Erin's lap or getting away from her when she opened the door to take him out.

"I haven't got that much luggage," she said. "I'll grab a couple of things, you can get Chester, and I'll come back later to get the rest of my stuff."

"Sounds like a plan Chester would agree to. Is that his leash on the floor in front of him?"

Erin nodded, went to the trunk, and picked up a tote bag and a small suitcase. When she closed the trunk and went back to get her purse, Kaely already had Chester out of the car. He immediately relieved himself on Kaely's yard.

"I'm so sorry," Erin said. "I've got plastic bags in the car that I use to pick that up."

"Oh, fiddle. Don't worry about it now. We'll get it later." Kaely laughed at her. "Noah and I do realize that dogs use the bathroom outside, you know."

Erin sighed. "I know. And thanks. I just don't want you to be sorry you invited us here."

Kaely frowned at her. Then she led Chester over to where Erin stood, and she put her arm around her. "You do know that I love you, right? Having you here makes me very happy, Erin. That's how friends feel when they get to spend time together. Don't you understand that?"

Erin stood there, staring at Kaely, unable to answer her question. She used to have friends. Before . . . that night. Had she forgotten what it was like to be close to another human being? She was so happy to have Kaely in her life, and she definitely considered her a friend. So why was it difficult to accept that Kaely actually wanted her to stay in her home? That it wasn't an imposition? That was the way she'd felt when Kaely was in Sanctuary. The truth was, Erin had spent so much time hiding in her apartment, and now hiding in a cabin in the woods, that maybe the concept of friendship had gotten lost somewhere along the way. At least the part about believing someone actually wanted her in their life.

"I . . . I'm glad to be here too," Erin said. "I've really missed you."

"I know." At Erin's surprised look, Kaely grinned. "I am pretty special. How could you not miss me?"

Erin laughed. "If only I had a snowball."

"Nah. I fell for that a couple of times when I was in Sanctuary. But we're not expecting any snowfall. At least not until the end of the week."

Erin's jaw dropped. "Seriously?" She'd just reconciled herself to the knowledge that winter was over, and she needed to embrace the seasons that followed.

"Gotcha."

Erin shook her head. "You're incorrigible. You really are."

Kaely laughed and led Chester toward the house while Erin followed behind. She'd been a little put out at the idea of having to come here and hide from some psychotic killer, but now that she was with Kaely, she realized just how thankful she was.

Kaely's house was nicely decorated. She seemed to have a gift that Erin lacked. It was one reason she was a little worried about changing things at the cabin. She had the ability to pick exactly the wrong things. She'd finally given up in her apartment in St. Louis. In the end, it had become nothing much more than functional.

She traipsed behind her friend, down a long hallway to a door at the end. "This is the guest room," Kaely said as she swung the door open. The room was beautiful. The furniture was white, and the bedspread and pillow shams had little blue flowers. They matched the frilly curtains. Accent pillows echoed the dusky blue paint on the wall. A rocking chair in the corner tied everything together perfectly, along with an overstuffed chair near the bed. There were fresh flowers on the dresser and a TV mounted on the wall. It was such a relaxing room. Frankly, Erin could barely wait to climb into the double bed. It looked so comfortable.

"Noah and I are upstairs, so we won't keep you up if you want to write—or just watch TV. There's nothing in the fridge that you can't have. Please just help yourself."

Chester, who had followed them, suddenly turned around. A large cat had come into the room. He sat down and stared at Chester with interest. He didn't seem upset or anxious about the large dog that gazed at him with curiosity.

"Chester, be good," Erin said, nervous about his reaction.

"How did you get out of the office, Hoovey?" Kaely asked, sighing. She shook her head. "I swear, that cat is too smart for me. You be good and make friends, you hear me?"

"He's huge," Erin said. "What kind of a cat is he?"

"A Maine coon." Kaely smiled. "And he has an attitude. He thinks this is his house and Noah and I are just here to serve him."

Mr. Hoover got up and walked over to Chester. He put his head up and sniffed Chester's nose. Chester backed up a little and crouched down, putting his legs in front of him. Then he laid his head on the floor, his tail wagging so fast it looked like a blur. Suddenly, he jumped toward Mr. Hoover, obviously trying to get him to play. Mr. Hoover's response was to fall over on his side and pat Chester's face with one of his furry front paws. Chester seemed unsure how to respond, but sensing that the cat wasn't going to join him in a game of chase, he began to lick Mr. Hoover's face.

"Well, there we go," Kaely said. "They're already friends."

Erin smiled, relieved that she didn't need to worry about either one of them. "Looks like it." She put her suitcases on the bed.

"I've never seen him react like that to anyone," Kaely said. "Especially a dog. I mean, he's fine with other animals, but he's never allowed any of them to lick him. This is amazing. I think I told you that he was left behind—just like Chester. He's had a lot of issues to work through." She frowned at Erin. "I guess they've both been abandoned. It's almost as if . . ."

"They're connecting because they've experienced the same trauma?"

Kaely shrugged. "That seems like a stretch, but look at them. It's like they already knew each other."

"Even with what he's been through, Chester accepts

people and animals easily. Well, you know how he is. Everyone's his best friend as soon as he meets them."

"Yeah, you're right. I'm just grateful they're okay with each other. One less thing to be concerned about." She leaned down and ran her hand over the large cat's gray and white fur. He purred loudly. Kaely straightened up. "You get settled in while I get the rest of your stuff."

"Are you sure?"

"Absolutely." Kaely started to leave the room but then stopped. "A friend of mine is meeting us after supper. Sheriff Skinner. He'll go over the information he has on the case. Even though you'll be questioned by the lead investigator at the command center at some point, I want you to be prepared. I know how you think. You're a lot like me. We both need time to engage our *little gray cells*."

Erin grinned. "Not sure I can hold a candle to Hercule Poirot, but thanks."

"I think you're incredible." Kaely smiled. "Only second to me, of course."

Erin shook her head. "Too bad I'm not as humble as you are."

"Funny."

Instead of leaving the room, Kaely stared at Erin with an expression that made her swallow hard. Although she was aware that Kaely and Noah believed a killer had used the MO from her book to murder someone, she still held out hope that they were wrong. Until Kaely's call, it really hadn't ever occurred to her that psychopaths read too. Finally, Kaely turned and left. Erin felt that she'd wanted to tell her something but had decided against it for some reason.

Surely there wasn't anything worse than what she already knew.

Rather than unpack, Erin sat on the edge of the bed. She felt spent, as if she'd just run a marathon. Was she actually responsible for the death of an innocent person? Could she bear the weight of another death?

She wasn't sure of the answer.

SIX

After Erin unpacked, she changed clothes. Her cargo pants were not only wrinkled—she'd accidentally dripped some caramel cappuccino on her lap. She'd bought the drink at a fast-food place on the way, not actually expecting much. Surprisingly, it was delicious, but the lid hadn't fit quite right. Her pants had paid the price. A fresh pair of jeans, a blue gauze blouse, and running a brush through her hair made her feel much better. Chester watched, his eyes following her every move.

"Everything's okay, boy," she said, kneeling down beside him. "When we're done here, we'll go home. I won't leave you behind. I promise. At some point, you're going to have to trust me."

His deep brown eyes gazed into hers. Would the pain of his abandonment ever heal? "I know how you feel, boy," she said softly. "Maybe we can get better together. How does that sound?"

Chester suddenly licked her cheek, and it made her laugh. "I think we have a deal."

Mr. Hoover, who had been watching them, jumped down

off the bed where he'd gone after Kaely left the room. He walked over to her and rubbed up against her leg. She reached down to pet him. Suddenly, he crouched and ran down the hall like his fur was on fire. Erin giggled. Cats were certainly different from dogs. When she was little, before her parents died, they would visit their aunt, who had a cat that entertained them with her weird behavior. She had her own ideas and couldn't be bothered by anything others wanted her to do. Erin and Courtney had enjoyed spending time with Cinnamon. Aunt Karen had named her that because of her coloring. At the time, Erin had no idea that, when she was ten years old, her parents would be dead, her older sister would take off, and Aunt Karen would take her into her home. Cinnamon was a comfort to her. Not long before she moved out, Cinnamon died. Although it sounded ludicrous, somehow, she'd convinced herself that Cinnamon had hung in as long as she could just so she could stay with Erin. That somehow, she knew she was needed. The thought of that silly cat brought tears to her eyes that she quickly blinked away.

Chester barked and ran to the door, his tail wagging. He looked back at her.

"It's okay," she said. "You can follow him."

Chester gave her another smile and trotted out, obviously wanting to see what his new friend was up to. Erin breathed a sigh of relief. His reaction was a good sign. He was actually able to leave her side for a moment. This trip might end up being good for him. Hopefully, he wouldn't be too upset when they went home. She had no plans to add a cat to their small family.

Clothes changed, her suitcase unpacked, she left the bedroom and headed down the hall. Something smelled great.

When she reached the living room, Kaely was there waiting. No sign of Mr. Hoover or Chester.

"They're in the kitchen," Kaely said, as if reading her mind. "I put the bag with Chester's food and bowls in there. Does he need to be fed now?"

"Yeah, actually he does." She smiled at Kaely. "Are you feeding me too?"

"Yeah, I assumed you'd be hungry after your long drive."

"Famished."

"Well, let's take care of everyone now," Kaely said. "I'll put Mr. Hoover in the laundry room so Chester won't be tempted to eat his cat food." She looked down at Chester. "Not that you would, you sweet, sweet boy." She reached down to pet him, and Chester quickly licked her hand. "Boy, you're really trying to wrap me around your furry paw, aren't you? Well, for the record, it's working."

Erin was a little surprised at how happy she was to be here. And to be around Kaely again, even though the reason for her visit wasn't a good one. Although the cabin was her safe space, getting away for a while gave her a sense of freedom. Not something she was used to feeling. Maybe she was finally getting better. Erin wondered if God could actually heal her. Was it possible? Kaely seemed to believe that it was. Erin still wasn't certain that the God of the universe cared about her, but there was one thing she *was* sure about. She wanted to find the God that Kaely knew. She'd seen the effect He'd had in her life. The peace. The love. She wanted that too. No, she *needed* that too.

She was also looking forward to meeting Noah. Kaely had told her so much about him, she was certain they would get along. She was happy that Kaely had someone like him.

According to Kaely, Noah was a good man. Erin hoped that was true.

While Kaely put Chester's food in his bowl, she checked out the kitchen. It was so warm and inviting—just like the rest of the house. Kaely certainly had a gift for putting her own imprint on her home. Looking at Kaely's choices, she was actually getting some ideas that she might be able use back at the cabin.

"I think I need you to come back to Sanctuary," she said to Kaely with a sigh. "I need you to help me redecorate."

"We don't actually have to be there," Kaely said. "If the pictures of the cabin are still online from when it was for sale, we can download them and then use an app to show you what your changes might look like."

"That would be awesome. If we get time, let's do that."

"Not sure how much of an expert I am," Kaely said, "but together I think we can figure it out."

After Chester and Mr. Hoover ate, she and Kaely sat down at the table in the kitchen. Kaely had made baked spaghetti that was so cheesy and delicious, Erin asked for the recipe.

"Since it's just me, I usually eat these already prepared meals I have shipped to me. But I could make this and freeze some servings for later. It's so good."

"Thanks. Noah loves it too."

"He's not coming home for dinner?"

Kaely shook her head. "They're working hard on this new case. Trying to write a profile for the Novel Killer."

Erin sighed. "Still?"

Kaely shrugged. "Don't judge me. You have a better name for him?"

"How about a low-down, dirty murderer?"

"That might be a little too long," Kaely said with a grin.

"What happened to simply calling him the UNSUB?"

Kaely sighed. "I'm tired of calling murderers unknown subjects. It has no flair. No panache."

"You're incorrigible, you know that?"

"So you say."

Kaely stood up. "Sheriff Skinner should be here soon. I thought I'd serve dessert and coffee while we go over the case. We could work in here because we have the table to lay everything out. Or we have a dining room, but we only use it on holidays."

As if on cue, the doorbell rang. Chester's ears perked up, and he ran out of the kitchen, headed for the front door.

"Chester!" Erin said. She got up and went after him. When she reached him, she pulled him back while Kaely opened the door.

A man stood there, dressed in jeans and a blue checked shirt. He was blond with eyes that were so blue they almost made her gasp. To say he was attractive was an understatement. Chester started to bark when he saw him.

"Chester, stop," she said again.

The man smiled and held out his hand. Chester stopped barking and sniffed the extended appendage. Then he looked up at the man and sat down.

"I think he likes you," Erin said, "but I can put him up if you'd rather."

He shook his head. "No, please don't. I love dogs. I think if I ignore him and don't make any sudden movements, we'll get along just fine."

"If you're sure."

He nodded. "I'm certain he'll be okay."

Kaely motioned to the man to come inside. "Erin, this is Sheriff Nick Skinner."

"Happy to meet you, Sheriff."

"It's Nick. Please." The sheriff walked into the living room, and Chester followed him.

"I thought we could sit down at the kitchen table," Kaely said. "I have coconut cream pie and coffee if you're interested."

Nick nodded. "You had me at coconut cream pie."

Kaely laughed and made her way back to the kitchen. Nick and Erin followed behind her. Nick Skinner certainly wasn't what Erin had expected. He was younger, hipper, and seemed rather casual about being the sheriff for Fredericksburg.

When he sat down at the table, Erin noticed the satchel he held onto with his right hand. He put it down on the floor next to him.

"Can I help with dessert?" Erin asked Kaely.

"Sure. That would be great."

Erin cut the pie and placed the pieces on the dessert plates already on the counter. She carried the plates over to the table while Kaely poured coffee and brought the cups over.

"I put a little sugar in yours," she said to Nick.

"Thank you for remembering," he said with a smile.

With the pie served and the coffee cups full, Erin and Kaely also sat down at the table. Nick took a bite of his pie and shook his head. "This is delicious, Kaely," he said. "Noah brags all the time about your cooking."

"I'm sure he doesn't say much about the first couple of years we were married," she said. "I had to learn. Trust me, not everything I made was a success." She shook her head. "Noah never complained. I hope his patience has paid off. At least now when he eats something I've made he doesn't have to choke it down while fighting to keep a smile on his face."

Nick laughed. "He's never mentioned anything like that. He only praises you." His expression changed for just an instant as he looked at Kaely. Although she couldn't be certain, Erin wondered if he was a little jealous of Noah. She glanced at the ring finger on his left hand. A gold ring.

"Are you married, Nick?" she asked.

Nick cleared his throat and put his fork down, not looking at her. "I . . . I was," he said. "My wife died about six months ago."

Erin felt incredible sadness for this nice man who hadn't been able to take his ring off yet. If he *was* jealous of Noah, it was for an understandable reason.

"I'm so sorry for your loss," she said softly. Erin wanted to ask how she'd died, but when she glanced at Kaely, she frowned and shook her head so slightly that only Erin would notice.

"Thank you," Nick said, obviously not seeing Kaely's warning. "It's an adjustment. I just put one foot in front of the other and try to make it through." He put the last bite of pie in his mouth and then washed it down with coffee. After that, he picked up the satchel on the floor next to him and removed a folder.

Erin's stomach tightened. She wanted to help catch the man who had killed three women, but knowing that the killer had taken a life based on something she'd written was . . . devastating.

"Nick can share the information from this file with us," Kaely said. "Noah can't do that. The FBI won't allow him to even remove case files from the building."

"I have to deputize you, Erin," Nick said. "Even though you'll be given some information at the command center, they might not give you access to anything outside of the murder that involves your book. But once you're deputized, you'll be working under my command, and I can show you anything I want to."

"I'm hopeful that being deputized will allow you more access to case information at the command. Updates. Things like that," Kaely said. "But I can't guarantee it. The Virginia State Police are in charge of the task force. It will be up to them."

Erin nodded. "I understand," she said. Having spent several years as a police officer, it felt a little odd to be deputized to work with Nick, but she really wanted to help.

Nick asked her to raise her right hand and swear to carry out the duties of a deputy sheriff for Spotsylvania County, which included Fredericksburg. Once she agreed, he reached into the pocket of his jacket and handed her a badge. Erin took it from him but was embarrassed that her hand trembled. It had been a long time since she'd had a badge. Her chest felt tight, and she had to remind herself that this was only temporary and had nothing to do with her previous life as a cop. She was surprised by her reaction. This was clearly a trigger. She took a deep breath to calm her rapidly beating heart. Thankfully, Nick didn't seem to notice.

She cleared her throat and smiled. "Thank you," she said. "I'll make sure I have this when I'm inside the command center."

Nick nodded and opened the file on the table. "A police investigator will want to talk to you. Since these crimes were just linked as serial killings, they're at the beginning of the inquiry. We were one of the first departments on the scene. That's why I have these. I sent everything to the Virginia State Police since, as Kaely said, they're the lead agency now. I printed these photos and reports from the files I emailed to them. I really don't want anyone to question why I shared this information with you. This way there's nothing online to track. I'm doing this as a favor to Kaely. Besides, Kaely said you prefer holding paper and photos rather than looking at them online."

"Yeah, I do. Not sure why. Might be because I spend so much time on my laptop writing. Having actual copies I can hold in my hands feels . . . more real. Thanks for doing this."

Nick nodded. "You're welcome." He pushed the contents of the file toward her. She was a little nervous about what she was getting ready to see. Right now, she wasn't certain she could write another book. Ever.

SEVEN

Erin hadn't noticed Chester come up to the table, and when he nudged her leg, she jumped. She had to get control of herself.

"Lay down," Erin said gently. Chester reluctantly flopped down on the floor. Mr. Hoover, who'd been freed from the laundry room, got up from his spot under the other side of the table and walked over to Chester. He turned around several times and then curled up next to his new friend. Erin and Kaely both laughed at their pets' antics, relieving Erin's tension a bit. She pulled some of the photos closer so she could see them.

"Kaely and I both want you to be prepared for what you'll experience tomorrow," Nick said. "This won't be easy, but we don't want you to be blindsided."

Erin nodded. "Thank you. I appreciate that."

Kaely and Nick were right. Ever since the night in St. Louis that had changed her life, situations that were new or uncomfortable could cause her to shut down. Even though she was still concerned about what Nick was getting ready to show her, she was grateful to Kaely for contacting him. She didn't want to have a panic attack at the command center. That would be incredibly humiliating.

"You said you'll go with me?" she said to Kaely.

Kaely smiled at her. "Yes, we'll go together."

It helped her to know Kaely would be there to support her. Although her agoraphobia had less of a hold on her now than it used to, she still struggled when going to new places. Especially when she was around people she didn't know. "So I won't be talking to anyone from the BAU?"

"No, the analysts only work on the profile. They don't do any investigation. Field agents handle that. Agents will be there, but you'll be questioned by someone from the state police department."

"Yeah, you told me that already. Sorry." Erin rubbed her hands together. "Feeling a bit anxious. I'm not only a long way from home, but I'm still trying to digest the fact that someone mimicked my book as a way to murder an innocent human being."

"You've got to remember that this isn't your fault, Erin," Nick said. "This UNSUB used other books too, and until he's caught, he may choose another author's work. This is on him. No one else."

"I know, and I agree with you," Erin said softly. "But it still messes with my head."

"Well, we could just outlaw all fiction. Maybe that will keep everyone safe."

Erin gave him a small smile. "Okay. I get it." She took a deep breath. "So, what should I look at first?"

Nick moved closer to her and lined the photos up. He pulled one toward her. Although there was a part of her that didn't want to look at it, she knew she had to.

"This is the first murder," he said. "It was taken from Dan Harper's book, *The Last Thing She Saw*. The unknown subject broke into the house of a young, single woman in Richmond. He came in through the back doors that led to her patio. The police believe they were unlocked. Family members told them she never locked them during the day. She liked to feed the birds and squirrels that frequented her yard. He entered through the gate attached to her privacy fence in the backyard just after dark. Unfortunately, none of the neighbors noticed anything. He tied her up, taped her eyes open, strangled her, and left a strange poem behind. It was grasped in her hand." He pointed at a photo of the note.

I am death, created by evil and fueled by hate.
I hold in my hands your ultimate fate.
You feel my presence as I draw near.
I feed on your anguish and relish your fear.
The Last Thing She Saw *was the look in my eyes*
as she realized today was the day she would die.

"Dan used poems in his book as well," Nick said when he was finished, "but this wasn't one of them. The killer wrote his own verse. As you can see, he emphasized the book's title. Also, the officers found a copy of Dan's book next to the body."

This bit of information made Erin shiver. This guy was scary. "Dan's the son of D. J. Harper, a really successful author," she said. "I think this is Dan's first book. What a way to start a career." She hesitated a moment before saying, "This poem is quite telling, actually. I think this guy wants us to know that his motive is some kind of revenge. He also wants everyone to believe that he's in charge. Not the authors and not the investigators." Erin looked at Kaely. "Do you agree?"

"Yeah, I do," Kaely said. "That's exactly what I told Nick and Noah. He agreed. The analysts at the BAU are looking over the poems now."

Erin finally looked at the crime scene photos. Everything was neatly staged. This was someone who was organized and meticulous. "I'll bet there weren't any fingerprints, right?"

Nick nodded. "Nothing left behind. Locard's Principle didn't work this time. He may have taken something with him, but if he did, investigators couldn't figure out what it was."

Locard's Principle of Exchange was a theory developed by Dr. Edmond Locard, referred to by many as the Sherlock Holmes of forensic science. The principle was known by everyone who worked in forensics. The idea was that criminals would not only bring something into a crime scene, they would also take something out. Crime scene analysts looked for trace evidence created from fingerprints, footprints, fibers, hairs, as well as other items that could point back to the unknown subject. Violent deaths could create blood spatter and physical injuries caused by the victim's fight for survival. This included skin from under the victim's nails which could reveal DNA. However, in this situation, it appeared that either the crime scene techs missed something, or this was an extremely thorough and careful UNSUB.

"You're probably wondering if investigators overlooked some kind of evidence," Kaely said as if reading her mind again. "The answer is no. The state police's forensics division is top-notch. Of course, mistakes happen, but I'd be surprised if it occurred this time. The police went out of their way to preserve evidence."

"I agree," Nick said. He pulled another photo from the folder and shoved it toward her. "This is the only other unusual thing investigators found. I mean, the item itself isn't unusual, but the woman's friends said she didn't own anything like it. Her parents weren't so sure about that, though. They said their daughter loved to frequent yard sales and sometimes bought things that she'd had as a child. There was a fire when she was young, and she lost all her toys. She liked to buy replacements when she could."

Erin studied the photo. There was an old Barbie doll lying on a table a few feet away from the body. She'd had one just like it when she was a kid. "It's not a real early one," she said. "It isn't rare or valuable, but I see why someone might like one." She frowned. "The victim was found in the living room and the doll was on the coffee table?"

"Yes." Nick shrugged. "The police didn't think it was connected to the murder. The killer in Harper's book didn't leave dolls behind. Just to be thorough, they talked to several people who'd held yard sales in the area, but no one could positively confirm that the victim had been there. One woman they talked to said she'd sold a similar Barbie, but she couldn't remember what the buyer looked like. All she could say was that it was possible the victim was the one who'd purchased her doll."

Erin nodded. "So, all three murders happened in Virginia . . ." She said this more to herself than to Kaely.

"Yeah, and that's strange," Nick said. "It's as if the killer wanted the FBI involved. As you can imagine, the police and the FBI work together all the time in Virginia. Quite a few police officers have attended the FBI's National Academy. It's an eleven-week leadership program for police from all over the world. There are four National Academies every year, with around two hundred officers attending each one. These are officers that the department believes will be assuming a leadership role in a few years or current chiefs of smaller departments who would benefit from learning new techniques, like how to talk to the media, how to handle major cases, and accessing available FBI resources. The reason I bring this up is because the Academy creates lifetime friendships between the police and the FBI. They actually enjoy working together. There's no fight for jurisdiction like there might be in other areas of the country. That's what makes setting the killings here . . . well, dumb."

"I've heard that the detective from the state police who is overseeing this operation attended the Academy," Kaely said. "Noah really respects him."

Nick nodded. "I doubt this guy will be able to hide from the task force for long. Too much talent and training against him." He frowned. "Of course, his ability to leave his crime scenes free of evidence is troubling."

"His comfort zone seems to be anywhere in Virginia," Kaely said. "It's a large area, but Virginia means something to him."

"I agree," Nick said.

"Is the FBI convinced that these are the only cases like this?" Erin asked. "Killings copied from novels? Have they checked out other areas of the country?"

"All the cases were run through ViCAP," Kaely said. "They searched for similarities, patterns, vehicles, suspect descriptions . . . anything that might help them find comparable crimes. Nothing current, although, as I told you, murderers have used scenarios from other books."

"That's true," Nick said. "It seems that sometimes killers are triggered by something they read. That's not widely known to the public, by the way. It's something law enforcement keeps under wraps for obvious reasons."

Erin sighed. "That's exactly what Kaely said. I find that not only frightening, but it makes me wonder if I should be writing about things like this."

Nick smiled at her. "Look, like I said, authors aren't responsible for the actions of psychopaths, Erin. We can't make it illegal to write books or produce movies that deal with certain subjects because some crazy person might use it as a way to express the evil inside them."

"Yeah, I know you're right, but still, it's really disturbing." She shook her head. "So, although the state police are the lead agency, they asked for the FBI's help." As before, Erin wasn't really asking a question, she was restating the information to herself.

"Yes," Nick said. "They requested that the Bureau assist the police under the Serial Killer Act."

"You told me once about the International Homicide Investigators' Association," she said, looking at Kaely. "Did the FBI contact them too?"

Kaely nodded. "They didn't find anything current that linked these murders to anything else either. Just like the ViCAP search, they didn't discover any other cases where a novel may have been the impetus for murders that were similar to these killings. No poems. No novels left behind. This UNSUB is unique. As you know, serial killers have a specific MO. A signature that links their murders to the killer's psychopathy. But that isn't happening here. Except for the poem, which is his way to put his own stamp on his crime and build up his narcissism, he's following the methods from the books to the letter." She sighed. "This is a tough one for the BAU. The UNSUB is hiding behind murders created from the minds of the authors he's mimicking. Seeing *him* clearly is tough."

"But isn't that a signature?" Erin asked. "Somehow, he's connected to these books for a reason. The BAU just has to find it."

"And that's what they're trying to do. But the three authors he chose have no connection whatsoever. Except for the serial-killer theme, there's nothing similar in their plots. I mean, absolutely nothing." She met Erin's gaze. "The only thing that stands out in the minds of the agents working the case? Your connection to me. Why pick an author who is close to a former BAU special agent married to someone in the FBI? The killer has to know that the FBI is investigating his crimes. That's why some of the people working the case wonder if you could be the key to finding this guy before someone else dies."

EIGHT

Erin took a quick breath. "Wow. I really hope I'm not the reason this UNSUB started killing." She frowned at Kaely. "Tell me the truth. Did you ask me here so I could help . . . or are you afraid I'm in some kind of danger?"

Kaely took a sip of coffee before meeting Erin's gaze. "I've been straight with you. It's for both reasons."

Erin reached for her own coffee cup and took a long drink. She wasn't certain what to say. It seemed to her that Kaely was more concerned for her safety than she'd originally let on. She appeared to be really worried about Erin, and Kaely didn't spook easily. Of course, if she'd been absolutely certain there was a threat, she never would have allowed her to drive alone to Fredericksburg.

"I'm sorry if you feel I should have been more forthright with you," Kaely said, "but to be honest, I could be overreacting. Noah and I are just erring on the side of caution. Look, for now, don't worry—at least not until we know we have something to worry about."

"She's right," Nick said. "Like I told you, this investigation is in its infancy. Don't make any assumptions yet. There's really no reason to fear the worst."

"I'll . . . I'll try not to." Erin took a deep breath and then let it out, trying to calm her jangled nerves. She frowned at Kaely. "Something is still bothering me. About all these killings happening in Virginia. Forget a minute about our relationship. Let's look at the other murders. Like you said, if he knows his actions will probably bring in the FBI . . . I mean, why would he want that? If he's as smart as it seems he is, he'd realize the FBI is more likely to help the police find him."

Kaely shrugged. "Maybe he's taunting them. You know, trying to prove he can outwit them."

"So Dan Harper has been notified about the similarities between his book and this crime scene. How did he react?" Erin asked.

"He wasn't happy about it," Nick said. "I think he was afraid someone might blame him for the murder."

Erin sighed. "I can relate. When Kaely first told me about the killer modeling his murder from my book, the first thing I thought about was needing an alibi. Not that I needed to worry. Being somewhat agoraphobic actually helps me, since I rarely go anywhere."

Kaely grinned. "I hear you, but I was fairly certain you weren't involved anyway."

"Fairly certain? Gee, thanks." Erin looked at Nick. "Are investigators looking at the authors as suspects?"

"They have to be cleared, obviously," Nick said. "But from what I've been told from the police working the case, so far none of them, including you, are under suspicion. Their preliminary investigation makes it pretty clear that none of the authors were anywhere near the location where the bodies were found. None of you reside in Virginia. Tomorrow, you'll be asked where you were when the killings happened, but since you live so far away, I think you'll be fine."

"I could have driven here, killed someone, and then driven back," Erin said.

Kaely grinned at her. "Doesn't that cute police chief check up on you from time to time?"

Erin felt her cheeks get hot. "I guess so."

"So, you think he's cute?" Nick asked, one eyebrow raised.

Erin shook her head. "I think I'll plead the fifth on that one."

Kaely laughed. "You buy groceries, Erin. Get mail. Didn't you tell me you recently had to put your car in the shop for repairs?"

She nodded.

"Then they would have written down your mileage. That should take care of any questions."

"Make sure you tell them about your car," Nick said. "It will prove you didn't make the drive to Fredericksburg . . . until today."

"Besides," Kaely said, rolling her eyes, "you're smart. You would have created an unbreakable alibi that would keep you from any suspicion. You would have come up with something to make it look impossible for you to have driven to Virginia . . . three times . . . to kill people you don't even know."

"Good point." Erin sighed. "Can't believe I'm actually even thinking about having an alibi. It's absurd."

"Of course it is," Kaely said. "I know you. And Noah trusts my instincts. The idea of you being involved never crossed our minds. Not even for a second."

"She's right. Please don't think about it anymore," Nick

said. "No one I've talked to seriously looked at you as a suspect. If I thought there was a chance of that, I wouldn't have deputized you."

"And I have a rule about not asking murderous psychopaths to stay in my guest room," Kaely said.

Erin laughed. "That sounds like a good rule. Look, I really want to help find this guy. I've been going over it and over it in my mind, wondering why he picked *my* book."

"I'm sure the other two authors are doing the same thing," Kaely said. "But the truth is, our UNSUB probably just picked three popular books with murders he felt he could pull off."

"Yeah, I guess so."

"Ready for the next one?" Nick asked

"Sure." Erin shoved the photos to the side, also trying to push the image of the young woman's horrified expression out of her mind.

"The first murder happened three months ago. This one is a month later." Nick pulled several other photos from the folder and laid them on the table in front of Erin. "This is copied from Toni Sue Smith's novel, *The Rosary Murders*. It happened in Virginia Beach. This woman was jogging in a local park. She was attacked and stabbed. Rosary beads were placed in her hands. She was found covered by a blue blanket and a lock of her hair was missing, just as in the book. Again, no trace evidence left behind."

Erin started to say something but stopped when Kaely held her hand up. "I already know what you're going to say. There should have been all kinds of trace evidence on the blanket. But except for grass and leaves from the park, there was nothing. And no prints on the beads. Investigators couldn't find out who sold the beads because they're so common. Trying to track the origin of every pair purchased in the state was an impossible task."

"This guy clearly knows what he's doing," Nick said. "Some of us have wondered if he's in law enforcement." He shook his head. "Not something I want to consider, but unfortunately, investigators are looking into law enforcement personnel in the areas where the murders occurred."

Nick took another photo from the stack and placed it in front of her. "He left another poem at this scene. This time it was found in the victim's pocket. Again, no fingerprints. Printed on cheap, common copy paper, just like the other one. Nothing there to help investigators. You'll notice that the beginning of the poem is the same as the other."

Erin pulled the photo closer. She read the typewritten words on a creased piece of paper.

I am death, created by evil and fueled by hate.
I hold in my hands your ultimate fate.
You feel my presence as I draw near.
I feed on your anguish and relish your fear.
The Rosary Murders *you quickly*
as you cling to your beads,
your fallen angels, and your blasphemous deeds.

Erin sighed. "Like you said, the first four lines are the same. He is establishing his hate for . . . something. But what? He really wants you to know that he's copying the books," she said. "It's important to him."

Nick nodded. "Yes."

Erin looked through the photos carefully, trying to find something that might lead to the killer, but there wasn't anything that made her think she was seeing something the FBI or the police had missed. This guy was slick. Erin pointed to one of the photos. "What's that?"

Nick pulled it over to where she could see it. "Oh, it's a Beanie Baby. Like I said, she was killed in a park. The police found several items left behind by families that frequented the park. Just to be certain, they dusted everything for prints and looked for DNA. Nothing. But it had rained for several days before the body was found. It's possible anything left on the items had been washed away."

"That Beanie Baby is called Amber the Tabby Cat," Erin said. "I had one of those too."

Kaely smiled at her. "You must have had a lot of toys."

Erin had seen many crime scenes, and none of them had included a toy she'd once owned. Now there were two of them. It felt strange, but Kaely was right. It was obviously just a coincidence. The killer was going out of his way to stay true to the books, except for the poems. He wouldn't leave toys behind. It didn't make any sense. She slowly pushed the photos away. The next killing was the one she dreaded the most. Kaely and Nick were quiet and waited until Erin nodded. Then Nick removed the final photos.

Erin swung her gaze toward the kitchen window and looked out at the trees in Kaely's backyard. Pear trees. They were full of white flowers. Not only were they hardy trees, they were extremely beautiful.

"Erin, you don't have to look at this if it's too difficult," Kaely said softly. "I can describe it."

Erin shook her head. "No. I need to see it. I mean, it's my fault."

Kaely reached over and grabbed her hand. "I meant it

when I told you not to go there. If you can't separate yourself from this, you can't help investigators. Whoever's behind this is the bad guy. Not you and not the other two authors. That kind of reasoning is the same as someone who wants to blame a gun or a knife in the hands of a murderer. A knife can kill someone, but it can also cut a piece of pie. A gun in the hands of a cop can save a life. Please don't let this guy get inside your head. That's exactly what he wants."

Erin took a deep breath. "Okay. I'll try not to let those thoughts in my mind. I really do want to help. But it's tough. Especially for someone like me. I'm pretty eager to blame myself for most things."

"I hear you," Nick said, "and I don't mean to sound as if I don't care, but we need someone who can see this dispassionately. So, what do you want to do? Play the victim or help us find this guy?"

"Wow. That's a little harsh," Erin said.

"I know, but it's true. This is your choice."

She wanted to be offended, but Nick was only trying to be straight with her. "Okay," she said. "Show me." She leaned forward. "Do you really think the UNSUB could be someone one of the authors knows?"

Kaely shrugged. "Maybe. When you talk to the investigator, they'll ask you about that."

"I . . . I hope that's not true, but the thing is, I don't believe it's possible in my case. I don't know anyone . . . really. I haven't talked to the people I used to work with for a long time. And I certainly don't keep in touch with the perps I've taken down."

"Look, finding you isn't tough," Kaely said. "You're famous. Like you said, this guy is full of hate toward someone.

Maybe a parent or a guardian? Yet, we still need to look for any connection to the authors." She sighed. "Maybe if we were all isolated from birth, we could stem the tide of destruction that twists the souls of human beings, but the truth is, even that wouldn't do it. Sick minds find reasons for hate. It doesn't have to make any sense. That's what makes it so hard to find them. Like the poem says, they're fueled by hate. Hate that is beyond human comprehension."

"You're talking about the devil, right?" A few months ago, Erin would have laughed at the idea of some kind of evil being whose goal was to destroy everything he could. Whose heart beat with hate and envy. Who detested every single human being on earth. But because of Kaely and the things she'd told her, Erin had started reading the Bible. Although it still sounded a little crazy, she had to admit that the presence of an evil being who hated God and everyone He'd created was beginning to make some sense. It would certainly explain some of the things she'd seen and experienced. As a police officer, she'd looked into the eyes of extremely violent criminals and could have sworn she'd seen something staring back. Something dark and malevolent. As if every trace of humanity was gone.

"Yes, I am," Kaely said. "But let's not talk about that now. I know you're new to the concept."

Nick sighed. "Working in law enforcement means we see the devil more than most people."

So Nick believed in the devil too? Interesting.

"You'd be surprised at what I'm beginning to believe," Erin said. She cleared her throat and looked down at the photos Nick had spread out on the table.

The first one was an exact replica of the murders in *Dark*

Matters. Only the top of the victim's head showed in the water. Then came the pictures after the woman's body was pulled from the lake. Her throat had been slashed. A concrete block was tied around her ankles, and her bright blue eyes stared up at the sky as if asking God why this had happened to her.

"The poem was found on a nearby picnic table. It had been placed in a plastic bag with a rock to hold it down. Again, no prints."

Erin picked up the next photo and read.

I am death, created by evil and fueled by hate.
I hold in my hands your ultimate fate.
You feel my presence as I draw near.
I feed on your anguish and relish your fear.
And by the time you wake up and see that **Dark Matters**,
you'll whisper my name while your life lies in tatters.

Erin jumped up from the table and ran to the kitchen sink where she threw up.

NINE

"I'm so sorry," Erin said again. "Please let me clean that up."

Kaely shook her head. "You sit still and drink your coffee. A little water and the garbage disposal will do the work." She smiled at Erin. "Good thing I set our plates on the counter. I usually rinse them and put them in the sink before placing them in the dishwasher."

Erin laughed lightly as she sat at the table, holding onto her cup as if it could somehow calm her. Kaely had seen this reaction before. Anyone in law enforcement understood a visceral reaction to the kind of evil in those photos. But this was different. Writing about death was one thing. Seeing your words lived out in reality was something else.

Kaely rinsed the sink and then briefly turned on the garbage disposal. When she finished, it was as if her friend hadn't just been violently ill. It appeared that everything was back to normal, but Kaely knew two things. Erin had been traumatized by those photos. And it would be a while before she made baked spaghetti again.

She went back to the table, pulled her chair next to Erin's, and gently took her hand. "Again, this isn't on you, Erin," she

67

said gently. "This is on the psychopath who is doing this. We need to use our talents, our experience, and our God-given ability to understand this guy so we can stop him. You have to remember that we're the good guys. We're on the side of the angels. This killer is spurred on by something dark. By the devil himself." She searched Erin's face, trying to interpret her expression, but she was attempting to be stoic. However, her breathing was too fast, and she was blinking more than normal. Signs of stress. "If it's too much, I'll understand and so will Nick. You can stay here, chill out, and head home whenever you're ready. Remember, the state police can't force you to talk to them. You're not charged with any crime. This is voluntary."

"There are top-notch people working this case," Nick said, concern written on his face.

Even as she and Nick tried to reassure her, Kaely was convinced that Erin wouldn't leave. She would stay and fight. That's who she was. Still, Kaely couldn't help but be concerned about the wounds in her friend's soul. They were deep. And now this. "Listen to me," she said. "If he hadn't used your book, he would have picked someone else's."

Erin took a big, shuddering breath. It was at that moment that Kaely's expectation was confirmed. Erin had no plans to run from this.

"Let's go over those photos again," Erin said, her voice shaking slightly. "I need to see them. I can't let this twisted piece of humanity beat me down. He's got to be stopped."

Nick got up and picked up the file that he'd shoved the pictures into after Erin's initial reaction to them. Then he sat down and opened it again.

As he did that, a part of Kaely wished she'd never contacted Erin about the murders. But if the killings had made it into the media before Kaely had a chance to break the news to Erin, it would have blindsided her, and that was something Kaely couldn't allow. Besides, if she hadn't called her, the police would have. And that would have been worse. Kaely felt compelled to keep Erin safe. She took a deep breath as Erin pulled the photos out again. She laid them side by side.

"The killer abducted a woman from a parking lot late at night," Nick said gently. "He took her to a lake, cut her throat, tied a concrete block around her ankles, then tossed her into the water with only the top of her head showing."

"How would he have known how deep the water was?" Erin asked.

"That wouldn't have been hard. The spot where she was found was near a dock. He could have measured it. Even jumped in himself to see how deep it was, just like the killer in your book. Although the police interviewed all kinds of people who frequented the lake, no one reported seeing him."

"Sure," Erin said. "Why would they? He was careful." She stared at Nick for a moment before saying, "Was this an area of the lake where swimming was allowed?"

He shook his head. "No, there's a roped-off area on the other side of the lake for swimming. Fishing was allowed, though."

"How long had she been in the water when they found her?"

"The medical examiner determined that death occurred approximately ten hours before a park employee discovered the body. That means she went in the water around nine at night."

"Where did this occur?"

"At Lunga Park, in Quantico," Nick said. "It's only open to active and retired members of the military and their families. There's no real reason to suspect any of the members, although they haven't been ruled out. Investigators are also checking out workers connected with the park, although, again, there doesn't seem to be anyone involved with the other murders. Some fencing that surrounds the park was under repair. Someone could have come in through there. It wouldn't have been difficult."

"I don't feel like this guy used this lake because it was convenient," Erin said. "This was planned down to the last detail."

"So, you think he knew about the repairs ahead of time? Used this lake because he could access it without being caught?"

"I do," Erin said. "Is the park closed at night?"

"Yeah. It closes at eight o'clock and opens at six in the morning."

"He could have put the body there to throw off the police and the FBI. With the fence making the park accessible, maybe he thinks investigators will believe he's not connected to the park."

"That's true," Nick said. "Like I said, they're working that angle as well."

Kaely noticed Erin's fingers tremble as she studied the pictures. "Who was she?" she asked finally.

Nick hesitated a moment before saying, "A waitress at a small coffee shop not far from here. Sophie Rogers. Single. Her only immediate family were her mother and her sister."

Erin didn't respond. Nick had just made the victim a real

person, but that couldn't be helped. She and Nick both knew that Erin would ask.

"So, all the victims have been female," Erin said. Kaely knew her brain was working, going over everything. "He hates women. Sees them only as the means to an end." She looked up from the pictures. "Similarities between the victims?"

"All single." Nick frowned. "None of them had two living parents. The first victim lost her parents a few years ago in a house fire. The second victim had a father but no mother. I realize that's not so odd in today's society, but the analysts at the BAU are looking that over to see if it's part of the UNSUB's signature. Even though he's copying murders from novels, they believe, and so do I, that his own proclivities have to be bleeding through somehow. But frankly, in my opinion, the family connection appears to be coincidence." He pointed at the picture of Sophie lying on the ground after she was taken from the water. "You can't tell it by looking since her hair is wet, but all the victims were blonde."

"That could be important," Erin said slowly.

Kaely looked at her closely. "You seem hesitant. Why?"

Erin sighed. "I have no idea," she said. "You know that feeling? The one where you sense something is right in front of your eyes but you can't see it?"

Kaely nodded. "You feel that way?"

"Yeah, but I can't explain it. I wish I could." She pulled the photo of the poem closer and stared at it for a moment. "This one's different," she said.

"What do you mean?" Nick asked.

Erin looked up at him. "All the other poems are written

about killing the victim. But this one says her life will *lie in tatters*. How can someone's life lie in tatters if they're dead?"

Kaely frowned. She didn't want to discourage her friend, but she felt she might be reaching. "Maybe he just needed something to rhyme with *matters*?"

"Maybe."

Erin didn't sound convinced.

Deciding that Erin had been through enough for one night, Kaely gathered up the pictures and put them back in the folder. "Look, let's take a break from this for a while." She clasped her hands in front of her. "This killer is different. Unusual. But the analysts at the BAU are the best. And they have us. We'll find him."

"We will," Nick said, smiling at Erin. "I have no doubt."

"I hope you're right," Erin said. "The one thing I'm sure of is that this guy isn't finished. Someone else is going to die if he isn't stopped."

TEN

Adrian was on the way home after a long day of handling complaints by neighbors fighting with neighbors, as well as trying to find missing dogs, cats, and even a pig. He'd sent two officers to Grady's General Store to scare the heck out of two kids who'd tried to steal candy. His mind kept drifting back to several months ago when a serial killer was operating in Sanctuary. Working with Erin Delaney and her friend Kaely Quinn had made him feel like an actual police chief. He'd moved to Sanctuary to get away from all the death and destruction he'd had to deal with in Chicago, so why was he so irritated with his job right now? His life was good. For the most part, Sanctuary lived up to its name. He really was happy here. But after helping to catch a serial killer, he now felt rather useless. An odd call from the FBI also had him worried and was probably the reason he was thinking so much about the past. He'd considered contacting Erin to let her know about it, but after sharing the contents of the call with his administrative assistant, Lisa Parrish, he'd changed his mind. Lisa felt that telling Erin about the call might make it harder for her to do what she needed to do now. Lisa was usually right, so he decided to keep quiet—for now.

He sighed loudly. "Stop it," he said to himself. Jake looked at him as if he were being chastised. Adrian reached over and patted his head. "I'm not talking to you. You're a good boy. I guess I'm the one who needs to straighten up, huh?" He took a deep breath. "You weren't happy in Chicago, Adrian," he mumbled. "You're not going to start complaining about Sanctuary. This is where you want to be. This is what you want to do."

As if he'd lost the ability to control his thoughts, his mind drifted to Erin. Her wide green eyes, her short blonde hair, and her incredible smile were burned into his mind. Was he missing the excitement of doing real police work, or was he just missing her? He couldn't answer that question. Not yet, anyway. Maybe someday. The truth was, Erin wasn't interested in him that way. She'd never given him any indication that they were more than friends.

He realized suddenly that his hands were gripping the steering wheel so tightly that his knuckles were white. He took a quick breath and loosened his hold.

Jake barked suddenly, and it made him jump. He looked over at his furry friend. "You okay?" he asked. "What's wrong?"

Jake barked again and looked out the window. They were passing Erin's cabin. "Sorry, boy. She's not there. Neither is Chester."

Jake pulled against the strap that kept him secure in the passenger seat.

"No," Adrian said sharply. "They're not home. Settle down."

Jake didn't listen, just kept barking loudly and squirming in his seat.

"Do you need to go outside?" Adrian asked. He'd taken him out before they left the station. He shouldn't need to go so soon again, but Adrian pulled over in front of Erin's place. Better to be safe than sorry.

He started to get out of the Jeep so he could take care of Jake when he noticed something unusual. Before she left, Erin had told him that she'd programmed some of the lights in her house to come on at six o'clock in the evening while she was gone, but the cabin was dark. He'd have to call her and let her know.

Suddenly, lights came on. He looked at his dashboard. It was eleven minutes after nine, a strange time to set a timer. He put the truck in gear and pulled into the driveway. Telling Jake to stay, he got out, grabbed his flashlight, and walked up to the house. He shone the light through the windows. Then he circled around the cabin, looking into each one, making certain everything was secure. Nothing seemed out of place.

When he was finished, he went back to the Jeep, planning to put Jake on his leash and give him a chance to do his business. But when he opened the door, Jake was sound asleep.

Adrian shook his head, got into the driver's seat, and headed home. He wanted to chalk Jake's behavior up to something else—maybe he saw a squirrel or some other animal, and it set him off? But his dog had started barking when they were near Erin's cabin. Had he seen something that Adrian hadn't? He tried to dismiss his concerns, but a soft voice inside him seemed to be whispering something different.

"You're just bored," he said, admonishing himself. Still, the timing of the lights seemed odd. He'd call Erin tomorrow and ask her about it. The anticipation of hearing her voice cheered him more than it should have.

As he drove home, he tried to push thoughts of her out of his mind. But they weren't easily vanquished.

The waitress brought Noah another cup of coffee. He thanked her and took a sip, hoping they'd made a fresh pot. His first cup had been closer to sludge than actual coffee. Unfortunately, this wasn't any better. Might even be worse. Tonight, he wasn't worried that the caffeine would make it hard to sleep. He was exhausted. He loved working for the BAU, but this recent rash of murders was keeping his team working late, trying to understand a serial killer who couldn't be understood. He was different. Copying murders from books wasn't a signature. Unless he had a beef with authors, but usually someone like that wouldn't buy books in the first place. Or they'd just leave bad reviews. Using their books to kill? It had certainly been done, but not like this. It wasn't just the method. He was writing poems that included the books' titles. He was detailed, organized, precise—and very angry. And he wasn't leaving any evidence. What they had now wasn't enough for the police and the FBI to go on. Although law enforcement had tried to keep the killings under wraps, it wouldn't be long before the media picked up the story. Then things would get much more difficult. The public could be helpful, but most of the time, panic set in, and law enforcement was overwhelmed with tips that only wasted time and resources.

He really just wanted to go home, but when he'd gotten a call from Lee Johnson, a guy who'd recently joined the men's group at church, he had to respond. He'd volunteered to mentor Lee. Well, actually, Lee had attached himself to Noah's side. He was the one who'd asked Noah for help. It wasn't that Noah didn't want to mentor him. He did. Noah was just concerned that he wouldn't be able to give him all the time he might need. But a commitment was a commitment. So, here he was at an all-night pancake house in downtown Dumfries, Virginia, instead of nestled in his comfy bed, sleeping next to Kaely.

Kaely's friend, Erin Delaney, was staying with them, but he was pretty sure he wouldn't be home in time tonight to meet her. Not that he could talk to her about the case anyway. The FBI was strict about things like that. Kaely had arranged for Nick Skinner to come by and clue her in. After he deputized her, she'd be able to officially help with the case. It would be easier for him to discuss things after that, but he still needed to be careful. The FBI realized it wasn't her fault that a killer had copied his last murder from her book, but they had to be absolutely certain she wasn't involved or that she didn't have knowledge that could help find this UNSUB. Sometimes people knew things they didn't realize were connected to a case. He'd seen that happen many times. There was some reason the UNSUB had picked her novel. Investigators needed to find out what it was.

"Here you go."

The waitress put two plates in front of him. Pancakes and a side of bacon. He'd missed dinner with Kaely. Baked spaghetti. One of his favorites. He suddenly realized how hungry he was. The pancakes smelled amazing.

"I'll get your butter and syrup," she said.

"Thank you," he said with a smile. "Maple please."

She'd just left when Lee walked in the door. Noah waved at him, and he headed toward the booth. Lee was the kind of man most people wouldn't notice. Everything about him was plain. Brown hair, brown eyes, medium build. He mostly wore jeans and T-shirts. But nothing too colorful. It was like he was there . . . but not there.

"Thanks for meeting with me," Lee said as he sat down.

"You're welcome. I told you to call if you needed to talk."

"You look tired," Lee said.

"Right now, I'm just hungry. Want anything?"

Lee hesitated, and Noah felt like an idiot. Lee worked for a lawn-care company and lived in a small apartment not far from the church. Noah had been inside his place. It was bleak. The paint on the walls was peeling, and Lee had been sleeping on an old mattress on the floor. Noah and Kaely gave him a new bed frame and mattress, telling him it was a bed they weren't using. It was true, but not completely accurate. They'd purchased it just for him. Kaely also sent him new sheets and a couple of blankets they had. Their pastor gave him odd jobs whenever he had something, which helped some. Lee utilized their food program, so at least he wouldn't go hungry. Didn't mean he had money to spend in a restaurant.

"My treat," Noah said, quickly. "I've got one of those two-for-one coupons. If you don't eat something, it will go to waste."

He really did have a coupon in his billfold, although he suspected it was expired. However, he wasn't certain, so again, it wasn't a lie. He wondered if he was playing a little fast and loose with the truth, but in his heart, he was certain God understood.

Lee smiled. "You sure?"

"I am." He waved to the waitress who came over and took Lee's order. He asked for the same meal Noah had. Noah wanted to warn him about the coffee, but before he could, Lee ordered orange juice. Good call. "Could you bring me a glass of orange juice too?" he asked the waitress. She nodded, made a note on her pad, and then walked away.

"The coffee is awful," he told Lee. "Wish I'd ordered orange juice from the beginning."

Lee smiled. "I can't drink coffee this late. It would keep me up all night."

Noah sighed. "When we're working a case that takes up so much of my time, no amount of caffeine affects my sleep. Takes a while to build up that kind of resistance, though. I don't recommend it."

The smile slipped from Lee's face. "I'm sorry. You should have told me you were too busy to meet me. The waitress hasn't turned in my order yet. We can cancel it."

Noah felt guilty again. Why had he said that?

"Don't worry about it," he said with a smile. "If I went home now, I probably couldn't sleep anyway." Now that statement was the truth. He'd lie in bed and worry about hurting Lee's feelings. Staying here was the only way to keep his conscience clear. Besides, being completely honest about it, the concentrated coffee sludge really had given him a bit of a rush. Probably not the healthiest way to get his second wind, but it was what it was.

"If you're certain," Lee said. "My apartment building is being fumigated. They sprayed this morning so I can't go back until tomorrow morning. We worked today, and I stayed after we were done so I could clean the mowers. I didn't realize it was this late. I shouldn't have called you. I'm sorry."

Noah glanced at the clock on the wall. A little after nine. Not late for most people. "It's okay, Lee. Really." Noah frowned at him. "What will you do tonight? Do you have someone you can stay with?"

He shook his head. "I'll just sleep in my car. I've done it before. I'm going to park in front of my building. At nine, I can get inside, take a shower, and go back to work." He smiled. "It will be fine."

Noah felt as if he should ask Lee to stay at their house. They had four bedrooms, but one was the home office he shared with Kaely, the guest room was where Erin was staying, and the other room had been turned into a nursery. A little prematurely, but he and Kaely had been convinced she would get pregnant. They planned to finish the basement at some point, but they hadn't had the time yet. Noah had only been accepted at the BAU a little over a year ago. Getting set up after the move had taken some time. Of course, there was the couch, but that wouldn't be very private. He and Kaely got up pretty early. It was then that he remembered they had a folding cot in the basement they could bring upstairs.

"Are you sure?" he heard himself saying. "We have company right now, but we could find a place for you. I have a cot I could put in our office, or we could put you on the couch."

Lee looked unsure. "I . . . I don't think that's necessary, but thank you. Like I said, I've slept in my car before. It's pretty comfortable, and it's not hot outside yet. It's just for one night."

Noah had seen Lee's car. A strong wind would probably

cause it to collapse. It looked as if it was held together by rust instead of metal.

The waitress walked up to the table and handed Lee his pancakes and bacon. Then she put two glasses of orange juice on the table, along with the bill, which she slapped down next to Noah.

"Anything else?" she asked.

Noah shook his head. "Not right now but thank you." As she walked away, Noah took a deep breath. "I'd feel better if you'd stayed with us, Lee. Really."

Lee stared at him for a moment and then shrugged. "You're very kind. I guess I could do that. Thanks, Noah." He frowned. "You mentioned *our* office. You share an office with your wife?"

Noah nodded. "We have four bedrooms. Our room, a guest room, and another room we've turned into a nursery. We're hoping for a baby one of these days. So, my office became *our* office. Kaely helps an author with research for her novels. We each have our own filing cabinets. She uses the office during the day if she needs to, and I use it at night and on the weekends. It might be problematic for some people, but it seems to work okay for us. We really haven't missed having our own space." Noah smiled. "So far our marriage is still intact."

Lee smiled. "That's all that matters."

Noah nodded as he stabbed another bite of his pancakes. He knew Kaely would understand. Still, he felt a little uncomfortable. He probably should have checked with her first. But his wife was the one with the big heart. He felt confident she would have extended the same offer. Lee was a nice guy. Everything would work out fine. Besides, it was just for one night. What could go wrong?

ELEVEN

I drove slowly by the large brick house. Things were progressing perfectly. The last killing was the most important, but they wouldn't realize it for a while. My next step? To shine the spotlight on my mission. My obsession. The world needed to know about me. I was something new. Something different. Even the incredible Kaely Quinn couldn't unmask me, but I looked forward to her attempt. I planned to get close to her—and to Erin. Closer than they could possibly imagine. People would be amazed at how brilliant I'd been. I laughed softly. What was it Sherlock Holmes used to say? The phrase popped into my mind, and I sighed with pleasure. Then I whispered, "The game is afoot."

Kaely and Erin were both in bed when Noah called. Erin was tired after her drive, and Kaely wanted to go over her notes about the case before she went to sleep. She'd grabbed her notebook and propped herself up in bed so she could read through them and add any thoughts that popped into her head. Although Nick had taken his files with him, Kaely could clearly remember what she'd seen. Although they might cause some people nightmares, Kaely was used to the evil that people were capable of. It probably wasn't a good thing, but in her mind, every crime scene was a puzzle waiting to be solved. Agents in the FBI, and especially in the BAU, battled wickedness daily, working hard to bring justice to those who needed it. It was a high calling. Something that God had summoned her and Noah to do. Even though she'd left the BAU because they wanted a baby, and Kaely felt the need to distance herself from the FBI so that could happen, she still liked to keep her head in the game. Working with Erin on her books had provided that for her.

She pushed her notebook away and got out of bed. Mr. Hoover opened one eye to check on her and then went back to sleep. Although he liked to snooze on the bed with them, he wasn't really a cuddler. Once in a while, he'd move closer, but if they tried to pet him too much, or God forbid, attempted to put their arms around him, he'd wiggle out of their grasp and move to the foot of the bed.

Even though tonight wasn't the best time for Lee to stay with them, Kaely agreed with Noah that allowing him to sleep in his car wasn't something they could accept while trying to be good examples of God's love. Helping him was something they felt they had to do.

She walked quietly downstairs, trying not to wake Erin. She looked forward to spending time with her, but she wished it wasn't under these circumstances. Although Erin was a fighter, it was obvious that looking at the photos and reading that awful poem had upset her. Erin was already dealing with a lot in her life. Adding this seemed like too much.

She'd prayed about it. Asked God to ease Erin's burden and keep her safe, both physically and emotionally. Although she hadn't heard His voice, a sense of peace had fallen over her as she'd prayed. Kaely took it as a sign that He would protect Erin and bring something good out of this horror.

When she reached the basement, she turned on the light and was able to quickly find their fold-up cot. It was actually very nice. Thankfully, they'd covered it with a blanket to keep it from getting dusty. She took the blanket off and carried the cot up to Noah's office. Fifteen minutes later, she'd put on sheets and a clean blanket, found a good pillow, and placed it at one end. The cot had a nice, thick pad that helped to make it comfortable. She looked around the room. None of Noah's notes were visible. She wondered for just a second if she should check to make sure his filing cabinet was locked. Although he wasn't allowed to bring files home from the BAU, he did make notes about his cases. He was pretty careful about keeping them locked up, so she decided not to worry about it. Besides, he had the only key with him, so there wasn't much she could do anyway. If it wasn't locked, he'd probably take care of it when he got home.

She left the office and went into the bathroom across the hall. She put out fresh towels and washrags. She also removed a fresh bar of soap from under the sink and put it on the counter, next to the bottle of hand soap. Lee might not want to take a shower, but just in case, he'd have what he needed. After she was satisfied that she'd done everything she could, she went back to their bedroom. She didn't know Lee very well, but if Noah felt okay having him stay in their house, she wasn't worried. Besides, she and Noah were trained agents and could handle themselves. After thinking about it, though, she got up, went to the closet, and unlocked the case that held her gun. She could have felt guilty, but she didn't. Being prepared was second nature to her and to Noah. It didn't mean she didn't trust Lee. It just meant that her training told her to always be ready for any potential problems. She sent Erin a quick text to let her know Lee was staying the night. They probably wouldn't run into each other, since the guest room was downstairs, and she used a different bathroom. However, she felt it was a good idea to let Erin know there was someone she didn't know in the house.

After that, she crawled back into bed, grabbed her notebook, and began to go over each murder in her mind, trying to find something that would make sense to her. This killer needed to be stopped before anyone else died.

After talking to Lee for about an hour, they finally left the restaurant and headed home. Noah was so tired he could barely think. When they reached the house, Lee parked his car in the driveway next to Noah's SUV. They went inside, and Noah took him into his office where Kaely had already set up the cot. He was grateful he didn't have to do it.

"It's actually pretty comfortable," he said to Lee.

"Looks great," Lee responded. "You have a beautiful home."

Noah felt a little guilty when he compared his home with Lee's gloomy place. Was Lee comparing his life to Noah's? Did he resent him? Noah hoped not, but if Lee did, he could understand it.

"Kaely said she put some fresh towels and soap in the bathroom if you want to take a shower. Is there anything else you need? How about something to drink? Soda? A bottle of water?"

"Water would be great," Lee said. "Again, I can't thank you enough."

"Seriously, it's nothing."

Lee looked down at the floor. When he looked up, Noah was surprised to see tears in his eyes. "I didn't used to think God was real. I told you about my father. How he always told me that only feeble-minded people believe in some kind of old man in the sky. He was a mean, mean human being. But you and Kaely have shown me who God is. He's someone who acts like you." He held out his hand. "You've made me believe. Thank you, Noah."

Now it was Noah's turn to get emotional. Here he was worrying about how tired he was, while God was using him to touch another human being with His love.

"You're very welcome," he said, shaking Lee's hand. "I'm happy we're friends. You've blessed me too." He couldn't think of anything else to say, so he just nodded and left the room, feeling embarrassed for only thinking about himself instead of realizing how much God was reaching out to a man who really needed Him.

He went downstairs to the kitchen, grabbed a cold bottle of water from the refrigerator, and then took it to Lee, who accepted it gratefully. Then he walked down the hall and opened his bedroom door, expecting to see Kaely sound asleep. But instead, she was sitting up in bed, scribbling in her notebook.

"What's going on?" he asked as he leaned down and kissed her.

"Just going over the murders," she said after she returned his kiss.

Noah took off his clothes, hung them up, and then pulled on his sweats and a T-shirt. "How's Erin doing?"

"I think she's freaked out," Kaely said. "I mean, wouldn't you be? She writes a book, and a serial killer uses it to murder someone? That would severely upset anyone."

Noah sat down on the edge of the bed. "I hear you." He sighed. "Full house tonight. Thanks for letting Lee stay here. He was willing to sleep in his car, but I just couldn't let him do it."

"You did the right thing. I wish we knew him a little better, though."

Noah sighed. "He told me tonight that he's learning to believe in God because of the love we've shown him. I really haven't spent that much time with him. Hard to believe that so little effort impacted him this much."

"I'm so proud of you, Noah," Kaely said, her eyes shiny with emotion.

"Well, don't be." He pulled the covers down and slid between the sheets. "At the restaurant, I was thinking about how tired I was, not how important it was to help him."

"What a shock," Kaely said, laughing lightly. "You found out that you're human?"

"Or selfish."

"You're not the least bit selfish, my dear husband," Kaely said gently. "You're just tired. Get some sleep."

Those were the last words Noah heard before he drifted off.

Lee listened at the door, waiting until he couldn't hear them talking anymore. Then he took a small flashlight from his pocket and began searching Noah's office carefully. When he tried the drawers to the filing cabinets, he was surprised to find them unlocked. He put the flashlight in his mouth and began to look through the files. When he finally found what he was searching for, he removed the papers from the file, laid them on the desk, and took pictures of each page. Then he returned them to the filing cabinet. After that, he put the flashlight, and his phone, back in his jacket pocket and lay down on the cot. It really was comfortable. He smiled as he waited for sleep to come.

TWELVE

Erin woke up early, disturbed by a weird dream that didn't make much sense. She'd been searching for something. In the dream she kept opening doors. Some of them were at the cabin and some of them here, in Kaely's house. But every time she looked behind the doors, nothing was there. Most of them opened into closets even though she knew they belonged to actual rooms like her bedroom at the cabin and the door to the office she'd set up. Another one was connected to a bathroom, and another was the front door of her apartment in St. Louis. A few of the rooms or closets were empty, but some of them were packed with junk. She recognized most of the items, but some she didn't. Her police uniform was there, along with her badge. Not hard to figure that out, but another door held things from her childhood. What was that about? Was it saying she hadn't dealt with her parents' deaths? She thought she had. A long time ago. She tried to push the images of the dream out of her head. She was still tired. The dream had made her restless and deprived her of sleep. Unfortunately, she was probably going to the command center today. This wasn't the day to be fatigued. But no matter how she felt, she'd have to push through and do whatever was required of her.

She finally got out of bed, went down the hall for a quick shower, and then dressed and headed toward the kitchen. She found Kaely sitting at the table.

"You could have slept longer," she said as Erin entered the room. "I hope I didn't wake you."

Erin shook her head. "You didn't. I had a weird dream and woke up trying to figure out what it meant. At least it wasn't a nightmare."

"Want to tell me about it?"

Erin shrugged. "I think most of it was obvious, but other parts have me stumped." She went over the dream while Kaely got her a cup of coffee.

"Not too hard to understand," she said when Erin finished.

After handing her the cup, Kaely sat down next to her. "You still have things hidden in closets that need to be cleaned out. No matter what door you open, hoping to get somewhere, those things are still there, blocking you."

Erin took a sip of coffee and frowned at her friend. "That makes sense. I'm doing a lot better since we were together in November, but I guess I still have work to do."

"But it appears your subconscious is aware of it, and that's a good thing."

"Yeah, but what about the room with things from my childhood? What does that have to do with anything?"

Kaely smiled. "I think it means that there's still pain from losing your parents, but you suspected that, didn't you?"

Erin sighed. "I guess. I really thought I was past it. It was terrible, but that was a long time ago."

"Truthfully, my friend? I think that situation began a pattern of pain in your life. That's probably when you learned to shut the things that hurt you behind mental doors because they were too upsetting to deal with."

Erin nodded. "I'm sure you're right." She smiled at Kaely. "What would I do without your insight . . . and your friendship?"

"God would have sent someone else. Erin, it isn't me. It's Him working through me. I hope that at some point you'll believe that."

Erin smiled. "I'm beginning to. Thanks for not pushing me."

"You're welcome." Kaely stood up. "Now, what can I get you for breakfast?"

"Cereal's fine. What kind do you have?"

Kaely grinned. "Sorry, my friend. No cereal this morning. You can have pancakes, waffles, scrambled eggs, or an omelet, along with bacon or sausage. Your choice."

Erin laughed. "For a second, I was afraid you wanted me to eat all of that. Whew!"

"I love you, but I don't even cook like that for Noah."

Erin was silent for a moment. Then, she met Kaely's gaze. "I love you too, you know."

Kaely's eyes filled with tears. "That means more to me than I can say." She grabbed a paper towel from a holder on the kitchen counter and wiped her eyes. "Now, before we both get too weepy, what are you hungry for?"

Erin sighed. "Oh my. How about scrambled eggs and bacon? I eat cereal at home so that would be a real treat."

"Coming right up."

"Hey, how did Nick's wife die?" Erin asked.

Kaely went to the refrigerator and opened it. She removed a carton of eggs and set them down on the counter. When she turned around, Erin could see the sorrow on her face. "She committed suicide," Kaely said. "She was a friend, and it was so hard to accept. Deanne seemed like such a happy person. I still can't understand it, but I learned that some people who are severely depressed hide behind a cheerful facade." She sighed. "The signs were all there. Noah and I used to talk about how she was always happy. No one is cheerful all the time—not unless something's wrong."

"That's so sad. Nick seems like a great guy."

Kaely nodded. "He is. He was devastated by her death. He's still having a hard time dealing with it." She turned around and started making breakfast.

As Erin took another sip of coffee, a man walked into the room. Erin was certain it wasn't Noah since she'd seen pictures of him.

Kaely, who was getting a pan out of one of her cabinets noticed him too. She smiled at him. "Hi, Lee. How about some breakfast?"

"I really appreciate that, but I need to go home and get ready for work. We were told we could get back into our apartments this morning."

"Lee is a friend of ours from church," Kaely said to Erin. She swung her gaze back to him. "Lee, this is my friend, Erin Delaney. Erin, Lee Johnson. He stayed here last night while his apartment was being fumigated."

"Nice to meet you, Lee," Erin said.

"You too." He nodded at her.

Erin couldn't help but notice that he seemed a little nervous. He wasn't maintaining eye contact and kept glancing toward the front door. She chided herself. She was too suspicious. Maybe he was just a little shy.

"Thank you for letting me stay," he told Kaely. "Will you also thank Noah for me?"

"Sure." Kaely frowned at him. "Are you certain your apartment is safe now?"

His head bobbed up and down. "The landlord is letting everyone back in this morning. I doubt if he'd do that unless it was okay." His smile was tight. "He probably doesn't want to poison us. He'd lose our rent."

Kaely laughed. "Good point."

"Bye. I'll see you Sunday morning."

He walked quickly to the door, opened it, and left.

"He seemed a little jumpy, didn't he?" Erin asked.

"I think he's just a little insecure. He's new to our church. He has a hard time making friends. Noah's been mentoring him."

"That's nice of him." She smiled at Kaely. "Is that what you're doing with me? Mentoring me?"

Kaely pointed her spatula at Erin. "You're my friend, not my project. Yes, I want you to know how much God loves you, but whether or not you give your life to Him, you will still be my friend. Does that answer your question?"

"Yeah, it does. Thank you." She hesitated a moment, wanting to ask a question, but not ready for any kind of commitment. Not yet, anyway. She decided to take a chance that Kaely would understand. She took a deep breath and said, "Kaely, I've known some religious people. When I was on the force, one guy was always trying to *save* me. When I told him to knock it off, he turned his back on me. Yet you love me no matter what I do. Is that how God loves us?" Her voice broke, and it embarrassed her, but she'd never met anyone like Kaely before. The way she presented God was different. Was it really possible that God could love her, no matter what she'd done? It was a hard concept to understand. How could a holy God overlook . . . unholiness?

Kaely took her frying pan off the burner and came over to the table. She sat down next to Erin and took her hand. "The answer is yes. That's how God loves us. He offers that same love to the worst person on earth. In fact, He loves every single one of us so much that He sent His Son to pay for the sins of every human being who ever lived. Jesus went to the cross so that we could come into the presence of a holy God and call Him Father. When we accept the free gift God gave us, our mistakes are all forgiven. Past, present, and future. We become His precious children, and He promises to never leave us or give up on us. God gave us the greatest gift ever given to mankind. All we have to do is accept it."

"Couldn't He have done it without Jesus going to the cross? Seems kind of cruel."

"That's a good question, Erin. I could talk about the Old Testament and the sacrifices for sin back then, but let me answer it like this. God is holy. Perfect. To come to Him, we must be holy too. Here's an analogy you should understand. When you were a cop, what happened when you arrested someone for a serious crime? A felony?"

"Well, he'd be put in jail, then eventually, he'd go before a judge for sentencing."

Kaely nodded. "Exactly. Say the judge sentenced him to life in prison, but someone stepped up and said, 'Judge, I'm here to serve his sentence.' The judge might say, 'But he's guilty. Why would you do that?' The answer would be, 'Because I love him.'"

"I doubt that any judge would allow that, but I get the point."

Kaely's example hit home. She'd arrested several people who, in her opinion, should never see the light of day again. It was hard for her to accept that they could . . . or should . . . be forgiven. She realized that Kaely wasn't saying hardened criminals should be released back on the streets. Man's laws might not allow that, but God seemed to work outside the boundaries set by human beings.

"In this case, of course, jail . . . or punishment . . . is being compared to eternal judgment," Kaely said. "Hell."

"How could a God who loves everyone send someone to hell?"

Kaely got up and went back to the stove where she put her pan back on the burner. After stirring the eggs a couple of times, she spooned some onto a plate. She carried it over and put it in front of Erin. "God doesn't send anyone to hell, Erin. He gave everything He had to keep all of us out of there. We decide to accept His incredible gift—or reject it."

Erin didn't say anything, but what Kaely said made sense. Was she really thinking seriously about going all the way with this God thing? A belief she'd sworn she'd never fall for?

THIRTEEN

Erin was just finishing breakfast when Noah came into the kitchen. He was tall, with dark, wavy hair and gray-blue eyes. He smiled when he saw her.

"I finally get to meet my wife's famous friend," he said. "We're glad you're here, but I wish it were for a better reason."

"Nice to meet you," Erin said. "You're right. It would be nicer if we were just getting together for the fun of it. I really hope you guys catch this UNSUB before anyone else dies."

"I do too." He walked over to Kaely and kissed her. "My wife is as good as it gets when it comes to writing a profile. With her help—and yours—I'm praying he'll be arrested soon."

"I know you can't share certain things with us," Erin said, "but can I ask how your profile is coming along?"

Noah poured a cup of coffee and sat down at the table. His deep sigh made it clear he was frustrated. "Well, we've determined that he's male. As you know, most serial killers are. Since the victims are women and were overpowered, this also points to a man. But beyond that, this one's tough.

He's different. Copying murders from novels? It may have worked well on TV, but in real life, serial killers just don't do that. They may get an idea from a book or movie, but their ego forces them to add a signature. A slightly different MO. Of course, we have the poems, but that's not really a signature. What we don't know is why he's killing. What is he angry about? What's driving him? Unless he just hates authors . . . or mystery novels." He shook his head. "What do our field agents and the police look for?" He smiled at her. "Any wonderful insight that will blow this case wide open?"

Erin laughed. "No, sorry. Besides, your wife is the one who has the talent. I'm afraid I'm just someone who walks in her shadow, hoping some of her brilliance will infect me."

It was Kaely's turn to laugh. "I think you just made me sound like a disease."

Noah grinned at her and put his hand on his chest. "Sounds about right. You make me sick . . . with love."

Erin giggled, and Kaely stuck her tongue out at him. "Hush up," she said. "Now Erin knows how corny you are." She grabbed a plate from the cabinet and put some food on it. Then she brought it to him.

"Thank you," he said.

Kaely bent down and kissed him. Then she went back to get his coffee.

Erin was impressed with them. It was obvious they really loved each other. She could not only see it—she could actually feel it. She was extremely happy for Kaely, but she couldn't help but wonder if she would ever experience love like that. Suddenly, Adrian's face flashed in her mind, and it startled her. She liked him, but they were just friends . . . right?

"Erin, while you're here, I'd love to invite a friend over to meet you," Kaely said. "Maybe for lunch. She's writing a book, and I've been helping her some. She's not published yet, but when I told her I knew you, she was really excited." Kaely held her hand up. "She's not the type of person to ask you for favors—in fact—Shannon's just the opposite. But she really admires you, and I think you'd like her too. Is it okay if I put that together?"

"I guess so," Erin said. "I suppose if you trust her, I'm okay with it."

Erin didn't really want to meet this friend who wanted help getting published. It wasn't something she could do, and most writers didn't understand that. But if it mattered to Kaely, she was willing to do it. She owed her so much.

Erin noticed that Kaely wanted to invite Shannon to her house rather than meet her somewhere else. Kaely had always encouraged Erin to get out of her house as a way to combat her agoraphobia. Was this another sign that Kaely was worried about Erin's safety? She realized investigators weren't sure if the authors were at risk, but was there something Kaely knew that she wasn't telling her? It made her a little nervous. Yet Kaely had always been honest with her. Maybe she was just feeling a little paranoid. Knowing that a serial killer had picked her book as a blueprint for murder had turned her life upside down. It was hard to know what to think.

"I need to get dressed," Kaely said. "Meet you back here in about fifteen minutes? Then we can talk more about the case if you'd like."

Erin nodded. "Sure. I've got to get ready too." She got up and started to leave the kitchen, but she stopped before she reached the doorway and turned around to look at Noah. "Kaely told me once that the first murder a serial killer commits is usually the most important one. I'm sure you've considered that."

Noah nodded. "We have, but so far, there's no rhyme or reason to his choices. We couldn't find anything or anyone connected to the writer, Dan Harper, that helped us. Doesn't mean it's not there." He put his coffee cup down. "Obviously, in the group of victims, there's one that was targeted for a reason. The police and the FBI are working hard to find it." He frowned. "Investigators want to talk to you. Kaely told you that, right?"

"Yeah. Do you know when?"

"I heard it was today, but I'm not sure." Noah shook his head. "They know you're staying with us. I assume they'll call me to make arrangements."

As if on cue, Noah's phone rang. He frowned and took it out of his pocket. "Hunter," he said. After listening for a few seconds, he rubbed his forehead and sighed. "Great. Not that we weren't expecting this, but I'd hoped it would take longer. Any idea where the leak came from?" He was silent as he listened to the person on the other end. "Okay. Thanks. Do you want me to come in now?" Another pause. Then he said, "See you soon." He hung up and looked at Kaely. "Well, we knew the media would get the story eventually, but it's out now. A news station in Richmond is reporting on it. The FBI is wondering if one of the authors leaked it to draw attention to their book."

Erin put her hands up in the air. "It wasn't me. You can check my phone and my laptop."

Noah smiled at her. "Relax. I know it wasn't you. Although,

don't be offended if the investigator you talk to at the command center requests those devices."

"I won't be offended. They may be a little bored, though. Not much happening in my life that would raise suspicions." She frowned. "Except my internet searches. When you write edgy suspense . . . Uh, oh."

Noah laughed. "I get it. Don't worry. I suspect my wife's laptop has lots of suspicious searches too." His face turned pink. "I . . . I mean about murder . . . you know."

His embarrassed expression made them both laugh.

"Don't worry, honey," Kaely said. "The only studs I look up would be horses or dogs. No actual men. You're the only stud for me."

As Erin giggled, Noah shook his head. "Not sure why you'd be looking up anything about horses or dogs either."

Kaely laughed lightly as Noah walked over to the kitchen counter and picked up a remote. He pointed it at a TV mounted on the wall in the living room. The open concept made it visible in the kitchen. He clicked a button, and the TV came on. A woman stood in front of a large brick building, doors behind her, with three large brick pillars holding up the roof over the entrance.

"That's the local police station," Kaely said.

Noah turned up the sound.

"We've learned that there may be a serial killer targeting Virginia women," the reporter said. "Allegedly, the killer is using plots from popular novels as a guide to carry out these murders. We've reached out to the police for clarification, but so far, all we've heard back is 'no comment.' We'll report any further information as soon as we receive it."

The scene switched back to a game show, and Noah turned off the TV. "Great," he muttered.

"Well, maybe this will help to make people safer," Erin said. "Women will be on guard."

"Or, it will cause the killer to lay low so we can't catch him," Noah said, his tone gruff.

"Hopefully, they won't discover the location of the command center," Erin said.

"They will, trust me," Noah said. "It happens quite a bit with high-profile cases. If someone involved in the investigation doesn't leak it, a reporter will follow one of our officers or agents to the site. We'll just start releasing daily updates to the media. That way we can control the dialogue."

"Control the dialogue?" Erin repeated.

Noah nodded. "We don't want the wrong information getting out. Trust me, our UNSUB will be watching. The last thing we need is to give him a heads-up as to where we are with the investigation. The other worry is that copycats will try to mimic our UNSUB's killings."

"That's scary."

"It happens more often than you might think," Kaely said. "If the task force can control the narrative, they have the chance to save lives."

"So, will you try to find out how the press got hold of the story?" Erin asked Noah.

"Well, *I* won't. That's not my job. But investigators might. If they have a leak, they need to find out who it is and plug it up. Psychopaths are narcissistic and love attention." He sighed. "Whoever leaked the story did him a favor. Investigators may need to find out why it happened and make certain our mole isn't connected to the killer. They will also have to find out how much they told him. If he knows what we know, it will make it much harder to stop him."

Erin didn't say anything, but as Noah left the room, his words only added to the apprehension she felt about the killer and his deadly reach.

FOURTEEN

Noah called not long after leaving the house to let Kaely know that Erin would be interviewed later in the afternoon at the command center.

"You're supposed to meet with the lead investigator at three o'clock," Kaely said after she hung up the phone. She could see that Erin was nervous about the appointment. Kaely had hoped Erin would have at least a day to relax before going to the center, but maybe getting it over quickly was for the best.

"You sure it's okay if Shannon joins us for lunch?" Kaely asked. "We can put it off if you want to. If it makes any difference, I think you two will hit it off. You're a lot alike."

"As long as she doesn't pressure me to find her an agent or a publisher, it's fine. You have no idea how many times people have emailed me or sent me letters asking for help. I can give her advice, but I can't do more than that. And I don't endorse books. For anyone. If I do it for one person, I'd be overwhelmed with requests."

"Don't get your panties in a bunch," Kaely said, grinning. "I don't think she would do anything that might make you uncomfortable. All Shannon wants is advice. She has no intention of asking you for a thing. Except for one favor."

Erin sighed. "Big surprise. What's the favor?"

"She wants you to sign her copy of your book."

Erin shook her head. "Well, I walked right into that one." She took a sip from her coffee cup and then set it down. "Sorry for being so crabby. I know you'd never put me in an awkward situation. I'm just sensitive about this kind of thing. The requests are overwhelming sometimes."

"I can understand that." Kaely leaned down to slide their plates into the dishwasher. "Believe it or not, I've been asked to sign a few copies of your book. I am mentioned in the acknowledgments, after all." She straightened up, patted her curly hair, and sniffed. "It's hard to stay modest when you're famous."

"If it wouldn't make a mess, I'd throw my coffee cup at you," Erin said, laughing.

"I'd make you clean it up, so it's a good thing you rethought that."

Erin picked up her dishes and carried them over to the sink. She rinsed them and handed them to Kaely.

"Thanks," she said, "but you don't need to help with anything. I want you to rest while you're here."

"Because it takes so much effort for me to sit around my cabin and write? Have you ever heard of writer's derriere?"

Kaely shook her head. "I think I can figure out where this is going, though."

Erin handed her a glass. "Yeah, not hard to understand. That's why I try to take Chester out for a walk every day. It helps both of us."

Kaely put the glass in the dishwasher. "You mean that walk you take with Chester and Chief Nightengale?"

"Well, yes." Erin shook her head. "I told you there's nothing going on between us. I'm not interested in Adrian Nightengale." She rinsed off a small plate and held it out.

"You can deny it all you want, but I saw the way you looked at him . . . and the way he looks at you."

Erin sighed. "If I wasn't certain you don't drink, I'd accuse you of being inebriated."

"Funny."

Erin had just rinsed off another plate when her phone rang. She wiped off her wet hands and pulled her cell phone out of the pocket of her jeans.

"You've got to be kidding," she said. "It's Adrian. You don't have this house wired, do you?"

"I'll never tell."

Erin smiled and shook her head. "Hello?" she said, into her phone. She walked into the living room.

Kaely went back to loading the dishwasher, trying to give Erin some privacy. Adrian was a good man. She was praying that Erin could overcome the trauma she'd been through. But until that happened, the possibility of a romantic relationship with anyone was improbable. Besides, Adrian was a Christian. She doubted he would consider becoming serious with anyone who wasn't. However, she could see that Erin was beginning to open up to the possibility of allowing God into her life. She needed Him. She needed Him desperately. All Kaely could do was to keep praying and say whatever she could without making Erin feel like she was hounding her. It was the Holy Spirit's job to draw Erin to faith. She'd made that mistake before—trying to do the Spirit's job. It usually didn't go well. She had no intention of messing things up this time.

She finished loading the dishwasher while Erin talked to Adrian in the other room. She'd just started it when Erin came back, a puzzled look on her face.

"Something wrong?" Kaely asked.

"I don't know. Adrian said my lights came on a little after nine last night. I programmed them to come on at six."

"Maybe it's just a glitch?" Kaely asked.

"It's possible. Or I did something wrong. I mean, it's my first time setting it up. Adrian checked things out. Everything looked fine inside. I guess if anyone had tried to enter my house, the alarm would have gone off and notified the alarm company."

"I'm sure it's okay," Kaely said. "If someone was trying to rob you, Adrian would have probably seen evidence of it. And like you said, a thief would have triggered the alarm."

"It's not like I keep stacks of money in my house," Erin said. "And almost all of the other stuff belonged to Steve. I'm pretty sure he didn't leave anything in the cabin that was really valuable."

Kaely nodded. "Okay, as long as you're not concerned about it, how about we get out of the house for a while? We could take Chester for a walk. He can work off some energy, and we can work on that writer's derriere."

Erin laughed. "That sounds good. I'd like to see a little more of Fredericksburg."

"There's a small park not too far away. Why don't we go there? There's a coffee shop across the street that makes great cappuccino. We'll grab some and then go to the park."

"Sounds great," Erin said. "Give me a couple of minutes to change my shoes."

"Sure. I'll feed Mr. Hoover and meet you back here."

As Erin headed toward the guest room, Chester hot on her heels after hearing the word "walk," Kaely went upstairs to her bedroom, put on a T-shirt, her holster, and then another shirt over that. She took down a box from the top shelf in her closet and removed her Glock. She slid it into the holster and then buttoned the top shirt to hide her gun. She didn't want to worry Erin, but until they knew exactly what they were dealing with, she was going to err on the side of caution. Although she'd feel better keeping Erin inside, she knew it wasn't fair to her friend. She felt okay going to the park since it was close by, and they wouldn't stay long at the coffee shop. If Kaely saw anything that concerned her, she'd get Erin back to the house. She'd suggested Shannon have lunch here because staying too long at a restaurant concerned her. If they started talking, it could make Erin an easy target. She and Noah had agreed to do whatever it took to keep Erin safe. Maybe this was overkill, but Kaely didn't plan on taking any chances with Erin's life.

FIFTEEN

Erin enjoyed her walk with Chester and Kaely. Fredericksburg was a lovely town. The houses in Kaely's area were so nice, and the park was beautiful. Chester made friends with a small white poodle named Frenchie and a large black lab whose name was Harvey.

When they arrived back at Kaely's house, Erin changed clothes and prepared for lunch with Kaely's friend, Shannon. Although she wasn't comfortable with people fawning over her because of her book, she sought reassurance in the knowledge that Kaely wasn't the kind of person who would allow someone like that to get next to Erin.

She was still a little nervous about her meeting with an investigator about the murder mirroring her book. The same thoughts kept rolling over and over in her mind. Did they suspect she was involved? Was she really in danger? Kaely had obviously felt they were safe taking a walk this morning, but Erin had noticed that she kept looking around them. Checking out the area. And she'd brought her gun along, although she'd obviously tried to hide it. If she wasn't worried, why was she armed?

Erin tried to stay positive. Being deputized and going inside a command center for a joint task force was actually pretty exciting. Fodder for future books. She realized she'd just had a thought about more books. Was she actually considering a future as a writer? *Dark Matters* was written just as a way to channel her love of law enforcement into something besides the job she'd left behind. The new book was written because she needed the money, and the publisher paid her a very nice advance. Truth be told, she really did enjoy writing it. Sometimes she wondered if she knew her own mind. One minute she couldn't see herself as an author, and other times she couldn't see herself doing anything else. Her dream of joining the BAU was still there, but working with Kaely and meeting Noah gave her an inside look at the life of a behavioral analyst without the responsibility of the job. She actually enjoyed the feeling of freedom she had now. When she was a cop, she was under someone else's command. Her life wasn't her own. Now, she had time to take walks with Chester and Adrian and spend time in her cabin just enjoying life. How could she go back to work and leave Chester behind? She loved sharing her life with him. She wasn't sure she'd trade that for anything.

She stared at her image in the bathroom mirror. She really wasn't sure what she wanted. Hopefully, at some point, her life would make sense. For now, she was just putting one foot in front of the other. Day by day. That's all she could handle.

She ran a brush through her hair, took a deep breath, and headed toward the living room. *Was Shannon here yet?* Erin had already decided to be as nice as possible to the woman. She was Kaely's friend, and the last thing she wanted to do was to offend either one of them.

She came around the corner, her smile already firmly in place. Hopefully, she looked natural. Her fake smile tended to look as if she had an upset stomach.

"Hello there," Kaely said. She was in the kitchen. A woman sat at the table. She had dark hair pulled into a sloppy bun with curly tendrils framing her face. She wore glasses—the kind of cool glasses Erin would choose if she ever needed them. Big and light pink. They seemed to be just for looks since the lenses appeared to be plain glass. Most people wouldn't notice, but Erin did. She'd just read an article that said some people who didn't need glasses were buying them as a fashion accessory. Erin thought it was silly, but truthfully, they looked great on Shannon.

"Erin, this is Shannon Burke."

"Nice to meet you," Erin said.

"I hope you don't feel pressured into this," Shannon said. "I told Kaely I didn't want to bother you."

"It's no bother." Erin hoped her tone sounded sincere. She really didn't mean what she'd just said.

"Sit down," Kaely said with a smile.

Erin pulled out a chair across from Shannon. Kaely had placed a beautiful spinach and cheese quiche on the table, along with a fruit salad, potato wedges, and blueberry muffins.

"Kaely, this looks delicious," Erin said. "Why didn't you let me help you? You obviously put a lot of work into this."

Kaely shook her head. "I'd already prepared the quiche, just had to pop it in the oven. The potatoes were frozen. Again, a few minutes in the oven. The fruit salad was easy, and although I'd like to take credit for the muffins, they came from a local bakery. Not much you could have done to help, but thank you anyway."

"It looks and smells amazing," Shannon said.

"I have coffee, tea, and caramel cappuccino," Kaely said to Erin. "Shannon asked for cappuccino."

"I highly recommend it," Shannon said.

"I'd love a cappuccino."

Kaely popped a pod into the single-cup brew machine that sat next to her regular coffeemaker. While it made the cappuccino, Erin studied Shannon. Besides being attractive, she wore her clothing well. Not designer pieces, but stylish and perfect for her body type. She was tall and willowy, relaxed, and she exuded confidence. She wasn't what Erin had expected. Although she worked hard to keep some distance between her and her readers, at the few public events she'd agreed to do under duress, those who approached her about their writing dreams had seemed rather frantic . . . and a little frightened of her. Erin wanted to be more social and hospitable toward people, but the trauma from her last days on the job had created strong emotional walls. Although they were there to protect her, she'd been using them to keep almost everyone out. The problem was, she had no idea how to change. How to become the kind of person she would like to be. Fear had made her a prisoner and caused her to become someone she didn't really like.

"I loved *Dark Matters*," Shannon said, breaking the awkward silence.

Erin smiled at her, hoping it was her sincere smile. Not the stomachache one. "Thank you. Kaely tells me you're a writer too."

Shannon's cheeks reddened. "I really don't want to bother you with questions or ask you for advice. Kaely is a lovely person, but if she made you think I planned to pressure you for some kind of favor . . ."

"No, she didn't do that."

"I only told Erin that she might be able to steer you in the right direction," Kaely said as she put a cup of cappuccino in front of Erin. "I've read some of her work, and it's very good." She sat down at the table. "For now, let's have lunch, and you two can get to know each other. We'll talk about writing when we're done. Sound okay?"

Shannon mumbled her assent. Erin could see that she was still uncomfortable about the situation, and Erin felt compassion for her.

"Tell me about yourself," Erin said. "How did you and Kaely meet?"

They spent the next hour eating the delicious lunch Kaely had prepared while chitchatting about Fredericksburg and how Shannon and Kaely met at a local coffee shop. Kaely had been carrying a copy of *Dark Matters* and Shannon had remarked to her how much she liked Erin's book. One thing led to another, and the two became friends. Erin was glad to see Shannon start to relax. She was a little jealous of the easy relationship the two women had.

Kaely had just brewed two more cups of cappuccino when Erin's phone rang. Brandon.

"I'm sorry," she said. "I need to take this." She glanced at her watch. "What time do we need to leave?" she asked Kaely.

"Not for another couple of hours," she replied. "You have plenty of time. You can go into the living room if this is a private conversation."

Erin wasn't sure how much that would help since the open floor plan didn't provide much privacy, but it probably wasn't important. She was fairly certain Brandon was just going to ask her if her manuscript would be turned in by the deadline.

He was concerned about her career, and rightly so, but she still wished he'd stop calling about it. The book was finished, but she needed more time for the edits. She intended to make the deadline.

Erin sat down in a chair next to the fireplace. It was the farthest point away from the kitchen she could find. She said "Hello" and waited for Brandon to greet her. He usually tried to sound upbeat unless he was asking questions about her deadline. When she heard his voice, she immediately knew something was wrong. He got right to the point.

"Erin, do you know someone named Christine Dell?"

"Yeah, I do. She's the manager of the lake that I used as a setting in *Dark Matters*. I needed a place to put a body, and I wanted to know if someone could access that lake after hours. She answered my questions and even gave me some helpful suggestions. I mentioned her briefly in my acknowledgments. Why?"

"She's the one I mentioned to you during our last call—the one who says you stole her story. She's planning to sue you, Erin. She says she has proof that the story is hers, and she also has information about the book you're working on now. She claims you stole that idea from her as well." Brandon paused for a moment while Erin tried to digest what she'd just heard.

Finally, she said, "That's ridiculous, Brandon. I might have spent ten minutes on the phone with her, and she emailed me a couple of times. That's it. How could she have *proof* that I stole the book from her. It's impossible."

"I'm not sure yet," Brandon said, "but the publisher is worried, and so is their attorney. Claims like this can catch fire, even if the allegations aren't true. There are individuals out there who harbor resentment toward anyone they believe is successful, especially if they're not. They like to spread stories like this. It's exciting to them. Publishers have been paying people like Dell off for years. They will probably try to do that in this case."

"I'm telling you, Brandon, it's a lie. I don't want them to give her one red cent. I mean it."

He sighed. "Look, don't worry yet. I'll dig a little deeper. Whatever you do, don't talk to anyone about this. Especially online or in the media. Do you understand?"

"Yeah, I . . . I guess so."

"Listen, Erin," Brandon said. "This isn't going away anytime soon. If we can't prove she's lying and she does go to the media, it could ruin everything you've worked so hard for."

SIXTEEN

After checking in with the owner of the local resort, Merle Hubbard, who once again wanted to lodge a complaint against a customer who'd taken all the towels from their room, Adrian decided to run by Erin's cabin again. The problem with the lights still bothered him. He planned to return to the cabin a little before six that evening to see if the lights came on when they were supposed to, but for now, he just wanted to make sure everything was all right. Although it seemed like a minor problem, something inside him just wouldn't let it go.

He was almost there when Jake started to whine. Adrian pulled his Jeep over, put a leash on him, and let him out. He realized he hadn't been outside since early that morning.

"Sorry, boy," he said as he followed the golden retriever into the woods where he immediately lifted his leg and relieved himself. Although he tried to fight the urge, Adrian's eyes shifted toward an area in the woods where two people died a few months earlier. Memories of the serial killer who preyed on innocent women fought for a place in his mind, but he pushed them away. Right now, he wanted to concentrate on Erin's cabin. Rehashing evil wouldn't help with that.

He was taken off guard when Jake pulled on the leash, letting Adrian know he was finished and they could go back to the Jeep.

A few moments later, they arrived at Erin's. When Adrian pulled up in front of the cabin, he looked carefully at the front of the structure. Everything seemed okay, but he decided to get out and look a little closer. He wanted to make sure the cabin was secure and that the problem with the lights was a fluke.

"Stay here," he said to Jake, who barked and stood up in his seat. "No," Adrian said in a stern voice. Jake wanted to go everywhere with him. In Jake's mind, asking him to stay in the car was a form of torture. Adrian couldn't help but laugh at the expression on his dog's face. "I'll be right back," he said. He got out of the Jeep and closed the door behind him. He could hear Jake's barking, but he just ignored it.

He walked up to the front door and checked it. Locked. He decided to walk around the cabin to make sure everything was secure. Maybe he was being overzealous, but his gut urged him to go the extra mile. During all the years he'd spent in law enforcement, he'd learned to trust his instincts.

He could still hear Jake's displeasure at being locked in the Jeep as he headed around the back side of the cabin. He looked through each window, but all of them were covered by shades or curtains. However, he could see into the living room from the double glass doors that led outside to the patio. He stared closely at the door handles and noticed scratch marks around the doorknobs. Someone had tried to open these doors. He took out his phone and started to take pictures when he heard a noise behind him. Before he had time to turn around, pain exploded in his head, and the world went black.

Erin tried to enjoy the delicious lunch Kaely had prepared, but she couldn't get Brandon's phone call out of her head. She hadn't known him long, but in all the time they'd been together, she'd never heard him sound as worried as he had just now. He was clearly troubled, and now, so was she.

She made an effort to join in the conversation, but it was difficult. Kaely looked at her and frowned.

"Shannon, can you give us a moment?" she said. Then she stood up and gestured for Erin to follow her.

"I'm sorry," Kaely said to Shannon. "We'll be right back."

Although Shannon looked a little confused, she smiled. "Sure," she said.

Erin went into the living room and found Kaely in the hallway that led to the guest bedroom.

"Okay, what's wrong?" Kaely asked as Erin walked up to her.

"We shouldn't leave Shanonn waiting alone," Erin said. "It's rude."

"We'll make it up to her. I've known you a while. I've never seen you react like that to a phone call. Tell me what just happened."

"It's probably nothing," Erin said slowly.

"You wouldn't be this upset if it was nothing." Kaely frowned at her. "You trust me, don't you?"

Erin sighed and leaned against the wall. "Of course I do.

To be honest, I'm just trying to process the situation." She repeated what Brandon had told her.

"Oh, Erin. It's a scam. I've heard of people trying to pull this off. They think publishers will pay them money to avoid a scandal. There's no way in the world she could prove you stole those books from her." Kaely put her hand on Erin's shoulder. "Don't worry about this. I'll help. My training with the FBI will come in handy. And Noah will help too. Might be a good idea to let this woman know you have friends in high places. Hopefully, it will scare her off."

"Brandon told me not to talk about it," Erin said. "If it gets out . . ."

"Well, I'm certainly not going to tell anyone. And Noah won't either. Now let's get back to our lunch. Put this out of your head for now. We'll talk about it later." She smiled. "There's a Bible verse that advises us not to worry about anything today and to let tomorrow worry about itself. In other words, just concentrate on today. This situation may not even be a problem by tomorrow. The whole thing could easily go away once this woman realizes she can't possibly prove her claim. If you spend today upset, it could be for absolutely no reason whatsoever." Kaely removed her hand from Erin's shoulder and gave her a quick hug. "Let's just enjoy today, okay? I promise you everything will be all right."

"How can you possibly promise something like that?" Erin asked. "You can't know how this will turn out."

Kaely let her go and put her hand under Erin's chin, raising her face so she was looking into Kaely's dark eyes. "I can promise that because I know you didn't steal that story. Or what you're working on now. I believe in prayer, Erin. And

I know that God will bring justice out of this. You don't know much about who He is yet, but I do. And I trust Him completely. This will turn out okay. You'll see."

Kaely pointed toward the kitchen, and Erin headed that way. She hoped Kaely was right. Would God really help her? She wasn't even sure she believed in Him. Why would He get involved in her life? Even as she asked herself the question, a spark of hope ignited inside her. Maybe Kaely was right. Maybe this really would be okay.

For a moment, Adrian thought he was still in bed. He had a headache and was thinking he should get up and take some aspirin. But then he realized he was lying on the ground. He pushed himself into a sitting position. The pain in his head almost took his breath away. It was then he realized he could hear Jake's frantic barks. He waited a minute or two until the world quit spinning. Slowly, he got to his feet and looked around. No one was there. He was alone. He leaned against the side of Erin's house, trying to get his bearings. He wanted nothing more than to get back to his Jeep, but he realized that before he made another move, he had to call the station and ask for help. Whoever hit him could still be nearby. His radio was on the ground, and he didn't want to reach down to get it. He was afraid he wouldn't be able to get back up. Instead, he reached into his pocket and pulled out his cell phone. He clicked on the station's number. Seconds later, Lisa answered. He mumbled into the phone, asking for assistance and praying she understood him.

"We're on our way, boss," she said. "Stay put."

He could hear the concern in her voice, but he had to get

to Jake. The dog was clearly panicked, and the fear he heard tore at his heart.

Adrian slowly moved around to the side of the house, using his arm to keep himself propped up. He finally reached the front of the cabin. The distance from where he was to the Jeep seemed like a million miles, but somehow, he had to get there. Jake needed him. It was then that he noticed the blood. It had dripped down onto his shirt. He put his hand up to his face and found it damp and sticky. When he pulled his hand away, all he could see was red. He stared at the Jeep for a few seconds and then launched himself off the side of the cabin and stumbled toward his vehicle, barely making it before he felt like he would pass out.

He opened the driver's side door and flung himself inside. Jake was all over him, trying to lick up the blood on his face in an attempt to help him. Adrian didn't want to push him away, but he had to. He was still battling with Jake when he heard the sirens. Help was here.

As he slipped into the welcoming darkness, he knew he would be all right.

SEVENTEEN

They'd just finished lunch when Kaely turned the conversation to Shannon. "Erin, why don't you let Shannon tell you about the book she's writing," she said. "It sounds really interesting."

"Kaely," Shannon said. "Please. I don't want . . ."

"Shannon, it's okay." Erin tried hard to make it sound as if she truly meant it. "Just give me a brief summary. I'd really like to hear about it." Although she wasn't a Christian, she'd been thinking a lot about God lately. She was fairly certain that lying was one of the big sins. But in this situation, she was simply trying to spare someone's feelings. Would that cover her fib? She wasn't so certain.

Shannon offered her a tremulous smile and took a deep breath. She rattled off a description of her book. It was romantic suspense, and the premise wasn't bad. Erin nodded at her when she stopped talking.

"I think you've got a great idea," Erin said, which she meant. "How far along are you?"

"I'm almost done," Shannon said. "I'm just having problems with the ending."

Please don't ask me to read it. Please don't ask me to read it. "I have to ask. Have you studied writing methods? There are several important techniques writers need to know that can help their book get noticed. I studied writing in college, but I still had more to learn before I started *Dark Matters*. Writing fiction is tricky, and to be honest, a lot of what I was taught in school wasn't beneficial."

"I've studied quite a bit. Hopefully, it will be enough."

Erin mentioned several books that had been helpful to her as Shannon took notes.

"Also, I'd recommend you have your book edited before you start sending it to agents," she added.

Shannon frowned. "I need an agent?"

"For the larger publishers you do. Trust me, a good agent is worth the fifteen percent they charge. If you'll finish your novel and have it edited, I'll give you the names of some agents I trust. I'd advise you not to search for one on your own. There are a lot of scammers out there."

"I didn't know that."

"Unfortunately, there are quite a few minefields out there for writers," Erin said. "I only avoided them because I did some research before I sent out queries."

"And that's how you landed the agent you have now?" Shannon asked.

Erin smiled. "No, I drove my first agent nuts. The one I have now is much more patient with me."

"Okay," Shannon said. "Thank you, Erin. Now I just have one other favor to ask you." She got up and grabbed the satchel she'd carried in with her. Erin prayed it wasn't her manuscript. Thankfully, she pulled out a copy of *Dark Matters*. She blushed as she handed it to Erin. "Would you sign this for me?"

Erin still wasn't used to the way people treated her because she was an author. She'd spent several years as a cop, putting her life on the line, saving lives and defending the populace. Yet most of the response in the neighborhood where she was assigned was negative. Sometimes hateful. She'd been spit on and called names more than once. Sure, some of the people who lived there appreciated the police and counted on their protection, but a lot of them were afraid to admit it. Powerful gangs kept families and older people locked inside their homes or apartments, afraid to leave because of the violence. Erin had been able to keep going because of the residents she knew needed her help. At least until . . . She caught herself thinking about that night again and forced her mind to concentrate on Shannon and signing her book. When would that night stop haunting her?

She wrote "Good luck with your writing, Shannon. Someday I hope to ask you to sign your book for me!" Then she added her name. When she handed the book back to Shannon, her smile told Erin that she'd written the right thing.

"Thank you," Shannon said. "I really appreciate everything you shared with me. I better get going. I know you both have somewhere to go."

She got up from the table and put the book back in her satchel. Kaely came over and hugged her. "I'll try to make it for coffee next week," she said. "If I have to reschedule, I'll let you know."

"Thanks, Kaely," Shannon said, her brown eyes tearing up. "And thank you, Erin. I can't tell you what this has meant to me."

"You're welcome. Hope things work out for you. And like I said, when you're ready for an agent, contact me. Kaely can give you my email address, or you can send me a message through my website."

Shannon nodded and scurried for the front door. After she left, Kaely grinned at her. "You mean the website you hate?"

"I don't hate it. In fact, it's wonderful. It wasn't something I initially wanted, but I guess authors are supposed to have them." Her first agent had insisted she have a website and recommended someone to set it up and maintain it. So, after a lot of work on his part, and very little from her, ErinDelaney.net was born. She ended up really liking it, especially since she didn't have to spend much time on it. "My webmaster has been incredible. I really don't know what I'd do without him."

Kaely grinned. "Sometimes I wonder why your agent and publisher even put up with you."

"I guess it's because I'm so incredibly talented," Erin said, raising her nose in the air.

"Now I'm thinking about dumping that cup of cappuccino on your head."

"The joke's on you," Erin said, laughing. "I drank every last drop. It was delicious."

Kaely picked up some of the dirty dishes on the table and carried them to the sink. Erin grabbed the rest. "Thanks for what you said about this lawsuit. I feel better, but Brandon really did seem concerned. He has a lot of experience in the industry."

"You haven't been with him long. Maybe he's just stressed. Having you for a client might cause that."

Erin shook her head. Kaely's lighthearted banter wasn't fooling her. She was trying to keep her from worrying. And it was working . . . somewhat. But for now, she had to concentrate on talking to the lead investigator at the command center. Although her agoraphobia was better, the idea of being in a large building full of people she didn't know made her heart race. And being questioned by someone who might think she had something to do with the deaths made it worse. *God, still not sure I believe everything that Kaely does, but if You're listening, I could really use some help.*

"I really think you should stay in the hospital overnight," the ER doctor said. "Just to make sure you're okay."

"You said you don't believe I have a concussion," Adrian said. "And you've stitched up the gash in my head. Except for a blinding headache, I'm fine. I need to get back to work."

The doctor, who according to his name tag was named J. S. Dunkin, sighed, and pulled a pad out of the pocket of his white coat. "I'm writing a prescription for something a little stronger than over-the-counter medicine. At least go home, take one of these, and get some rest." He wrote out something on the pad, tore off a sheet, and then handed it to Adrian.

"Thanks, Doc." He put the prescription in his pocket but had no plans to have it filled. He needed to find out who had attacked him at Erin's cabin. And why.

After the doctor left, Lisa said, "You have no intention of obeying the doctor's orders, do you?" She pushed back a strand of her strawberry blonde hair off her face. "You know, there are other people in our department who could follow up on what happened."

"You're right," Adrian said, struggling to smile even though it felt as if his head was getting ready to explode.

"About the first part. We're going back to Erin's. I want to see if we can find anything helpful. I also want to make sure her automatic lights come on when they're supposed to this evening."

"We can do that. Please go home and rest."

He shook his head, even though it hurt. "I need to find out who hit me. I want him."

Lisa sighed loudly. "Okay, boss. Whatever you say. But only if you stop by the pharmacy and get that filled. I want to know that you'll have it tonight if you need it."

Adrian started to protest, but she raised her hand. "No. And I mean this. I'll tell everyone at the station to ignore you. And you know they'll listen to me if I convince them it's the best thing for you. You also need to follow up with Doc Gibson. I'm sure the emergency room doctor is good, but Doc Gibson is *your* doctor. He needs to take a look at you. You call him, or I will."

"You call him, and I'll fire you."

She didn't react, she just stared at him. He had no doubt she would do everything she'd just threatened to do. "Okay. This evening I'll stop on the way home and have the prescription filled. But no Doc Gibson. I mean it. He's too bossy."

Lisa didn't acknowledge what he'd said. "You've also got to call Erin, you know."

"I will. But I'm just going to tell her that I think someone may have been hanging around the cabin. I don't want to alarm her. She needs to stay where she is. Especially after this. I have no idea why I was attacked. It could have been Erin instead of me. We need to find this guy before she comes home."

"I think you should tell her the truth," Lisa said. "But whatever you decide, we'll all back you."

Adrian got up from the exam table. He had to hold onto the side of the table because the room started to spin. He smiled at Lisa as if everything was okay. He was determined to find out what was going on at Erin's cabin. He had to make certain she was safe. That was more important to him than the pain in his head. He would do everything he could to protect her.

EIGHTEEN

WEDNESDAY AFTERNOON

I stared down at my next offering. I didn't want to be too obvious. I was leaving clues, but so far they didn't seem to get it. I planned to keep going until . . . well, until the last one. It was coming soon. Would they figure it out in time? I laughed, but the woman lying on the ground didn't join in. Even though she was smiling, I'd had the last laugh.

Erin tried not to let her nerves take over on the drive to the command center. She clasped her hands in her lap, squeezing them tightly as a way to redirect her apprehension. Would she be okay, or would she act foolishly in front of the people manning the center? The fear of having a panic attack in front of strangers was almost enough to cause one. Until the night Erin watched Scott die during a gang war and one of her own stray bullets hit and kill a young girl inside her own apartment, she'd never experienced a panic attack. They were truly awful. Something she wouldn't wish on her worst enemy.

As if knowing how she felt, Kaely said, "Please don't worry about this. I'll be with you every step of the way. If you want to leave after you're interviewed, we will. However, since I'm a consultant and you've been deputized, we can hang around."

"I'm not sure what they want from me," Erin said. "I've seen the crime photos. I don't know any more than they do."

"That's just the evidence," Kaely said. "Now, they're writing a profile and looking for suspects—people who knew the victims. You may have a connection you don't even know about. They're just trying to be thorough. You know how this works."

"They're checking out the authors in case they might be involved."

Kaely looked over at her. "Sure, but they already know you had nothing to do with this."

Erin sighed loudly. "You've told me that several times, Kaely. But how could they know that? They haven't even talked to me yet."

Kaeley was quiet for a moment. "Investigators followed up on your whereabouts. You were right. It wasn't difficult. They know you never left Sanctuary."

Erin looked over at her. "And how did they do that?"

"They called Adrian. Since you both walk your dogs almost every day, it was easy to put you miles away from each murder. They also checked with the people who worked on your car. They confirmed that you didn't make a quick trip to Virginia to kill anyone."

Erin had squeezed her hands until they hurt. Why hadn't Adrian told her about the call? "We don't walk the dogs every day," she said through clenched teeth. She wasn't certain just why she was so upset, but the idea of people talking about her without letting her know made her angry.

"I know, but the days you did walk your dogs happened to fall on the same days the women were murdered." Kaely glanced over and met her gaze. "Are you upset because they called Adrian?"

"I don't like people doing things behind my back." Erin turned her face away. "Why didn't you tell me?"

"I just found out about it. Besides, the police and the FBI are kind of funny about stuff like that. I was trying to follow protocol." Kaely sighed. "I'm sorry. I guess I should have told you. Don't be mad at me."

Even though Erin understood protocol from her days with the police department, she couldn't seem to let go of her anger. What was wrong with her? She took a deep breath and let it out. This was stupid. She'd spent several years in law enforcement. Being so nervous was ridiculous, and it made her feel weak. Maybe that was the real reason for her anger. She used to be brave. Fearless, even.

Suddenly, Kaely pulled off the road and brought the SUV to a stop. She put the car in park and turned toward Erin. "We can reschedule this for later, you know. I want to catch this guy, but I care more about you than I do this investigation."

Erin leaned back against the headrest. "You said the other authors have been interviewed?"

"Yes, Dan Harper and Toni Sue Smith have both been interviewed by their local police departments."

"Their reports were sent here? To the local task force?"

Kaely nodded. "They work together, not only on the case, but also in how to handle the media."

"And I'm the only one who will be interviewed by the task force at the command center?"

"I assume so." Kaely frowned at her. "But like I told you, you're the only one in Virginia. Are you really that nervous about this?"

Erin grunted. "Just call me a coward."

"You are absolutely not a coward," Kaely said, emphatically. "In fact, you're one of the strongest people I've ever met."

Erin looked at Kaely like she'd lost her mind. "Are you kidding? I can barely leave my house. I avoid almost everyone. The other day while I was in town buying groceries, a car outside the market backfired, and I fell to my knees. I pretended like I'd dropped something, but I'm pretty certain anyone watching knew the truth."

Kaely reached over and put her hand on Erin's arm. "And that's my point, Erin. Regardless of everything you've been through and are still going through, you're here, aren't you? That's what real courage is. Can't you see that?"

Although she still didn't feel very brave, Kaely's words impacted her. It was true. She could have refused to come to Virginia and talk to investigators at the command center. Maybe she had a little more backbone than she'd realized. She hoped it was true. She wanted to feel like herself again. The person she was before that night in St. Louis.

"I'm going to take a chance here," Kaely said gently. "Don't get angry with me, but could I pray for you? It won't be long or very religious. I just want to pray for peace and ask God to give you strength."

Erin still wasn't certain if there was a God who cared anything about her, but she nodded. To be honest, she was surprised by her reaction. She hadn't planned to agree, she just . . . did.

"Dear God," Kaely said softly, "please touch my dear friend Erin with Your peace, and hold her up with Your strength. I ask this in the name of Your Son, Jesus. Amen."

That was it? Erin had expected her to address God using Thee or Thou. But this was simple. As if Kaely were talking to a friend. It was at that moment Erin felt something. Something real. Peace. But not the kind of peace she was used to feeling, the kind of peace she'd only experienced when everything was going right in her life. This wasn't that. This was . . . a person. She felt . . . Someone. It wasn't until Kaely took her hand that she realized tears were streaming down her face.

"What . . . what is that?" Erin whispered. "Is . . . is that . . . Him?"

"What do you think?" Kaely asked with a smile. "Did you think I was just delusional? I worked for the FBI. I know how to analyze data. I'm not the kind of person who would fall for something that wasn't real, am I?"

Erin shook her head. "No. No you're not." A sob tore through her. "He's real. This is . . . real."

Kaely unbuckled her seat belt and reached for Erin. She leaned over and put her head on Kaely's shoulder and wept for a while. When she could gain control of herself, she sat up straight in her seat. "We're going to be late," she said, wiping away her tears with a tissue Kaely handed her.

"Only a little bit. And it's totally worth it."

"When we get back to the house, will you . . . you know . . . help me pray?"

"To ask God into your life?"

Erin nodded.

"We can do it then . . . or even now. There's no special prayer or ceremony, you know."

"I figured that," Erin said. "But I don't want to rush it. And I don't want to get so emotional that the police and the FBI change their minds and decide I really am a serial killer."

Kaely laughed. "I don't think that will happen, especially since most serial killers are psychopaths and don't cry, but if you want to wait, I completely understand." She'd just put the SUV in drive and pulled back onto the road when Erin's phone rang. She looked at the caller ID.

"It's Adrian," Erin said. She took a quick breath to calm herself and then answered her phone.

"Hi," Adrian said. "I hope I'm not bothering you."

"We're on our way to the command center where I'll be talking to an investigator. We still have a little way to go. Is everything okay?"

When Adrian hesitated, Erin started to tense up again, but this time she dismissed it. She wasn't letting go of the peace she was experiencing. It felt so . . . good.

"I saw someone hanging around your house this morning. He ran off before I could stop him. Your house is fine, but I thought you'd want to know. We're going to keep a close watch on things until you get back."

"Do you think he was trying to break in?"

"No way to tell, but if your alarm is on, I don't believe you have anything to worry about. Like you said, if anyone does try to get in, the alarm company will be alerted."

"I know I set the alarm, so everything should be okay. Maybe it was just someone checking out the cabin. It wasn't that long ago that it was for sale."

"You could be right," he said. "How . . . are you doing? Any way I can help?"

"Can you come here and pretend to be me? That would make things a lot easier."

Adrian's laugh wafted through Erin's phone. She loved his low, husky laugh.

"Not sure I could fit into your clothes," he said. "And I certainly wouldn't be as attractive."

Erin was glad Adrian couldn't see her. She was sure her cheeks were red.

Kaely reached over and touched her arm. "We're almost there," she said softly.

"Adrian, I have to go. Thanks for looking after my cabin." Something suddenly occurred to her. "Hey, maybe I should give you the password and the code for my alarm. My password is 4397. It has to be entered when I come in, and again when I leave. I also have a code in case the alarm accidentally goes off. If it isn't used within thirty seconds, the alarm company will send someone out to investigate."

"Okay," Adrian said. "I promise to keep this information safe."

It was Erin's turn to laugh. "I'm really not worried about it. You don't seem like the type to break in and pillage my cabin."

"Pillage? Not even sure how to do that."

Erin noticed Kaely turning into the parking lot of a large, abandoned warehouse. This had to be the command center.

"My code word is Jake."

"From your book?"

"Yeah," Erin said. "My character and your dog. Thought it would be easy to remember."

Kaely drove behind the warehouse where there were other parked cars.

"I'm here, Adrian," she said. "Thanks for letting me know there was someone skulking outside my house."

"Erin, there's one other thing. I wasn't going to tell you because I didn't want to worry you, but . . ."

"Someone called you to ask about my whereabouts during the past few months?" She could hear him breathe a sigh of relief.

"Yeah. I'm glad you know. I feel better. Thanks."

"You're welcome. If anything else happens, let me know?"

"I will," he said. "Bye, Erin."

Erin realized that talking to Adrian had helped her get her mind off what was coming. At that moment, she wished he was with her, helping her get through this. Although she didn't want to have feelings for another man after Scott, she finally admitted to herself that it was already too late.

NINETEEN

"Why didn't you tell her the whole truth?" Lisa asked. Adrian looked up. She was standing in the doorway of his office again. He hadn't noticed her there.

"Don't you have anything to do?" he asked crossly.

She didn't answer him. Just continued to stand there.

He sighed loudly. "Because she might have felt she needed to come back." He frowned at her. "Do I need to run all my decisions by you?"

"No, boss. But when she finds out you were attacked, how do you think she's gonna take it?"

"I hope she'll realize what I was trying to do. Look, we're going to keep a close watch on the house. She just gave me the codes for her alarm system. If I feel like I need to go inside to check things out, I can do that now."

"Whoever hit you was serious about stopping you," Lisa said. "He could have just run away. Attacking you took this to a whole new level."

"I know. Look, let's just pray he's moved on."

Lisa didn't respond, but she had a habit of rubbing the back of her neck when she was troubled. She did that now.

"You don't think he's done, do you?" Adrian asked.

"No. No, I don't. And I don't want anyone else injured while we're watching the house. Boss, I don't think you should send our officers out there alone. How about two cops whenever they check out Erin's cabin?"

Adrian thought about what she'd said. She was right. He'd asked Lisa more than once if she might be happier as a police officer, but she always said no. She loved her job and had no desire to change things. Too bad. She was as savvy as any officer under his command. Thankfully, though, she was here and available to him and the department. He felt ashamed for speaking to her so harshly. Thing was, she never got offended. She always believed the best of him. Even when he didn't deserve it.

"I think you're right. Can you send out a message letting everyone know that? And assign times and match officers to do surveillance?"

"How many times a day, boss?"

Adrian shrugged. "You decide. You know what needs to be done." He met her gaze. "Sorry about snapping at you."

"Did you snap at me?" she asked, grinning. "I didn't notice. I'll take care of the surveillance schedule right away." She turned and left his office.

Adrian went back to the reports on his desk, but it was almost impossible to concentrate. Why had someone been checking out Erin's house? And what about the scratches on the back doors? Since the alarm was set, whoever was sneaking around couldn't have gotten inside without setting it off, but still, it was troubling. Had the assailant's encounter with him run the guy off for good? Lisa was right. Assaulting a police officer was serious. This guy had been willing to put his life on the line for some reason. Thank God, Erin hadn't been there. Adrian had to make certain things would be safe before she came home. If anything ever happened to her . . . He pushed the thought away. He needed to concentrate. It seemed like every time he thought about Erin, his mind refused to let anything else in.

He pulled the first report closer and forced himself to focus on the papers in front of him, instead of the short girl with deep green eyes and a smile that made him feel happy inside.

"Like I told you, the command center is almost always set up in an abandoned building," Kaely said once they'd parked.

"Why not house it at the marine base, or CIRG?" Erin's research into the FBI's Critical Incident Response Group was extensive. It seemed as if keeping the investigation in-house made more sense.

"Not enough room for everyone. Just wait until you see the inside."

"Boy, you weren't kidding about it being hidden," Erin said. "From the front of this warehouse I would never imagine there were people inside." Erin frowned. "I can see setting something like this up if it's a national security issue, but a serial killer?"

"It's not only because they need the room, but they also want to keep their information from prying eyes. They don't want the killer to know what they know."

"But the media is already talking about it."

Kaely nodded. "True. And like Noah said, the press will

probably find the command center before long. They're like bloodhounds."

"The UNSUB will love the attention."

"That's true, but trust me, if law enforcement doesn't control the narrative, the media will run wild with speculation—that will feed his narcissism even more."

"What if someone from the press tries to get inside?"

"First of all, everyone must be on an approved list," Kaely said. "And each and every person will have to sign in when they try to enter. A police officer or a deputy will check their ID. Also, look at the windows."

Erin turned her head to see that all the windows of the building were obscured with something.

"Every window is covered with brown paper so no one can look inside and see what's going on. Investigators use dry-erase boards for notes. And computer screens have information that investigators want to keep private." Kaely shrugged. "It might sound like a primitive solution, but it works."

"I hope attention from the media doesn't encourage the UNSUB to kill again in an attempt to gain more notoriety."

"It might," Kaely said, her tone solemn. "But to be honest, I think he already has."

Erin's gut told her that Kaely was right. She nodded. "Narcissistic personality. He craves attention. Enjoys creating fear. He has everyone on edge. He can't allow too much time to go by before he strikes again. He's afraid to be out of the spotlight too long."

Kaely smiled at her. "You would have made a great analyst. You've got good instincts."

"Some of it comes from being a cop, but most of it's because of you. You've taught me so much." Erin looked away for a moment. She was experiencing a wave of unexpected emotion. In the past, it would have made her feel too vulnerable, but now . . . Now she was just grateful she could feel again. She'd shut herself off for so long, protecting her mind and emotions, she'd also trapped the pain inside with her. She looked over at Kaely and saw the compassion in her eyes. "Thank you," Erin whispered, her voice breaking. "Thank you for . . . for being here for me. For being my friend. And for telling me that there's a God who loves me regardless of all the mistakes I've made."

Kaely reached over and took her hand. "You're welcome. And thank you for being my friend as well. You bless me more than you realize." She blinked away tears that filled her own eyes. "Now, before we cry ourselves into wet messes, let's go inside."

Erin laughed lightly and wiped her eyes. "Sounds good. I only hope I can really help with the investigation."

"I know you will. Not only with your own story, but your instincts and knowledge will be a great asset."

Kaely started to open her car door, but Erin stopped her.

"Give me just a second," she said. She took several deep breaths, trying to calm her nerves.

"Hey, I'm right here," Kaely said. "I'll stick close to you until you're interviewed."

"You won't be able to stay with me during the interview?" Erin's anxiety level rose some and she tried to force it back down.

"No, but I'll be nearby. Really, Erin, you've got this." Kaely frowned. "If the investigator who interviews you is too harsh, remember . . . I'm packing heat."

Erin laughed. Of course, she wasn't *packing heat* today. Kaely had made it clear that no guns were allowed in the building unless you were law enforcement. It felt strange sometimes, not having her gun, even though she hadn't carried it for a couple of years now. As a cop, it was almost part of her body. But that body part had been excised the night Scott and Sarah died.

As they got out of the car and headed toward a large metal door, Erin's heart began to beat harder. What did these people want from her? Although she really wanted to help, she was apprehensive. A serial killer knew who she was, and he had killed in her name. No matter what Kaely said, she felt responsible. And guilty. At that moment, she wished she'd prayed with Kaely and asked God to come into her life before facing what was ahead of her. She craved the peace she'd felt earlier. As if Kaely knew what she was thinking, Kaely reached over and took her arm. Once again, it was as if Someone she couldn't see began walking next to her, reassuring Erin that she wasn't alone.

TWENTY

Lisa had set up schedules for Adrian's officers to drive by Erin's cabin. He looked over her work and approved it. She'd done a perfect job. He and Lisa were both concerned about their suspect's motive for attacking him. There was no way to know if he'd be back, but until they could figure out why he was there in the first place, they were in the dark. He struggled with what to say to his officers. He didn't want them to react hastily should they encounter someone on the property. The idea that an employee from the electric company, just there to read the meter, could end up shot was a concern. His officers weren't really used to confronting criminals who wished them harm. Eventually, he told them the truth but admonished them to use extreme caution. He didn't overemphasize the danger, yet he wanted them to know that, should they encounter someone on the property who didn't belong there, they had to assume they might be armed. In the end, he had to trust their discretion and training.

The truth was, someone without ulterior motives wouldn't have hit him. The nagging voice in his gut was telling him that this might not be over. He also wondered if Erin would be upset with him when she learned the truth. For now, he'd have to take his chances. If he and the officers under his command couldn't keep one property safe, they had no business serving in law enforcement. Besides, they weren't that busy right now. Sure, the number of thefts was up, but that always happened during the tourist season. Although it would get more hectic later, since many people liked to visit the Smokies in the spring. It really was beautiful here. Merle Hubbard, over at the Sanctuary Resort, had called again about more missing towels and robes. He was losing his patience with Merle. Adrian had advised him more than once to simply charge the missing items to the guests' credit cards, but he still called, wanting Adrian to know every time something disappeared. He wasn't going to send his officers out to track down people who thought taking amenities from the resort was expected. It was silly. He felt bad that Merle had to keep replacing stolen items, but it wasn't exactly grand larceny. So, he just kept trying to soothe the enraged innkeeper while reminding him once again to charge their cards.

"You call Doc Gibson yet?"

Adrian jumped. He hadn't noticed Lisa standing in his office doorway again. That woman should be on a surveillance detail. She could sneak up on anyone without tipping them off. How would she react if he suggested she wear a bell around her neck?

"I told you no an hour ago," Adrian said, frowning.

"And what did I tell you?" she fired back.

Adrian shook his head. Another thing about Lisa—she was incredibly stubborn when she thought she was right. And at that moment, he wondered if he should have listened.

His head was still pounding. He'd been swallowing over-the-counter pain relievers like candy. It wasn't helping.

"You told me that if I didn't call Doc Gibson, you'd call him yourself," he said.

"That's right."

He raised an eyebrow and tried to look threatening. "And what did I tell *you*?"

She smiled beatifically. "That you'd fire me if I called him."

"That's right."

Lisa turned and looked down the hallway. Then she waved her arm. Doc Gibson stepped past her and into Adrian's office.

"What's this I hear about you gettin' a head injury and not comin' to see me?" Doc said, his bushy eyebrows knit together like two hairy caterpillars locked in battle. "I don't have time to do house calls."

That was something Doc Gibson always said, yet he did a lot of house calls. Adrian pointed at Lisa. "I'm supposed to be your boss, yet you never listen to me." He tried to sound angry, but he couldn't. Frankly, he was glad to see Gibson. Maybe he could help.

Lisa shrugged. "You're never going to fire me. First of all, you know I'm right, and secondly, you know you can't get along without me." She smiled at the doctor. "He was hit hard. Passed out, has a large gash on his head. He went to the ER and got stitches, but I'd feel better if you checked him over, Doc. Don't let him try to tell you he's okay. He's in a lot of pain."

"Didn't they give you a prescription for somethin' to help your head?" Gibson growled at Adrian.

"Yes, they did," Lisa said, "but he hasn't had it filled yet."

"I said I'd take care of it on the way home," Adrian snapped.

Gibson held out his hand. "Let me see it."

For just a few seconds, Adrian thought about telling Gibson to stay out of his business, but he couldn't say that to Doc. He'd been taking care of the citizens of Sanctuary for over forty years. He was a curmudgeon, but underneath his gruff exterior, he really cared. And he was a really good doctor. Sanctuary was blessed to have him. He handed Gibson the prescription.

He looked at it and snorted. "This ain't gonna take care of your pain. Them ER doctors are afraid of gettin' in trouble so they never prescribe anything strong enough to really help."

Adrian had always wondered how it was Gibson made it through college and medical school, yet he still talked like a hillbilly. He'd decided years ago that it was best not to ask.

Gibson crumpled up the prescription and tossed it into Adrian's trash can. "I'm gonna call the pharmacy. Your medicine will be ready within the hour. You leave here, go pick it up, and then go home, take it just the way I prescribed it, and lay down for a while, ya hear me?"

Adrian nodded. He had no doubt that he'd get relief from the pain that held his head in its viselike grip. His concern was being able to get out of bed within a day or two.

"You get that today," Gibson said, wagging his chubby finger at Adrian. "I'll know if you don't. Jenny Nickerson at the pharmacy will call me if you don't show up."

Adrian gave in to the inevitable and just nodded. "Okay, Doc. I'll pick it up."

"And?"

He sighed. "And I'll take them. At least some of them."

Doc didn't move. He just stood there and gave Adrian the evil eye. Adrian sighed again. "Okay, I'll take all of them."

The chubby doctor stayed right where he was, staring at Adrian as if he were a small child who'd just spilled a cup of milk on the floor.

"As prescribed," Adrian said under his breath.

With that, Gibson picked up the worn, black leather medical bag he'd carried in with him. Before leaving he pointed his finger at Adrian one more time.

"When are you gonna grow up and come to see me when you need somethin'? I swear, you're just like your grandpa. He made light of bein' sick up 'till the day he died." He grunted. "Bein' manly doesn't mean you shouldn't seek help when you need it, ya know." With that he left the office.

Adrian leaned back in his chair. He wanted to feel annoyed at Lisa and Gibson, but he couldn't. They cared about him, and although it was sometimes irritating to be ordered around, he wouldn't want it any other way. They were family. Maybe not by blood, but by something much stronger. By choice.

Kaely punched some numbers onto a keypad next to the metal door. Erin looked away, not sure if she was supposed to see the sequence. She didn't feel as if she belonged here. She wasn't FBI or ex-FBI, she was just an ex-cop and the author of a silly book.

There was a loud click, and Kaely pulled the door open. On the other side of the door, a large man stood. He wore a police uniform, and his expression made it clear that getting past him wouldn't be easy. Kaely took out her driver's license and showed it to him. Erin quickly fumbled for her ID and held it out as well. Then, not sure if she was supposed to, she showed him the badge Nick had given her. The man glanced at them and then at their IDs.

Suddenly, his scowl faded. "You're Erin Delaney?" His eyebrows raised, and he broke out into a big smile. "I loved *Dark Matters*! It was great. You're the only author I know who gets it all right."

Erin was so surprised, she just stared at him. "Well . . . thank you," she said finally. "I'm glad you liked it."

"Can't wait for the next one. When will it be out?"

Never? "Not sure. Just finished writing it. Still has to go to my publisher. It might be a while."

"Well, I'll be the first one in line, waiting to buy it." He hesitated a moment. Erin was pretty sure what was next, and she was right.

"If I bring my copy of *Dark Matters*, will you sign it for me?"

There it was. She glanced at his badge. Officer Brad Spencer. She smiled. "Of course, Officer Spencer. I'd be happy to."

"Please, just call me Brad. Will you be here tomorrow?"

She looked at Kaely. "She should be," Kaely said, "but if not, she can sign it and give it to my husband. Noah is working here."

"The BAU guy?" Brad asked.

Kaely nodded. "You know him?"

"Sure. Everyone does. Great guy."

"Yeah, I think so." Kaely smiled at him.

"I have to check your bags before I let you in," Brad said. "Sorry, it's just protocol."

There was that word again. Erin had a feeling she was going to hear it often from now on. Kaely handed him her purse. He looked through it and handed it back to her. Then he checked out Erin's tote bag, which included her laptop and her phone. She'd also stuck her wallet inside so she wouldn't have to carry her purse.

"The investigator wants to go through my laptop and my phone," she said. He probably already knew that, but she felt compelled to explain. Again, that odd feeling of guilt. As if she'd done something wrong.

"I understand," he said. "You two go on in. We're being extra careful today. We got a tip that some reporter from a station in Richmond thinks he can worm his way inside the building and write a story." He shook his head. "I respect good reporters, but some of these people would actually put lives at risk for a headline."

Kaely thanked him and walked away. Erin followed her.

Her gaze swept the room. Although she was aware that the command center had just been set up, it didn't look like it. There were groups of stations where people sat in front of computers and huge dry-erase boards at the back of the enormous room. Also, there was a large area off to one side with tables and chairs. Several people sat there, eating and talking.

"How do these people get food?" Erin asked. "I can't imagine they go out and pick it up if they're trying to stay hidden from prying eyes."

"Sometimes they do, but most of the food comes from organizations and churches. Quite a few of them respond when law enforcement officers are working cases like this. Someone from the local police, FBI, or sheriff's department probably contacted them." Kaely smiled. "Regardless of what you hear in the media, most people are very supportive of law enforcement."

"That would be a good way for a reporter to sneak in, wouldn't it?" Erin said. "They could pretend to be a church member bringing in food."

"They're not allowed inside. The people working here accept the food outside and carry it in. Unless someone in this building lets him in, and they won't, that reporter from Richmond has no chance of getting through the door."

A man walked up to them, his expression stern. "Can I ask who you are?" he said.

Kaely introduced herself and then turned toward Erin. "This is Erin Delaney. She's here to talk to someone. Your UNSUB copied one of his murders from her book."

"I'm Detective Herrington with the Virginia State Police. I'll be interviewing Ms. Delaney." He stared at Erin for a moment, then said, "Would you follow me please?" He pointed toward the area with the tables and chairs. "You can have a seat over there, Ms. Hunter. I'll send her your way when we're done."

Erin looked at Kaely, who shrugged and nodded at her. "You'll be fine," she mouthed, making sure the detective couldn't see. Even though Kaely had warned her that she probably couldn't stay with her during the interview, Erin felt her body tense.

"All right, Detective Herrington," Kaely said with a smile. She met Erin's gaze. "I'll see you when you're done."

"Come this way, Ms. Delaney," the detective said. His words were curt and to the point. It was clear that he was the kind of person who didn't suffer fools gladly.

As Erin followed him, she was not only certain he wasn't going to ask for an autograph, she was beginning to feel as if he actually believed she might be guilty of something. Erin tried to ignore the sudden paralyzing rush of agoraphobia that whispered to her that she was shut inside this building with no means of escape. She swallowed the sour bile that filled her throat. If she got sick now, everyone would see her, and they'd think she was weak. She looked back at Kaely, who hadn't moved. She was watching Erin and gave her a big thumbs up. Erin wanted to respond in kind, but fear had tightened its tentacles around her chest, and she felt as if she might pass out.

TWENTY-ONE

Erin had just taken a seat in front of the desk where the dour detective stood, staring at her, when a woman in a police uniform came up and whispered something in his ear. The detective's face made it clear that what she'd said had upset him.

"I need you to stay here," he said, looking at her. "I'll be back."

Erin nodded at him. He walked away and was quickly joined by several other people, some of them in uniform. One man, who looked to be in charge, was clearly angry about something. It was then that Erin noticed Noah was part of the group. After a brief conversation, a few of the people left the building, including Detective Herrington. Now what? Should she just stay here? Noah left the people still standing there and came over to the desk where Erin waited.

"Sorry," he said to Erin. "Something's happened."

"What's going on, Noah?"

Kaely's voice from behind her made Erin jump.

"Sit down," Noah said to his wife, under his breath.

Kaely grabbed a nearby chair and pulled it up next to Erin. Noah sat down in the detective's chair.

"They've found another one," Noah said, his voice low.

"Do you have any details?" Kaely asked.

Noah shook his head. "Call came in from the local police department. Body was discovered just north of Fredericksburg. The police took pictures and notified the state police. We'll get more info soon since we're working on a profile. But they did give the state police the name of an author. Patricia Long. They found a book with her name on it at the crime scene. Just like the other murders. Have either of you heard of her?"

"I have," Erin said. "In fact, I met her once. Before I wrote *Dark Matters*, I went to a book signing at a store in St. Louis. I've read all her novels. I'm a huge fan."

"What genre does she write?" Noah said.

"Crime thrillers. I think it's been a few years since she's had a new book, though. I read she'd decided to take some time off from writing. That she was burned out."

"So, you read her last books?" Kaely asked.

"Yeah. You're wondering if I can tell you how the killer in her last book did the deed?"

"You see right through me," Kaely said with a smile.

"What can you remember?" Noah asked.

Erin ran the last book through her mind. What was it about? "Okay, her main character is a tough-minded detective named Austin Blake. The last case was . . ." What was it? Before writing books, Erin used to read . . . a lot. "Okay, I believe he chased down a killer that . . ." Suddenly, the cover of the book flashed in her mind. For the second time that day, she felt as if she might lose her lunch. Or breakfast.

Kaely leaned over and looked into her face. "What is it, Erin?"

"*Grin*," she said, her voice shaky. "The name of the book was *Grin*. There's a large bloody grin on the cover."

Noah took out his phone and began to tap on his device.

"The killer used a knife to carve a large smile on his victim's face," Erin said slowly, "using the corners of a woman's mouth to create his . . . monstrosity. He also . . ."

"I just pulled it up," Noah said. "He slit their throats and carved a smile on the victim's chest." He shook his head. "That's awful."

Erin nodded. "Yeah, it was. Some people think the story was a little too personal. It was taken from a series of murders that happened in Pennsylvania where Patricia lives. The killer was called the Joker because he made his victims look like the Joker in the Batman movies. I think he killed six women before getting caught."

"She stole the idea?" Noah asked.

"No, not really. Just the method of killing. She never used the killer's nom de plume. Besides, the murders happened over twenty years ago so it was fair game. She did mention the previous crimes in a foreword. There was supposed to be a movie about the book, but after several delays, the idea was scrapped."

"You know a lot about that movie," Kaely said.

"I think it was because I enjoyed Patricia's books so much. I was looking forward to the movie. When she stopped writing, I was really upset. She was a great writer."

"We'll know more about it after they get back from the crime scene," Noah said. "But for now, you'll be talking to me. Detective Herrington asked me to do the initial interview with you. This is just preliminary. You'll still have to talk to him, and that will probably happen tomorrow, okay?"

Erin felt momentary relief. She wasn't as nervous talking to Noah instead of the surly detective. After being here today, she was certain she'd be better prepared tomorrow. She nodded. "That's fine, Noah. So, what do you want to know?"

He looked down at the tote bag she'd brought with her into the command post. After removing her wallet, she handed it to him. "My laptop and my phone," she said.

Noah nodded. "Thanks. I'll clone your phone and copy the files from your laptop while you're here. You'll be able to take them home with you."

"Okay," Erin said. "Of course, you've ruined the great excuse I had for running behind on my edits." She smiled at Noah. "How many authors get to tell their editors that they can't send in their manuscript because the FBI commandeered their laptop?"

Noah laughed. "Sorry. I could try to hang on to it a while longer if you want."

"That's okay. I wouldn't want you to get in trouble."

"We'll be looking through your emails, texts, and social media to see if anyone who contacted you or posted about you might be a suspect. This would be someone who has a fixation on you. They might be praising you beyond what's normal or even criticizing you. Does anyone spring to mind when I say that?"

Erin tried to run through some of the comments she'd received through her website or on social media sites. She really didn't spend much time looking at them so that made it harder for her to answer his question. "I . . . I can't think of anything. There's been criticism, yes, but I've found that most authors get that. There was the woman who didn't like the color red on my cover. But I don't think that means she's a psychopathic serial killer. A few that made me a little uncomfortable with their praise, but again, nothing that sticks out." Something popped into her mind. She couldn't believe it was connected to the murders, but still . . .

"You look like you just thought of something," Noah said.

"I don't believe it's linked to these murders, but . . . Well, you're talking about the way people react to my writing." She told Noah about Christine and the attempt to blackmail her publisher. As she talked, Noah took notes. When she finished, she said, "Her number is on my phone, and her address is in my emails. I asked for her address so I could send her a copy of my book. But seriously, Noah, Christine isn't a serial killer. Just a greedy woman who thinks she can make some money by lying. She told my publisher that she can prove her allegations, but that's impossible. She had nothing to do with either book, except for giving me some information about a lake in Missouri that I used in *Dark Matters*."

"We still need to look into her." He smiled at Erin. "Maybe being questioned by the police will make her change her mind about trying to squeeze money from your publisher." He shook his head. "You'd be surprised by all the ways scam artists dream up to make money. People like your publisher pay them off to avoid bad press. Unfortunately, it just encourages thieves."

"Trust me," Erin said, "I saw my fair share in St. Louis when I was a cop. Some of the stores just watch thieves walk out with merchandise because too many people have guns. It's very discouraging for those of us in law enforcement." She realized what she'd just said and felt her face flush. "Of course, I'm not in law enforcement anymore. But you know what I mean."

"Yeah, I do. But you know what? Once a cop, always a cop. Law enforcement is something that gets in your blood, and it never goes away. You're just living it through your writing."

"Yeah, I guess so. Sorry, I guess we need to get back to this interview."

Noah nodded and made some notes. When he stopped typing, he said, "So where did you get the idea for this book?"

"I . . . I don't know. Just from my head, I guess. I didn't pattern it after any case I ever worked or anything I read or saw on TV."

"So, you just imagine stuff like this?" Noah asked. "Think I'll start sleeping with one eye open."

Erin laughed. Noah had helped her to feel calmer, and she appreciated it more than she could say.

He asked her to go through the plot of her book, in particular how the murders were committed, which she did. Then he asked the name of her publisher and then her agent.

"Now, what about public events? Book signings? Did you meet anyone who seemed . . . unusual?"

"That's a loaded question," Erin said. "Some fans are certainly unusual. In awe of meeting me. But most are just there because they enjoyed my book and wanted a signed copy. I used to do the same thing." She shrugged. "People are people. There wasn't anyone that made me think they were psychotic."

"So, no strange fan mail? Emails? Anything? I know I already asked you about this, but you've had some time to think. Anything pop into your head?"

She shook her head. "Not that I can recall, but to be honest, I don't see it all."

"I know you've seen the crime photos," Noah said, "but let's pretend you haven't. The state police can be very territorial. Is it all right if I show them to you again?"

Erin nodded.

"If you see anything that sparks something you didn't notice before, or that links you to the victim or the crime, let me know."

Erin sighed. "You mean other than using my plot to take a human life?"

"Yeah, that. Please look closely at each photo. Tell me if there's anything different between the way the killer staged the crime scene and the way you wrote it."

"Well, for one thing," Erin said, "there wasn't any poem. And of course, there wasn't any reference to a book."

Noah nodded. "We're aware of that. We've come to believe that those elements are our killer's signature, although it's very unusual. However, his intentions are more elusive. We're trying to understand his motives. Any other differences in the crime scenes might help us to find why he kills this way."

Even though she didn't really want to see the photos again, Erin took a deep breath and squared her shoulders. She was determined to do anything she could to help them find this guy. Noah brought the photos up on his computer. He went slowly through each one, asking her when to move on. She looked carefully at each one, trying to take in everything in case there was anything that might spark something that would help investigators find the guy who had caused so much pain and anguish. It was so weird to see something she'd created in her mind displayed in reality. It made her wonder if something inside her was twisted. How could she have imagined this kind of perversion? Murder *was* perversion.

No one had the right to snatch away someone else's life. It wasn't theirs to destroy. Every time a human being was killed, other people died as well. Children, grandchildren, and great grandchildren. Generations of humans who would never be born. It was monstrous.

As she stared at the carnage, something caught her eye. "Wait a minute," she said, pointing at the screen. "I didn't notice this before. The screen makes the photo larger. It's this. Her bracelet."

Noah frowned. "I don't understand. What about the bracelet?"

"It's a . . . what was it called?" She thought for a moment. "Jelly bracelets. Glitter jelly bracelets. They were popular around 2000–2001. I don't see them much anymore." She looked up at Noah. "This is the third time there's been some kind of toy, or in this case, a piece of jewelry worn by kids, at the crime scenes. There was an old Barbie at the first murder. A Beanie Baby at the second. The police chalked it up to something accidentally left behind by some kid who visited the park. But now there's this bracelet. It wouldn't be that concerning if they were somewhat contemporary. But these are all older."

"Looks like a pattern to me," Kaely said.

Noah was quiet for a moment before saying, "I believe the people analyzing these crime scenes felt the Barbie and the Beanie Baby were incidental elements. Not germane to the murders."

"I understand," Erin said. "But some old toy at each murder? I don't think it's coincidence. I think the killer is sending a message. This could be the actual signature you've been looking for. These items just might be a clue to the killer's identity."

TWENTY-TWO

Kaely sensed that Erin was right about the killer sending some kind of message, but what was it? He had a bad childhood and was killing out of anger? He didn't get enough toys? That didn't make sense. There was something else going on here, but she wasn't certain what it was. She could tell that, even though Noah was being as laid-back as he could be in a situation like this, the stress was getting to Erin. She clearly wanted to help, but seeing something she'd written played out so violently was difficult for her. When Noah glanced her way, she nodded her head slightly and frowned, trying to send a message that Erin needed some time to decompress. His return nod was barely noticeable.

"Let's take a break," Noah said. "I need a cup of coffee." He smiled at Erin. "How about you? I have to warn you first, though. It's truly awful."

"Oh, Noah," Kaely said, grinning. "It's not that bad. You're just used to mine." She pointed at him. "You told me a church brought doughnuts in this morning. Any left?"

"There are. Jelly-filled doughnuts and some great cheese

Danish. Can I interest you in one?" He directed his question to Erin.

She nodded. "I love cheese Danish. That is unless the church brought some Mallomars."

Noah laughed. "Sorry. I don't think they did." He stood and headed to the back of the building, where the tables and chairs were set up.

Kaely moved her chair closer to Erin. "You're doing great," she said. "Seeing that bracelet and connecting it to the other deaths? That's amazing."

"Someone else would have noticed," Erin said. "The Barbie and the Beanie Baby might have been regarded as superfluous. But with the bracelet . . . well, it seems these old toys are important to the UNSUB."

Kaely nodded slowly but didn't say anything.

"What are you thinking?" Erin asked.

Kaely turned her head to meet Erin's gaze. "What do the doll, the Beanie Baby, and the bracelet have in common?"

"Well, they're all old. I mean, I know Barbie and Beanie Babies are still around, but that Barbie was popular around twenty years ago."

"How do you know that?" Kaely asked.

"It's a special edition. A holiday Barbie. I really wanted one when I was ten. Never got it, though. My parents died right before Christmas. I always thought my mother planned to buy me one, but after the accident, there weren't any Christmas presents found in our house. Mom was really good about preparing for Christmas, but I guess with Courtney's problems, she just didn't have time to shop." She shook her head and looked away. While they were working together on Erin's first book, she'd told Kaely how her parents had died on ice-covered roads while rushing to the hospital after her seventeen-year-old sister had once again overdosed. Kaely felt such empathy for Erin. They'd both had very rough childhoods. Kaely felt it was one of the reasons that Erin had felt safe enough to open up to her. Erin turned her head and met Kaely's gaze, her expression tense. "You're the profiler. What do you think the toys and bracelet mean?"

"Well, it must have something to do with his childhood. But the doll, the bracelet, maybe even the Beanie Baby—they all seem more . . . feminine. Maybe he has a beef with a female sibling? I've seen that before." Kaely shook her head. "I need to think about it a little more. It's hard to focus here." She frowned and leaned back in her chair. "Okay, moving on, what do mystery and suspense authors have to do with the murders? Is he simply copying the authors so he doesn't have to think up MOs on his own?"

"That doesn't sound right, does it? I think we already decided that he's extremely intelligent, organized, and narcissistic."

"Yeah, you're right," Kaely said slowly. "He's clearly creative. The poems make that obvious." She frowned at Erin. There was another possibility tickling the corners of her mind, but she wasn't certain if she should voice it.

"What?" Erin said, her tone somewhat cross. "I can tell when you're thinking something, but you're not sure you should tell me."

Kaely raised an eyebrow. "So, you think you can read me, do you?"

"It's not that hard. The more time we spend together, the easier you are to understand. Please, tell me what's on your mind."

Kaely hesitated, unsure of what to say. The last thing she wanted to do was to frighten Erin. She knew she was tough, but she'd been through a lot. Kaely didn't want to add to her paranoia. Talking to the task force was clearly stressful enough.

"I have to wonder," she said slowly, "if the UNSUB is targeting authors for a reason. Maybe the toys and the poems are just a distraction. Perhaps one author is his actual target. The others are just designed to hide his real objective."

"Target?" Erin said. "You think he intends to kill one of us?"

"I think it's possible. And I'm certain Noah and the other special agents with the BAU have considered that as well."

"So, is this guy targeting authors or someone from his childhood?" Erin retorted. "Which is it?"

"Hey, it's okay," Kaely said gently. "I'm just tossing ideas around. I didn't mean to upset you."

"I . . . I'm sorry." Erin rubbed her forehead. "I haven't been around this many people for a while. It's making me uptight."

Kaely noticed Noah headed their way. "Maybe we could finish the interview at home later."

Erin shook her head. "No. I appreciate your concern, I really do. But I need to get through this. I can't run away or let you coddle me, even if your intentions are good. It's time I stopped being so afraid. I don't even recognize myself anymore. Besides, I doubt that Detective Herrington would appreciate it." She offered Kaely a tight smile. "The person I've become? That's one of the reasons I need God in my life. I still haven't been able to heal from what happened in St. Louis. I truly believe I need His help to get better. I'm tired of being scared of life, Kaely. And I'm tired of being trapped in that one night. I have the rest of my life to live. I need to move on."

"But it's not really just that night, is it, Erin?"

"What do you mean?"

Kaely smiled at her. "Before that night, you lost your parents and your sister. Your aunt. Then you found out that the man you loved was cheating on you. Those losses are bad enough, but not long after that, you watched him die. And you accidentally killed that young girl, Sarah. That's a lifetime of pain. Really hard for one person to bear."

Noah had almost reached them, but Kaely waved him away. He stopped in his tracks, then turned and went back to the place set up for people to eat. She was glad he was sensitive enough to realize that she needed some time alone with Erin.

"The truth?" Erin said.

"Please."

She turned her tear-filled eyes to Kaely. "I know this might sound . . . crazy. But sometimes I feel like years ago I shattered into a thousand pieces that are now rattling around inside me, like broken glass inside a jar."

Kaely pushed her chair up next to Erin and put her arms around her. "I'm making you a promise," she said softly. "If you give Him the chance, God will put all those pieces back together so that the cracks won't even show."

Erin tried to hold back a sob. "I'm holding you to that," she said. "I just want to feel joy again."

"You will." Kaely hugged her and then motioned for Noah to come back. She had no fear that God wouldn't do what she'd promised because He had done the same thing for her.

TWENTY-THREE

Adrian had planned to drive to the resort so he could talk to Merle. Sometimes it was the only way to calm him down. But Lisa told him to stay put and called Thomas, one of his officers. She asked him to go in Adrian's place. Arguing with Lisa was fruitless. Especially when they both knew she was right.

He had half a mind to leave work now, pick up his prescription, and crash on the couch. The pain wasn't getting any better. He was close to telling Lisa he was leaving, which would have delighted her, when the phone rang. The sound made his head pound so he picked up the receiver as quickly as he could. He could turn the sound down on his cell phone, but not on the landline. It was old school, with a cord, but he was used to it. He was a creature of habit.

"Chief Nightengale," he said.

"Chief? It's Dale. Lonzine and I drove by Erin Delaney's cabin. Something weird is going on."

Dale Robinson was a fine officer. Young, kind of inexperienced, but he made up for it with determination. He loved being a police officer, and his wife, Alice, and their two kids were more than proud of him.

"Define weird," Adrian said.

"Something about the front door didn't look right," Dale said. "So, we decided to check it out. It wasn't locked, boss. We pushed it open. The alarm was turned off. The house looks fine from what we could see from the porch. We didn't want to go inside until we talked to you first, though. We called the alarm company, and they told us that whoever opened the door had the code. They assumed it was Miss Delaney. But that can't be right, can it? Didn't you say she's still out of town?"

"Yeah, she is." Adrian sighed. "Look, stay there. I'm on my way. Don't go inside until I get there."

He hung up. Now he had no choice. He had to tell Erin about the break-in. This was her house. Her life. She had to decide what to do from here. He couldn't make that decision for her. First, he wanted to check things out himself. He got up from his chair a little too fast. The pain in his head made him sit down again. He opened his desk drawer and grabbed his bottle of over-the-counter pain reliever. It would have to do for now. He picked up the phone again and called Detective Sargeant Timothy Johnson. Tim was trained in forensics.

"Yeah, boss," Tim said.

"I need you to go with me to Erin Delaney's place. There's been a break-in. I want fingerprints, trace evidence, anything you can find."

"Sure, boss. I'll grab my kit and meet you outside."

Adrian popped several pills into his mouth and then swallowed them with the bottle of water next to him. Then he slowly stood up again. Those pills the doc ordered were sounding better and better every minute.

He was on the way out of his office when Lisa stepped inside again, blocking his way. What was it with this woman? Was it possible she really could read his mind?

She put her hands on her hips and stared at him. "You finally listening to some sense and going home?"

"I'm headed there," he said.

"When?"

He frowned at her. "I'm not sure you know who works for who here. As I've told you more than once, I don't have to check in with you."

"Actually, it's who works for *whom*." She didn't move, just kept staring at him. He knew that look. There wasn't any way to get past it.

He sighed. "I'm stopping by Erin's cabin because there's been a break-in. On the way, I'm going to pick up my medicine. After I'm done at Erin's, I'm going home to lay down and knock myself out with Doc's pain pills. Hopefully, I'll wake up again. Someday soon, anyway."

Lisa finally smiled. "I don't think Doc's plan is to send you into a drug-induced state of unconsciousness and a lifelong addiction to pain pills. I'm pretty sure you can trust him."

"Yeah, that's what all drug addicts say about their doctors."

Lisa laughed. "Hey, boss. If you're not feeling up to it tomorrow, stay home at least one day? I can't remember you ever missing a day of work. We can get by for a day or two without you."

Adrian winked at her. "That's what I'm afraid of. Finding out you don't need me."

He walked out of the station, Lisa's light laughter following him.

Erin quickly ate the cheese Danish and chased it down with coffee. The coffee wasn't that bad. Although she didn't normally like strong coffee, at that moment, it was exactly what she needed. Noah waited patiently until she was finished.

"Let's continue," she told him after wiping her mouth with her napkin.

"I know I seem to be repeating myself, but one more time, is there anyone you know who might be behind this?" Noah asked. "Do you have any enemies who would go to these lengths to target you? Someone not connected to your book. Maybe someone from your past?"

Erin grunted. "I was a police officer. There were a lot of criminals who would like to see me dead, but most of them are drug addicts, thieves, or both. And none of them could come up with something as intricate as this. Besides, even if it were possible, I left the force a long time ago. Why would they wait two years to target me? Doesn't make sense."

Noah shot a quick look at Kaely. What was that about? He cleared his throat, a sign of nervousness.

"Just ask it, Noah," she said. "I'd rather talk to you than to Detective Herrington."

"Kaely told me about the young girl who was shot accidentally during a gang war in St. Louis before you left the force. Could someone from her family be involved?"

Erin thought back to Sarah's father. He was angry at first but later let her know he'd finally realized it was an accident and that he didn't hold any ill will toward her. She could still see his grief-stricken face in her mind. It really never left. But she'd never noticed anything about him that would make her think he was capable of something like this. Besides, that was in St. Louis. The murders were happening in Virginia. And even if he wanted her to suffer for Sarah's death, he would never kill innocent people to make his point. He was a good man who'd been through a terrible tragedy.

"No, her father would never do something like this. He's a good man."

"Still, I need his name," Noah said.

Reluctantly, Erin gave it to him, along with Mr. Foster's address. "I really hope you don't bother him. I guarantee you he's not involved."

"So, this is the famous Erin Delaney," a deep voice behind her said, startling her. She turned around to find a tall man with brown hair and dark eyes staring down at her.

"Erin, this is Sargeant Paul Jackson with the Virginia State Police," Noah said. "He's working the case too."

He stepped up next to Erin and smiled. "I'm happy to meet you. Sorry you've been dragged into this. We're all hoping you can help us find this guy."

"Not sure I'm much help," Erin said. "But I'm trying."

"Hi, Kaely," Paul said. "Good to see you."

"It's been a while, Paul," Kaely said. "How are you?"

"Good. Just busy trying to find this UNSUB. We're all working on adrenaline and caffeine. I know you understand that."

"Yeah, I do," Kaely said.

"Paul, I'd like to talk to you, but I'm interviewing Erin right now," Noah said. "Maybe we could catch up later?"

Paul frowned at him. "Where's Herrington? Isn't he supposed to be conducting the interview?"

"He left to go check out another murder that might be tied to the others."

Erin noticed Noah's jaw tighten. He wasn't pleased with this interruption.

"Shouldn't someone from our department take his place?" Paul asked. "This is highly irregular."

"Look, Paul, your boss asked me to do it. I realize it's unusual, but you'll have to take that up with him when he returns, okay?"

"You bet I will." He offered Erin a tight smile. "It was nice to meet you, Miss Delaney. Kaely, good to see you."

Erin just nodded at him. Rather than leave immediately, he stared at her for several seconds before turning around and walking away. There was something about him that made her uncomfortable.

"Sorry," Noah said when Paul was out of earshot. "Jackson's very territorial. Frankly, he can be a jerk. He's certainly interested in you, Erin. As soon as I got here, he wanted to know when you were going to be here. I'm surprised he didn't ask you to sign his book. I know he has a copy. I saw it on his desk."

"I'm sorry he's upset," Erin said, "but I'm grateful you're doing the interview. I'm so much more relaxed with you than I am with Herrington."

Noah smiled. "I'm glad. However, like I told you, Herrington will probably still talk to you. Go over my notes."

"I know. Hopefully, I'll be better prepared to handle it."

"You're doing great," Kaely said. "And you'll be fine with Herrington."

"I appreciate your faith in me," Erin said. "I wish I felt the same way."

Kaely put her hand on Erin's shoulder. "Just remember that you're not alone. We're here, and we'll be here if Herrington interviews you."

Erin took a deep breath and smiled at Kaely. "Thanks, that helps more than I can say. I don't know what I'd do without the both of you." She squared her shoulders, and Kaely withdrew her hand. "So, let's get back to what we were talking about. The toys?"

"Yeah, the toys," Noah said. "They make some sense, something from the UNSUB's childhood. This makes us wonder if his anger is with a parent. God knows we've seen that before with serial killers." He shook his head. "And I agree with you. Sarah's father doesn't sound like a suspect. The toys would be newer. Something Sarah owned." He met her gaze. "Someone may contact him, Erin. I'm not sure what leads the police and the FBI are following."

"Well, I truly hope they don't bother him," Erin said. "He's been through enough."

"I hear you." Noah leaned forward and lowered his voice. "Was there anything you noticed from the other cases? I mean besides the toys?"

Erin considered his question for a moment. "The women who died all looked different, but they all had blonde hair. The authors look different. The first book copied was written by a man. That doesn't mean that the killer isn't targeting authors, but I think his choices point more at the victims."

"But you have blonde hair," Kaely said. "Are any of the other authors blonde?"

Erin thought for a moment. "I'm going from the author

photos on their books. Dan Harper has gray hair. Toni Sue Smith . . . I can't quite remember, but I think she has brown hair. Patricia Long had brown hair with blonde streaks. Of course, that was a few years back. I have no idea what her hair looks like now."

"I just can't see the connection with the authors," Noah said. "Why pick these particular writers? Was it because he felt he could pull off the murders he read about in their books?"

"Could be," Erin said. "I can't really answer that question, but I'm certain of one thing. He had a reason for picking us. This guy is very organized. He has a definite plan."

"I agree," Kaely said.

Noah nodded. "I do too. He has a strategy, a design, and he'll stick to it." He smiled at Erin. "Kaely is right. You would make an incredible behavioral analyst. You have great insight."

Erin was gratified by his statement, but it also hit her hard. That had once been her dream, but that was over. Her behavior after the shootings made it clear that she didn't have what it took to work for the BAU.

"Thank you," she choked out, "but I think it comes from Kaely. She's taught me so much." She cleared her throat as a way to push back the emotions that threatened to overwhelm her. It was the stress of this situation and her proximity to the career she'd always wanted that made her feel so emotional.

"Noah's right," Kaely said. "Maybe I had something to do with teaching you about profiling, but no one can teach the kind of instinct you have."

"Do you have any other ideas about these murders?" Noah asked.

"She's tired, Noah," Kaely said. "Erin will be with us for a while. Why don't we give her a break? If she comes up with something else, she can talk to you at home."

"That's fine," Noah said. "I'll give Detective Herrington what we have so far. I'll talk to him when he gets back. Maybe he'll accept what we have and call it good. But if not, I'll let you know, okay?"

Erin was about to tell him that she understood. The truth was, she hoped that didn't happen. She was uncomfortable around the brusque detective. Before she could respond, the back door of the building, the one she and Kaely had entered through, suddenly swung open. Erin watched as Detective Herrington walked in with a woman. As they came closer, she realized the face was familiar. It was Patricia Long. She thought she was the only author who was going to be here in person. So, what was Patricia doing here?

TWENTY-FOUR

"That's Patricia Long," Erin whispered to Noah and Kaely.

"You said you met her once?" Kaely asked.

"Yeah, she was doing a book tour and came to St. Louis. I was thrilled to meet her." She shrugged. "I'd written a couple of books for a small publisher. When I went to the book signing, it was the first time in my life I wondered what it would be like to be a bestselling author. Until that moment, the only thing I'd ever wanted was to be a cop." *And a behavioral analyst for the BAU.*

"Excuse me for a moment," Noah said. He got up and walked over to where Detective Herrington and Patricia Long stood. As they talked, Erin looked over at Paul's desk. He sat there, staring at her. She was worried he might try to cause a problem for Noah, but then she remembered that Herrington was the one who'd asked Noah to finish her interview. She wasn't certain who had more authority, Herrington or Paul Jackson. It would be interesting to see what happened now that Herrington was back. Erin noticed a copy of her book on Paul's desk. If he came back for a signature, she would be as nice as possible. Maybe she could help to smooth things over. She smiled at him and turned her attention back to Noah. A couple of minutes later, he came back to where she and Kaely waited and sat down.

"Seems she's in Virginia visiting her daughter," he said. "She goes to college here. They want to question Ms. Long."

"That's quite a coincidence," Kaely said, frowning. "She just happens to be in Virginia where the murders happened?"

Erin nodded. "I was thinking the same thing."

"Don't get ahead of yourselves," Noah said. "Some coincidences are just that. Coincidences."

Erin knew he was right, but it still set off alarm bells in her mind. Seemed odd. But maybe she was trying to see something that wasn't there. She felt you could get to know someone through their writing. An author's personality bled through the pages. She'd never noticed anything in Patricia Long's writing that would make her think the author could be a serial killer. Besides, the killer they were looking for was a man. If by chance she was female, she'd have to be extremely strong. The victims had probably fought back, and most women wouldn't have been able to overpower them, although it wasn't impossible. She frowned and pulled the photos back toward her.

"What are you thinking?" Noah asked.

"I'm sorry," Erin said. "I realize you found no evidence at the crime scenes. No DNA under the victims' fingernails. But were there any defensive wounds?"

"No. Nothing," Noah said.

"Could they have been drugged?"

Noah stared at her. "You're wondering if a woman could have killed our victims?" He was quiet for a moment before saying, "Nothing suspicious in their tox screens."

"There are some things that don't stay in the system that long," Erin said. "Like insulin. An overdose might not show up because it is absorbed quickly. And insulin is something naturally found in the body."

"Actually, there are quite a few things like that," Kaely said. She stared at Erin. "You're wondering if a woman could have drugged or poisoned the victims and then been able to kill them without resistance?"

"Yeah."

"I'm sure Herrington is wondering the same thing," Noah said. "Trust me, he'll check to see where Miss Long was when the other women were murdered."

Erin cleared her throat and nodded toward Herrington and Long as the two of them walked toward them.

"Ms. Delaney, I thought you might like to meet Patricia Long," Herrington said. "Our latest victim was killed using the MO from Ms. Long's book."

Herrington's tone wasn't necessarily sarcastic, but there was definitely a sharp bite to it. Why? Surely, he didn't actually suspect either one of them in the murders.

"Ms. Long is uncomfortable talking to us," Herrington said, suddenly making the situation clear. "I thought maybe since you're both in the same line of work, she would be more comfortable if you sat with her while I interview her."

"Herrington," Noah said, "why don't we give Ms. Long a little time to decompress? It's up to you, of course, but maybe some coffee and a little conversation would help before she talks to you?"

"Fine, but you know the rules," he said, looking at Erin. "No sharing anything about the case that we're trying to keep private."

Erin nodded. "Of course." She wasn't quite sure what he was talking about, but she wanted him to think she did.

"All right, I'll be back to interview her soon. I'll need my desk back." Herrington turned around abruptly and walked away.

"Sorry about that," Noah said in a low voice. "He's a little tightly wound. Of course, he has every right to be. We're trying to find this guy. If we'd cornered him sooner, maybe he wouldn't have had the chance to use your book as a road map to murder."

"Trust me," Patricia said, "I want him caught too. The idea that he took something from my book to kill someone makes me furious."

"I understand," Erin said. "He did the same thing to me." She held out her hand. "I'm . . ."

"Erin Delaney," Patricia said, shaking her hand. Erin remembered her low, throaty voice from the book signing. Very distinctive. Although she was about ten years older than Erin, Patricia didn't look it. She was a striking woman. Her brown hair was expertly streaked with blonde highlights. "I loved *Dark Matters*, Ms. Delaney. Perfectly written. Very suspenseful."

Erin opened her mouth to say *I love your books too* but suddenly felt like it would sound insincere. Instead, she said, "I met you six years ago when you did a book signing in St. Louis." She laughed nervously. "I wanted to tell you how much I loved your writing, and that you inspired *Dark Matters*, but I was afraid it would sound disingenuous. And it's Erin. Please."

For the first time since entering the building, Patricia smiled. "I can tell from your writing that you're a very straightforward person. And it's Pat."

"Thank you, Pat." Erin pointed toward the tables set up in the back of the building. "Would you like to share a cup of coffee with me? Maybe we could talk a little bit? I mean, we're both going through the same thing."

Patricia sighed. "Yes. Yes, please. The police showing up at my daughter's dorm room, insisting I come with them because some psycho used a book I wrote to commit murder? Yeah, I've been a little upset. I'm not quite sure what to think. Maybe talking to you will help."

"Would you rather we wait here?" Kaely asked. "I'm Kaely Hunter," she said to Pat, "and this is my husband, Noah. He's working on this case."

"Kaely Quinn-Hunter?" Patricia said with a smile. "I always look at the acknowledgments inside the novels I read. I guess it's because of all the people who've helped me with my books. You worked for the BAU, right?"

"Yes, and now my husband works there."

"I could tell that the research in Erin's book was spot-on. Now I know why. It's nice to meet you, Mr. and Mrs. Hunter."

"Kaely, please." She held out her hand, and Pat shook it.

"And Noah." Pat shook his hand too.

Patricia smiled at them, but Erin could see the weariness in her face.

"Let's go get that cup of coffee," Erin said. She stood and shook her head at Kaely and Noah, who nodded in understanding. Erin felt it would be better to talk to Pat alone. She was really upset. Erin headed toward the back of the building, Pat following behind her. Erin wasn't certain just how she could help. What could she say that would calm Pat's nerves when she was already fighting with her own?

TWENTY-FIVE

Adrian and Tim got to Erin's cabin as soon as they could. They found Dale and Lonzine, standing next to their car, awaiting Adrian's arrival. Almost every day he thanked God for the both of them. Dale was as steady as they came, always trying to do his best for the department and for his boss. Lonzine Lee was the officer every department should have. Tough, committed, yet compassionate when consoling victims. Adrian suspected that if he ever left Sanctuary's police force, Lonzine would be the next chief. She deserved it. The truth was, she could easily work in a larger town where her gifts could be used more often. But her grandmother lived here, and Lonzine took care of her. She would never leave the woman who raised her when her own mother died at a young age.

He and Tim got out of the Jeep and walked up to the officers. "So, the door was open when you got here?" he asked them.

Dale nodded. "We assume someone's been inside. We don't know if they're still there. After we called you, we waited out here. We knew you didn't want us to contaminate the scene."

"You're attacked, and now this?" Lonzine said to Adrian. She frowned. "Someone's after something, boss. I think we need to try to figure out what it is and if he finally got it."

"I agree," Adrian said. He walked up to the entrance of the cabin, and his officers followed him. "Tim, I need you to look for evidence that will lead us to a suspect. Fortunately for us, not that many people have been inside. You'll probably find prints from Erin, her friend Kaely, me . . . and maybe even from Steve Tremont since he owned the cabin before Erin. Anything else we find could belong to whoever broke in here." He frowned. "I'd love to know how our intruder knew the code for Erin's alarm system." He pointed at Tim's bag. "Booties and gloves for all of us."

Tim set the bag down, opened it, and took out the items Adrian had asked for. They all put booties over their shoes and pulled on latex gloves. Adrian wanted to do everything they could to make certain Erin would be safe when she came home. He'd been following the Novel Killer's crimes on the news, although reports were sketchy. The investigation was new, and he was certain the police were guarding their information as much as possible. He knew Erin was being protected by Kaely and her husband, and that the state police and the FBI were probably keeping an eye on her as well. She should be safe, but something in his gut kept nudging him. Why? Could the person behind the killings be connected to what was happening here? So many questions filled his mind. Now, he needed answers. And he had to keep Erin up-to-date about what was happening in Sanctuary, just in case it had something to do with the murders. He'd call her right after they searched her cabin.

"Boss, how many places do you want me to dust?" Tim said.

Adrian sighed. "I'm not sure. Use your own discretion. I'd certainly dust the front door, back entrance, and the alarm keypad. You'll need to retrieve Erin's fingerprints from the system so we can exclude them. And Kaely's would be helpful too."

"I agree," Tim said.

"We need to search upstairs," Dale said. "I'll look around. See if anything looks out of place."

Adrian nodded. "Sounds good. We'll focus our search down here."

As Dale headed up the stairs, Lonzine said, "Look, I know you don't want to put more pressure on Erin, but you've got to tell her everything that's happened, boss. Everything. Maybe she can tell us what someone might be looking for. We've got to find this perp and arrest him before someone gets seriously hurt."

Adrian was just about to respond when three shots rang out.

"You'd think I could approach this with a little more composure. I mean, I researched crimes, criminals, and death for years." Pat held out her hand. It shook.

"I understand," Erin said softly. "I was a cop in St. Louis for three years. The violence, the hatred, the gangs. I thought I was immune to it. I mean, you have to develop a thick skin when confronting the things I saw. Add to that, hatred for the police. The name-calling was bad enough, but I've had at least a dozen people spit in my face. Still, there were the people we helped. There are good, innocent people who live in fear because of the criminals that take up residence in certain neighborhoods. Most of them can't afford to move. There were elderly people who had no one to watch over them, protect them. I felt it was my job to help them. To be there when they needed me."

"And were you able to do that?" Pat asked.

"Sometimes," Erin said. "But not as well as I would have liked to."

"So, you left the force and decided to become a writer?"

Erin took a sip of the coffee she'd poured for them. Thankfully, someone had just made a fresh pot. She put her cup down and took a deep breath. "No, I left because one night, while we were trying to shut down two gangs fighting in the streets, my partner died, and a bullet from my gun went through the wall of an apartment building and killed a little girl."

Erin's chest felt tight, and she gulped for air. The sign of an anxiety attack. *Not now. Please, not now.*

"Look at me, Erin," Pat said. She put her hands on either side of Erin's face. Erin met her gaze. "Now, breathe with me. Slowly." Erin forced herself to breathe along with Pat. "Slower," she said. "No one except me knows what's going on. It's just us. Breathe, breathe, breathe," she said as she took in air and slowly let it out. Erin felt her body relax. The fear of not being able to catch her breath was the worst part of a panic attack. The second was making a scene in front of other people.

"I'm okay," Erin said softly as the symptoms faded. "I'm okay," she repeated. "Thank you."

Pat took her hands off Erin's face and smiled. "I've had my

share of panic attacks. Are you stressed about the method of murder the killer used from your book? Or is it something more?"

Erin looked around the room, wondering if anyone had noticed her little meltdown. Either they were all busy with something else, or they were trying to act as if they hadn't seen anything. She was relieved.

"After I left the department, I shut myself up in my apartment," she said, leaning back in her chair. "I only felt safe there. Nowhere else felt secure. I know it doesn't make sense . . ."

"Yes, it does," Pat said. "It's called agoraphobia, and I wrestle with it too. This place? I mean, it's huge inside. But if I'm not careful, I could begin to feel trapped. Like I can't get out. Of course, I can—the fear isn't real. But that isn't how it feels. It's like the world is outside of these walls, and I can't get to it." This time when she smiled, it was real, not forced. She seemed more comfortable. Maybe misery really does love company. The two women now had a bond. Not one they really wanted, but one that they both understood.

"Yes, it's a feeling of being out of control," Erin said. "Like you said, trapped, or unsafe. I'm actually better than I used to be. Kaely has been a great help. I rarely have attacks now." She shook her head. "I . . . I'm sorry for putting you through this. Kaely is the only other person I ever shared that with. My reason for leaving the department, I mean."

Pat looked down at the table for a moment. Then she lifted her head and met Erin's gaze. There were tears in her eyes.

"You mentioned that I haven't written a book in a while. I . . . I had a stalker. A man who became obsessed with me. With my books. First, there were the emails. When it started, they were just comments praising my books. Then he wanted to meet me. They became a little inappropriate. I stopped responding to him. Blocked him where I could." She wiped away a tear that ran down her cheek. "He found my address. Do you know you can find almost anyone's address online?"

"Yes, unfortunately, we don't have much privacy anymore."

"He started sending letters," she said, her voice cracking. "Angry letters. I called the police. They said they couldn't do much because he hadn't done anything wrong." She grunted. "I guess someone has to hurt us before they can be stopped. Found out he lived about twenty miles away from me, so I got a restraining order. And then, one night, I woke up to find someone in my house."

"You didn't have an alarm?"

Pat nodded. "He'd actually gotten a job at the alarm company. He was able to get inside, reset the alarm, and come upstairs to my bedroom."

Erin wanted to say something. Wanted to tell Pat how sorry she was, but at that moment, she felt she should stay quiet.

"I heard him on the stairs. I lived alone so there shouldn't have been anyone in the house. I . . . I knew it was him. I'd bought a gun for protection." The expression on her face broke Erin's heart. "When he came into the room . . . I shot him." She smiled sadly. "Some people ask the police why they don't shoot an armed person in the shoulder or the leg? At that moment, it doesn't occur to you. You're just trying to neutralize the threat against you. I fired several times. He died. Turned out he was a disturbed man who'd needed help but never got it."

"It's not your fault."

"I know that," she said. "But killing someone? It changes you. No matter what anyone says, I took a life. That's why I quit writing. And now someone is using my last book as a map to murder?" She shook her head. "I wish I'd never written a book in my life. And I don't plan to ever write another one."

Hearing Pat voice Erin's own thoughts shook her. At that moment, she wondered once again if she should ever write another book.

TWENTY-SIX

Adrian sat in the waiting room. Perfect name for this place. Waiting. Dale's wife was next to him, trying to be brave. Trying not to fall apart. Dale was in surgery. He'd been shot twice before returning fire. The intruder had escaped out of an upstairs window, landing in the bushes below. Dale thought he might have hit him, but he wasn't certain. He couldn't describe him more than to say that he was male, white, and wearing a dark hoodie. After that, he'd lost consciousness. Adrian and his officers had been so busy attending to him, no one had chased the intruder. Later, they'd try to find him, but for now, Adrian was focused on Dale. Still, Adrian wanted the man who had shot his officer. Who was he, and why had he been in Erin's house? What was going on?

His mind was still trying to process what had happened. None of his officers had ever been seriously injured on the job before. He'd seen it happen in Chicago, but moving to Sanctuary had allowed him to let his guard down. They should have had their guns drawn when they went inside the house. Why hadn't they done that? Dale and Lonzine hadn't noticed anything that made them think someone was still inside. No car. No movement. Nothing that made them suspicious. Standard procedure was to draw your weapon anytime you entered a building that had been breached. Why hadn't he followed his training? He'd been attacked outside Erin's cabin, yet he still failed to encourage his officers to protect themselves. Even as he asked himself the question, he knew the answer. It was because this was Sanctuary. Not Chicago. Yet just a few months ago, they'd encountered evil. Adrian had seen it as a fluke. He even chalked up the attack on him as something unusual. His mistake may have cost Dale his life. He vowed to never take another chance with his officers' lives again. Even if it made them feel paranoid. He wiped tears from his eyes as he prayed silently yet fervently for Dale's life.

He looked across from where he and Alice sat. Lonzine, one of the strongest people he'd ever known, was also wiping away tears. To her, everyone in the department was family, and now she was suffering. He could hear her whispered prayers for Dale. So could Alice, who seemed frozen, unable to process what was happening. He'd seen this before. An officer in Chicago, a friend of Adrian's, was shot by a druggie who thought he was the devil coming to take his soul. Adrian had sat with his wife, just like this. She'd been like a statue, unable to move, unable to speak. When the doctor in Chicago came out into the waiting room, Adrian knew his friend had died by the look on the surgeon's face. It was only then that Kim fell apart, overwhelmed with emotion. He prayed as hard as he could that it wouldn't happen a second time.

"Mrs. Robinson?"

Adrian had been so lost in his thoughts that he hadn't

noticed that the doctor had stepped into the waiting room. But Alice had seen him. Her eyes were focused only on him. She didn't blink. Just stared.

"Will you come with me?" the doctor said. "We have a room where we can talk."

"No!"

Alice's response startled him, but the doctor appeared to take it in his stride. He was probably used to this.

"Tell me now," she said through gritted teeth. "Now."

The doctor nodded. "Dale came through the surgery just fine. Both bullets passed through without causing major damage. He'll need some time to recover, but he'll be able to resume his duties in a month or two."

Alice looked at Adrian. "I don't want him on the force anymore. I almost lost him. I won't go through this again."

Adrian didn't say anything, just nodded. He knew how she felt at that moment, but after Dale was better, she would probably see things differently. Dale loved his job. He'd be back. But now wasn't the time to talk about that.

"I'd really like to speak to you about what to expect during his recovery," the doctor said. "Now can we go somewhere to talk about that?"

Alice nodded, got up, and followed the doctor without a word to Adrian or Lonzine. He wasn't offended. He nodded at Lonzine, and they got to their feet.

"I think it would be best if we leave her alone for a couple of days," he said. "We'll send flowers and check in with her when she's had a chance to process what happened."

"But what about Dale? I'd like to let him know we're thinking of him," Lonzine said.

"Let's call him tomorrow. Today, we need to find out who

was in Erin's home and why. What was he doing there? Was it a simple robbery? Or was there more to it?"

"Okay," Lonzine said. She frowned. "Odd to shoot at a police officer over a simple B&E. He would have been arrested, maybe spent a little time in jail, but nothing major. Why take a chance at throwing away your life by trying to kill a police officer?"

She was right. "Well, we're going to have to find the answers to those questions, aren't we?"

His phone rang and it startled him. "Just a minute," he said. It was Tim. He listened, thanked him, and hung up. "They found blood at Erin's house. Outside in the bushes and along a path where a car had been parked behind the cabin, hidden in the trees. The tire tracks are fresh."

"We looked back there," Lonzine said, "but we didn't see a car."

"It was well hidden. Besides, you weren't searching for a vehicle in that location. Easy to miss."

By the look on her face, Adrian could tell that she felt guilty about not finding it. If she and Dale had discovered the automobile when it was parked back there, they would have entered the cabin with guns drawn. Dale might not have been shot.

"Tim took samples of the blood," Adrian said. "He sent it for DNA testing. The lab promised to get back to us later today. Maybe we'll get lucky."

Lonzine nodded. "Good." She frowned at him. "Have you called Erin yet?"

Adrian shook his head. "I was going to tell her that someone was in her house. Now, I have to tell her that Dale was shot there." He sighed. "This is one phone call I don't want to have to make."

Erin was thankful that Detective Herrington was going to allow her to sit with Pat while he interviewed her. It was obvious how nervous she was. It was also clear that Herrington wasn't going to get what he needed unless he could find a way to calm her. He hadn't shown her the same understanding and allowed Kaely to stay with her. Either she'd hidden her apprehension well, or he'd decided he needed to change his tactics. He pulled another chair up to his desk and gestured for Erin to sit down.

"I know this will be difficult," Herrington said to her, "but I need you to look at some photos." He cleared his throat, proving that even for a seasoned investigator, these murders were disturbing. Having to tell the truth to this uneasy woman was proving to be a challenge.

"How do you know this murder was based on my book?" she asked.

"The murder follows your plot exactly," he said. "And he left a copy of your book along with a poem."

Pat swallowed hard. "Read the poem, please." She reached over and grabbed Erin's hand. She was fairly certain Pat had done it subconsciously.

"All right," Herrington said, clearing his throat again. "In every murder, he's left behind a poem that includes the title of the novel. We found this one written on a piece of paper that was folded and placed inside your book. It reads:

"I am death, created by evil and fueled by hate.
I hold in my hands your ultimate fate.
You feel my presence as I draw near.
I feed on your anguish and relish your fear.

As your life drifts away, I make you **Grin**.
Now we wait while investigators uncover your sin."

Pat gasped and squeezed Erin's hand harder. "It doesn't make any sense. What sin?" Her voice shook. She took a shaky breath, clearly trying to calm herself. "Look, our books are based on research, not firsthand knowledge. But I believe serial killers have a signature. A reason to kill. Unless he's a frustrated novelist whose manuscripts have been rejected, what's his motive? Why pick these books? My book?"

"I've brought up the same thing," Erin said. "Of all the serial killers I've studied, there's no motive here that makes sense. We know he's angry, but we have no idea why. This makes it very difficult to profile him. To understand him."

She noticed Herrington's irritated glance but decided to ignore it.

"I'm not asking you about motive," he said to Pat. "I want to know if you know anyone who might have done this. Anyone who had a reason to copy the murders in your book. I need you to look over these photos and tell me if you see anything that might help us locate our unknown subject."

"You can say UNSUB, Detective Herrington," Pat said. "I know what it means."

He let out a small sigh. She glanced over at Erin and rolled her eyes. Herrington didn't seem to notice. He clicked open a file on his computer and turned the screen toward her. Although she thought she was prepared, Erin was shocked by the pictures. The first showed a woman lying on the ground, her face disfigured by the killer's attempt to turn her mouth into a grotesque smile. Her throat was cut, and her blouse was open, another smile carved on her chest. It was immediately clear that it was created after she'd been dead for a while. There wasn't much bleeding from that wound. The cut on her throat had killed her. The rest, her chest and her face, were done later.

"It's . . . it's horrendous," Pat said. "When you write something like this it's . . . not real. My imagination never envisioned this." She frowned. "Is this my *sin*? That I wrote this book?"

"I understand, Pat," Erin said. "But writing a book isn't a sin. He's trying to make you feel guilty. All of us. The authors. He wants us to believe we're responsible for his madness. But we're not. This is on him and him alone."

"I know you're right, but this is . . . monstrous."

Erin nodded her assent. This killer really was a monster. It was then that she noticed something. "Her hair is blonde too," she said. She looked at Herrington. "That's important. All of the victims have been blonde. You can now be certain that he's hunting a type."

"You're right," Pat said. Herrington clicked through the additional photos, including one of the poem and another one of the book. "No fingerprints?" she asked.

Herrington shook his head. "We think he's wearing gloves. So far, we have no evidence that could lead us to him."

"No sexual assault?" Patricia asked. She'd let go of Erin's hand and her voice was steadier.

"No. Not with any of the victims."

Pat shook her head. "I'm sorry, Detective, but I can't help you. This UNSUB has almost perfectly re-created the murders in my book. And I can't think of anyone who could have done this. There was one man, but he's dead."

"We know about Jerry Jasper," Herrington said. "We've

already started checking out family members and friends. He was an only child, and his parents are dead. And Jerry didn't have many friends. He was a weird guy."

"Was there any kind of toy at the scene?" Erin asked.

"Toy?" Herrington shook his head. "No, nothing like that. I know you think the UNSUB is leaving twenty-year-old toys behind, but that didn't go anywhere. We don't think they have any connection to the crime."

Erin was a little surprised and even more disappointed. She thought she'd found something linking the killings.

Herrington suddenly got a strange look on his face and clicked open another file on his laptop. He looked at Pat.

"These are shots of her clothing," he said. He pointed to something next to the woman's discarded jeans.

Pat looked at the photo and shook her head. "This doesn't mean anything to me. I have no idea what it is." She glanced over at Erin. "Do you recognize this?"

Erin scooted closer to the screen. What she saw made it hard to catch her breath. "It's a My Little Pony sticker." She looked at Herrington. "This proves that he's leaving children's toys at each scene. This is how you'll catch him."

TWENTY-SEVEN

"Can I ask you a favor?" Erin said after they'd gotten into the car and were getting ready to head back to Kaely's.

Kaely nodded. "Of course, what is it?"

Erin hesitated a moment before asking, "Could we go to the lake where Sophie Rogers's body was found?"

Kaely frowned at her. "You know the scene was thoroughly processed, right? I guarantee you that the crime scene techs did a thorough job."

"I'm not saying they didn't. I just . . . I just want to see it. Sometimes looking at the scene in person helps me to understand more about a murder."

Kaely was quiet for a moment. "Erin, I could make that happen, but isn't it possible it might make it harder on you?"

"Maybe, but I really want to do this," Erin said. "I know you said it was a private lake."

"I have a friend who can get us in. The police have released the scene." Kaely stared at Erin for a moment longer before taking her phone from her purse. She placed a quick call and then hung up. "Okay. My friend left our names at the gate. We can get in . . . if you're sure."

Although somewhere inside, Erin wasn't completely convinced this was a good idea, for some reason she felt drawn to the site. She nodded at Kaely. "I'm certain."

About thirty minutes later, they were pulling up to the entrance of the lake. The man at the gate verified who they were and let them in. The park was quiet. It was April, but it was still chilly this time of the year in Virginia. Kaely drove around the outer perimeter of the lake and then parked. They got out of the car and walked over to where a large dock stretched out from the shore and into the water.

Erin was silent as she walked to the end of the dock. This was where Sophie Rogers died. Or at least where her body was dumped. The medical examiner's report said they didn't find any water in Sophie's lungs, which meant she was dead when she went into the lake. Seeing this place . . . knowing that someone had died this way because of what she'd written . . . Erin suddenly felt a little faint and swayed. Kaely quickly put her arm around Erin's waist, helping to steady her.

"I think we need to go home," Kaely said.

"I wish I'd never written that book," Erin said softly.

"No, you don't. It was a good book. Again, he could have used someone else's plot. The fact that he picked yours? A big mistake." Kaely pulled on Erin's shoulders until she was facing her. "You're going to help catch him, Erin. Don't you see that? I'm glad it was your book, because we're going to put him away for good."

Erin looked back at her friend and thought about what she'd said. Although she was still battling feelings of guilt, Kaely's logic made sense. Maybe she was right.

Erin stepped away from her friend and gazed around once more. Being here hadn't brought any new revelations, but it had made Sophie's death seem more real. And it had also made her even more determined to see justice done. She wouldn't stop until the Novel Killer was either in prison or dead.

After collecting all the evidence they could from inside and outside Erin's house, Adrian called the alarm company to make sure everything was secure. Then he increased the number of times his officers checked out the cabin, making certain it was closely watched until Erin returned. Although he had no idea what her schedule was, he felt he had to call her right away. When she answered the phone, he asked if it was convenient to talk.

"Sure. We're back at Kaely's house. It was a long day. I have to admit that I'm pretty tired."

"I'm sorry," Adrian said, "but I have to give you some rather bad news." He took a deep breath and went over the events of the day.

She gasped when he brought up Dale. "Is he okay?" she asked.

"Yes, he's going to be fine." He had no plan to tell her about the attack on him. Not now. It wasn't important. Maybe when she came home. "We didn't catch whoever was in the house, Erin. I've contacted the alarm company. They know that no one should go inside the house until you return. I told them either you or I will contact them once you're headed home. We've locked everything up tight, and we're watching it closely. No one will get in again. But . . . do you have any idea what this guy might be looking for?"

"No," she said. "Like I said, I don't have anything of real

value inside. No safe. No cash under my mattress. Maybe he realized I was out of town and took it as an invitation to break in and look around. He probably thinks I have a lot of expensive things because of my book."

"Yeah, that could be right." Although her assumption made sense, his gut told him something different. This guy hit him and then shot an officer. He wasn't just prowling around, looking for something to steal. No one would take the chances this guy had unless he was trying to get his hands on something really valuable. He was committed and had a goal in mind. Adrian couldn't tell Erin what he was thinking. He didn't want to frighten her any more than he already had.

"Look," she said, her voice tight. "It would be difficult for me to come home right now. Are you certain everyone's safe? I don't want anyone else hurt."

He noticed that she didn't ask about her house first. She was more concerned about his officer than she was her possessions.

"Don't worry. Everything will be okay from here on out," Adrian said. "You just do what you need to do."

"I really appreciate that," she said. "I wish I could tell you why this is happening, but I honestly don't have a clue."

He could hear how tired she was, and he knew this wasn't the time to push her. He really wanted to know what it was inside the cabin that the intruder was looking for. Obviously, Erin had no idea. He wanted this guy stopped, but most of all, he wanted him arrested and in jail for shooting Dale. Adrian intended to do whatever it took to see that happen.

"Do you know when you'll be back?" he asked.

She sighed. "No. Today was the first day at the command

center. I think I may have to go back again tomorrow. To be honest, I'd like to help with the investigation if they'll let me. I've been deputized, can you believe that? Kaely believes I will be safer here, in Virginia, with them. After what you just told me, she may be right." She paused for a moment, then said, "That guy couldn't be looking for me, right? I mean, it's fairly obvious that I'm not there."

"I can't be sure, but I agree with you. If he was interested in hurting you, he would have made sure you were in town first. Besides, he went out of his way to make certain no one was in the house before he went inside."

"How did he manage to not trip the alarm?"

"I don't know," Adrian said, "but I think you need to change your code immediately. It's possible he has it. Can you do it from there?"

"I'm sure I can," Erin said. "I'll take care of it right away."

"Good, that will make me feel better. Why don't you text me your new code once it's changed."

"I will. And Adrian, thank you for watching over the cabin. I'm so, so sorry about Dale."

"Me too, but the important thing is that he's going to be okay."

Adrian wanted her to come home, but she was probably right. Staying with Kaely and her husband was the safest thing to do right now. He was certain they'd take good care of her.

"Will you let me know when you're on your way back?" Adrian asked.

"Sure. Like I said, I'm not certain how long I'll be here. I'd like to wait until they catch this guy. We'll have to wait and see what happens."

"We've seen some of the news reports," Adrian said. "Are they any closer to finding him?"

Erin sighed. "I don't know. There's been another one. I don't think the media has it yet. This time he stole his idea from Patricia Long's book *Grin*."

"I read that book," he said. "It was good, but she hasn't published anything for a few years. I've wondered why."

"She's here," Erin said. "She was visiting her daughter in Virginia when they found the body. I know why she's not writing now. I'll save that story for when I get back, okay?"

"Sure. Not a problem." He hesitated a moment, but something was bothering him, and he felt the urge to share it. "If I remember right, Long lives in Pennsylvania, right? Her stories were all set there."

"Yeah, that's right," Erin said. "Before you mention that her being here is a strange coincidence, I've already thought about that. But if you met her, Adrian, you wouldn't see her as a suspect. She's just not the type. Besides, investigators are pretty confident the killer is a man. It would be hard for a woman to overcome these victims. I'd be worried that Pat might be a target, but the first murders happened when she was still in Pennsylvania. It really seems like coincidence that she's here. Maybe this guy found out and decided to kill again just because she was in the state? I don't know. My mind is working overtime. Forget what I said. I'm really exhausted and a little overwhelmed with everything."

"You need to get some rest," he responded. "Well, like I said, don't worry about your place. Truthfully? I think whoever broke in is long gone. A confrontation with the police makes intruders nervous. I'm sure everything will be fine from here on out."

"Please give Dale my love, will you? Tell him I'm praying for him."

"I will."

Adrian disconnected the call, but he was struck by a couple of things. First of all, he didn't completely believe her when she said she didn't suspect Patricia Long. He knew her well enough to hear a shadow of doubt in her voice. Secondly, she just said she was going to pray for Dale. That was new. He sat at his desk and stared at his phone, wishing he was in Virginia, not here worrying about Erin from so far away. All he could do was pray that God would watch over her and keep her safe. He cared deeply about her, but there was no indication she felt the same way. He tried to push thoughts of her out of his mind, but it wasn't easy.

"I'm coming back."

"Did you get what we need?" Lee asked, shielding his mouth over his phone. He was trying to keep his voice down so that the old lady inside the house couldn't hear him. He hadn't yet finished trimming this grouch's lawn. She had an outside camera and was watching him through her window as he took the call. He didn't want her to call his supervisor and complain. He had to have this crappy job. It was all he had. For now, anyway. He glanced her way then turned his back to her. Stupid witch. It was only April. It wasn't like the grass was that long anyway.

"Yeah, I got it. But that cop shot me, man. *Shot me!*"

"You didn't go to the hospital, did you? They have to report gunshots."

"I didn't go to the hospital. I'm not an idiot. It's not that bad. I took care of it myself. Besides, I paid him back. I don't think he'll be causing anyone problems again."

"You shot a cop?" Lee said. He glanced back and looked at the old lady, who finally walked away from the window. She was probably watching him on her camera now. "Are you insane? The police will be all over this now. That was really stupid."

"If you want out, I'll gladly finish the job. Just tell me. I could do a lot with all that money."

"Okay, okay," Lee said. "I think we have everything we need. Come on back." He sighed. Things were really complicated now. He shouldn't have teamed up with Pilcher. He really was nuts. "We have to finish this," he said through gritted teeth.

"You better be willing to see it through. You promised me."

Lee grunted. "I have no intention of letting her out of this now. Erin Delaney's gonna pay. And pay big time."

TWENTY-EIGHT

When Kaely and Erin got back to the house, Erin sat down at the table in the kitchen while Kaely poured them both a glass of iced tea. She'd been upset about Dale and a little worried about her house. She'd called the alarm company and changed the code. Then she'd texted the new code to Adrian. On the way home, Kaely had asked if she could pray for Dale. Listening to her pray in a way that made it clear she believed that God not only heard her but would answer had given Erin some peace about the situation.

After handing Erin her glass, Kaely sat down next to her. After taking a sip from her own glass, Kaely put it down. Erin had stayed with Pat as Herrington asked her the same questions Noah had gone over with her. But except for her dead stalker, there wasn't anyone who had ever made Pat feel uncomfortable enough to be a suspect. Nor did she have any idea who could have committed the murders. Pat also handed over her phone and laptop. Hopefully, the police would find something that could help. Pat was concerned about getting her items back, but when Erin showed her that hers had already been returned, she seemed to relax.

"You said you wanted to ask God into your life when we got home," Kaely said. "Are you ready to do that?"

Erin nodded. She felt the need to say something, but for some reason she couldn't. It was as if the words were stuck in her throat.

"There are some things I want you to understand before we pray," Kaely said. "Some people believe God is in charge of everything. That nothing happens that isn't His will. That's wrong. He created a beautiful world for us, but people decided to disobey Him and let evil in. That wasn't what He wanted. He gave us free will, Erin. We're not puppets on strings. That's why it has to be our decision to turn our lives over to Him. To allow Him to come inside of us and change us into the person He created us to be. Do you understand that?"

Again, Erin nodded. She felt tears welling up in her eyes, but she didn't care. She felt something again. Like she had earlier. There was a presence in the room. Something warm, sweet, and loving.

"I talked to you about Jesus before, but I want to make sure you understand this too. Jesus is the Son of God. He came down to the earth to live as a man among people. He felt the same things we do and was tempted the way we are, but He was sinless. Perfect. He came for one reason. To pay the price for the sin that led us away from God. All the sin that ever existed. He paid the price for any sin you ever committed and any sin you ever will commit. This is hard to imagine, but this perfect Man not only paid the price by giving His life as the only sacrifice ever needed for the world . . ." Now it was Kaely's turn for tears. She choked them back. "He *became* sin on the cross." She turned her head away for a moment.

A deep sob forced its way from somewhere deep inside her. Then she took a deep breath and turned her tear-filled eyes on Erin's. "I . . . I can't imagine how that felt. He became the most disgusting, despicable sin you can imagine. For us. It must have been beyond torturous. Even His Father had to turn His face away from His Son, something Jesus had never experienced before. That's why He cried out, 'My God, my God. Why have you forsaken me?' When Jesus took His last breath, the curtain that separated men from the inner part of the temple in Jerusalem tore in two. From top to bottom. It symbolized that there was no more separation between God and man. Jesus paid the price so that today, you can become His child. His own beloved daughter. Your spirit will come alive, and you'll be one with God. He will always see you as righteous." She gazed deeply into Erin's eyes. "Do you understand what I've said?"

"Yes," Erin whispered. Even though it was difficult for her mind to comprehend, inside she knew what Kaely had said was true. There was no doubt in her mind that God was real and that Jesus had done exactly what Kaely had told her. The understanding of what Jesus had done on the cross became more real than anything else in her mind. And she wanted God with all her heart.

"All you have to do is accept what He did on the cross," Kaely said gently. "And exchange your sin for His forgiveness. In fact, it's called the *great exchange*. Do you want me to pray first and then you can repeat what I say?"

Erin shook her head. She wanted this to be from her own heart. From her own lips. She closed her eyes. "Dear God," she said, her voice shaking. "I want the new life Jesus died to give me. I accept the forgiveness He purchased for me. I'll do my best to follow You the rest of my life. Let Your Holy Spirit live in me and through me. And thank You for Your incredible love. I will cherish it . . . and You . . . forever."

It was at that moment that the feeling that was all around her came inside. She felt the most incredible love. It flowed through her. She was suddenly different. She could tell that she was no longer the same person she'd been before. She wasn't alone anymore, and she never would feel that way again. She scooted her chair closer to Kaely, put her arms around her friend, and sobbed until she couldn't cry anymore.

Kaely held her until Erin gently pushed away. "Thank you," she whispered. "I'm so happy. I'm not sure why I'm crying."

Kaely smiled at her. "Sometimes joy drips out of our eyes."

Erin laughed. "That is so corny."

"I know. I was sorry as soon as I said it."

Erin started to giggle and couldn't seem to stop. Kaely laughed along with her. Finally, Erin leaned back in her chair and shook her head. "I feel like a wrung-out dish towel. I'm exhausted . . . and hungry."

Kaely nodded. "I've got to go to the store and pick up some groceries. I forgot to take anything out of the freezer before we left. I'd planned to stop on the way home, but I forgot to do that too."

Kaely started to say something else, but suddenly the doorbell rang. "Stay here," she said to Erin. She got up and went to the front door.

Erin listened as the door opened. She heard a woman's voice. After a brief wait, Kaely came back into the kitchen. She was with Shannon.

"Shannon has something to tell us," Kaely said.

"While you two were gone," Shannon said, "I drove past the house and noticed a man snooping around. I turned around and pulled into the driveway. I asked if I could help him. At first, he was evasive, but then he started asking questions about you, Erin. Where you were. If you were staying here. Then he actually offered to pay me for what he called your *story*. That's when I realized he was a reporter who wanted to know more about this serial killer the police are looking for and the location of the place where they're working. I lied to him. Told him you'd been here but that you'd gone home." She shook her head. "I didn't know what else to do. I hope I didn't do the wrong thing."

Kaely put her arm around Shannon's shoulders. "I don't usually advise lying, but in this case, it may have been the only thing that would have sent him on his way. Thank you, Shannon."

Shannon looked at Erin. "If I see him again, I'll let you know. I'm sorry you're going through this."

"Thanks, Shannon. I really appreciate it."

Shannon smiled at her, said good-bye, and left.

"Wonder if it was that reporter from Richmond," Erin said once the front door closed.

"It's possible." Kaely paused for a moment. "He might be back. I think it would be a good idea to put your car in the garage. Noah can park in the driveway when he gets home. If that reporter hasn't thought to check the license plates on our cars, let's hide yours before it occurs to him."

"Good idea."

Kaely opened the garage door, and Erin went outside. She drove her car into the garage. Chester ran to the front door and watched her. He was probably confused as to why Erin got into the car without him. He stayed calm, though. Since spending time around Mr. Hoover, he'd settled down quite a bit. Didn't seem as nervous. Who knew the big Maine coon would have that kind of effect on him? Erin's resolve about adding another furry creature to their home was shaken a bit. But not enough that she actually changed her mind.

Once her car was in the garage and the door was closed, they went back inside. Chester's tail wagged when she walked into the kitchen. Then he plopped down next to her as she took a seat at the kitchen table.

Kaely had just joined her when her phone rang. Kaely picked it up and looked at the caller's name. "Noah." She answered the phone and said, "Hello, honey."

Erin tried not to listen, but Kaely's expression alarmed her. She didn't say much, but when she finally disconnected the call, Erin could tell something was wrong. She didn't want to question her since whatever Noah told her might have been personal. However, her instincts told her it was something else.

"Everything all right?" she asked, hoping it didn't sound like she was being nosy.

Kaely sat back down in her chair. "I don't know. Patricia Long is missing."

TWENTY-NINE

"Missing?" It was the last thing Erin had expected to hear.

"Noah said they're not panicking yet, but she's not answering her phone, and no one knows where she is. The officer who took her to her hotel after she left the command center went back to check on her. She's not there, but all her stuff is still in the room. They're searching the hotel again now, just in case they missed her the first time around. There are two restaurants inside as well as a bar and several restrooms. She wasn't supposed to leave the premises. Investigators planned on having her return to the command center tomorrow."

"Maybe she went to see her daughter," Erin said. "Is her car still there?"

"I don't know. Noah didn't mention her car, but I'm sure they checked that right away. The daughter says she hasn't seen or heard from her."

"Maybe she got a cab or an Uber?"

"It's possible, but where would she go?" Kaely sighed. "I just pray she's all right."

"I do too. I like her."

"What's your gut telling you?" Kaely asked. "You spent the most time with her. Do you think she left on her own? Or do you think it sounds suspicious?"

It was almost impossible for Erin to answer that question. She'd only spent a couple of hours with Pat. She told Kaely that.

Kaely frowned. "I've never known anyone who could read people as well as you can, Erin. Just give me your first impression."

"I . . . I can't see her running away," Erin said slowly. "I mean, she had a really bad experience with a stalker. It's why she quit writing. I'd think she'd stay in a location where she felt safe. Like the hotel. She seemed really nervous but committed to helping with the investigation. Based on the short time we had together, I don't think she'd take off without telling anyone. And she'd certainly contact her daughter if she was leaving the hotel. I got the impression that they're really close."

Kaely got up and took some cups out of the cabinet. She added water and tea bags and then put them in the microwave. "I think she's in trouble," she said.

"You sure you're not being paranoid?" Erin asked.

"Maybe, but better safe than sorry." Kaely hesitated for a moment, staring at Erin as if she was unsure about what to do next.

"Maybe the whole thing was just too much for her. She could be holed up in a different hotel somewhere."

"I guess that's a possibility," Kaely said. "But she would have taken all of her things. Plus, the police have been checking her credit cards. So far, there's been no activity. And from what you say, I don't think she'd worry her daughter like this."

Kaely shook her head. "I just don't buy it." When the microwave dinged, she took out the cups and handed one to Erin.

"You're the one who taught me about serial killers. If the first murder wasn't the most important one, then maybe Pat was the reason behind his spree. His last murder. I certainly hope he hasn't taken her."

"Yeah, me too."

Erin could hear the uncertainty in Kaely's voice. "You need to do your profiling thing again."

Kaely looked at her with one eyebrow raised. "My profiling *thing*?"

"You know what I mean."

"Maybe when I get back from the store. I've got to pick up a few things. It's not far away. You want to come with me?"

Erin shook her head. "I don't want that reporter to see me in case he's watching the house . . . Besides, I need to finish editing my book. I've got to get it done and turned into my publisher by the deadline."

"I'm certain your publisher would show you some grace. I mean, people loved your first book so much."

Erin grinned. "You might be right, but after what I put them through with *Dark Matters*, I probably shouldn't push it."

Kaely took a sip of her tea before saying, "With Patricia missing, I'm not sure I should leave you."

"Don't be silly. I'll be fine. We're not sure if Pat's really in trouble and, as far as we know, all the other authors are okay. I really don't think anyone's coming after me. Besides, like I said, I don't want that reporter to find out I'm here. If that gets out to the public, the media and lots of lookie-loos could make life miserable for me, you, and Noah."

Kaely didn't move. Just kept staring at her.

"Okay," Erin said. "If I get my gun, will you feel better?"

She nodded. "Much."

Erin sighed and got to her feet. It only took her a couple of minutes to go to the guest room, unlock her gun from its case, load it, and get back to the kitchen. She showed it to Kaely. "Okay?"

She smiled and nodded. "You know, now you have more than your gun protecting you. You have angels standing guard."

Kaely's words gave her chills. She wished she could actually see angels. How cool would that be?

"Could you do me a favor before you go?" Erin asked. "Would you take Chester out? I'd do it but . . ."

"I get it. If the reporter really is out there, he'll see you," Kaely said.

"Exactly."

"I'd be happy to." Kaely got Chester's leash and called his name. The border collie loved going outside. Sometimes it was hard to get him back in.

Erin finished her tea while Kaely and Chester were in the front yard. She really wanted nothing more than to go to bed, but Kaely planned to make supper, and Erin didn't want to hurt her feelings. Besides, she really did need to work on her edits. She could do that while Kaely was gone and then wait until after they ate to tell Kaely she needed to get some sleep. Hopefully there wouldn't be any more weird dreams tonight.

"He did everything he needed to," Kaely said once she let Chester off his leash.

Chester came over to Erin, wagging his tail, as if he was

proud of doing his business on Kaely and Noah's front yard. "Good boy," she said, stroking his soft head.

Kaely went over and picked up her purse from the kitchen counter. "If there's anything else I can do for you, just let me know, okay?"

"I can't think of anything right now." She sighed. "I know I've told you this before, but without you, these books would never have been written."

Kaely grinned. "I know. I'm indispensable."

"I think you mean indefensible, don't you?"

Kaely laughed. "I take exception to that. Look, you keep the doors locked. Don't let anyone in this house except me, understand?"

"So, if Noah comes home, I should refuse to open the door?"

Kaely sighed dramatically. "Yes, you can let Noah in. Although he has his own key." She pointed her finger at Erin. "Like I said . . ."

Erin shook her head. "I promise to be good. I'm going to sit here at the table and edit. I won't open the door. I won't even move from this spot. And I'll keep my gun close by."

"Good. Set the alarm code after I leave."

Erin frowned at her. "Well, I'd have to get up."

"Very funny. Set it. I mean it."

"Seriously? Don't you think you're overdoing it a bit? The door will be locked. I'm right here."

Kaely, who was almost at the door, turned and looked at her. "Look, I realize I might be obsessing, but after what happened in Sanctuary, Patricia's disappearance, and that reporter nosing around . . . I don't know. Something feels . . . wrong. I just can't put my finger on it."

"You know, we talked about this. I mean, about Patricia possibly being the killer."

"You just told me you couldn't believe she was involved."

"I know," Erin said. "Frankly, I'm just trying to put the pieces together. So, let's say it is her, which I seriously doubt. She hasn't tried to hurt any of the authors involved in this thing. *If* she's the killer, wouldn't she be planning her next murder? Not backtracking to hurt me?"

"You could be right," Kaely said. "I just don't want to take any chances."

Erin sighed loudly. "Would you just go? The grocery store will be closed by the time you finally leave."

Kaely looked at her watch. "It's a little after seven. They're open until eleven. Even I'm not that slow. It's nearby. I should be back in about thirty minutes."

"Okay, I'm hungry, and I need to work. Now get out of here."

Kaely smiled and rolled her eyes. "Yes, your majesty. I'll hurry. Cheeseburgers and sweet potato fries okay for tonight?"

"Well, I was holding out for filet mignon, but I guess if that's the best you can do." She looked at Kaely through narrowed eyes. "We still have plenty of Mallomars, right?"

"Since you're the only one eating them, I'm hopeful that four boxes will keep you for a while."

"I guess so."

Kaely shook her head and walked out the door. Erin got up and reset the alarm. As she did, she heard Kaely get into her car and drive away. Then she retrieved her laptop from the coffee table where she'd left it and began working. She had doubts about this story. It wasn't easy to come up with new ways to kill someone. Especially with what had been going on with the Novel Killer. She'd already changed things once because her killer too closely resembled the UNSUB in Dan Harper's book. Hopefully, what she had now would work. It was pretty inventive, but since giving her life to God, she wasn't certain she was comfortable with it. She stared at the words on the screen, wondering how to combine faith along with death.

She remembered an interview she'd read featuring Patricia Long years ago where she was asked a similar question by a reporter. The reporter had asked how writing about serial killers could be seen as a positive contribution to society. Patricia had answered that the kind of books she wrote brought together the battle of darkness against light. Evil against good. "In the end, good wins," she'd said. Her detective, Blake Monroe, always brought the killer or killers to justice. Funny, Erin had forgotten that until now. It helped to ease her mind. Still, the mode of killing in this book . . . It might be creative, but was it over the edge? She wasn't certain. Erin wanted to add a story of redemption to the book. Would her publisher reject it? In the end, did it matter? She'd refused to sign a three-book deal originally because she wasn't certain she wanted to write more than *Dark Matters*. If the publisher didn't like this book, she could adjust it. Give them what they wanted. Then if she continued to write, Brandon could find her another publisher. One that would allow her to create the kind of stories she wanted to write now. Stories that would give people hope. Make them think about God. Maybe even call on Him the way she'd done this evening.

She'd just started looking over another chapter when her phone rang. *Brandon*. She sighed and answered the phone.

"I'm working, I'm working. I plan to make my deadline..."

"I'm not calling about that, Erin," he said. "Although I'm relieved to hear it. I got a call today from Christine Dell's attorney. They're asking for quite a bit of money, and your publisher is willing to pay it."

"That's ridiculous, Brandon," Erin said. "I told you I didn't steal *Dark Matters* from her. And I certainly didn't steal her idea for the one I'm working on now."

"The attorney described your new book pretty closely. There were a few differences," he said, sounding tired. "But it was close enough." He quickly went over the description of the manuscript Erin was working on now. As he repeated what the attorney had said, Erin's mouth dropped open.

When he finished, she said, "Did you share the plot with my publisher, Brandon?"

"No. I mean, I took this from the synopsis you sent them when we signed the contract."

"Listen, Brandon," Erin said. "Tell the publisher not to settle. Not to do anything until you hear from me. Do you understand?"

"I . . . I guess so, but I think we need to cut our losses . . ."

"We won't have any losses," Erin said. "Trust me. I'll get back to you in the next couple of days, I promise. Just hold off."

"Okay, but you'd better be right about this. If they think we're holding back, they might . . ."

"They're not going to do anything, Brandon. I guarantee it."

After she disconnected the call, she stared at the words on her laptop and slowly started to smile.

THIRTY

Erin tried to concentrate on her manuscript, but she couldn't. The minutes ticked by like hours. When the front door finally opened and Kaely came inside, she couldn't wait to tell her what she'd learned.

Kaely reset the alarm and carried her shopping bags into the kitchen. "I'll start supper right away."

"Not yet," Erin said. "We need to talk."

Kaely left the bags on the counter, pulled up a chair at the table, and sat down. "Sounds serious. Everything okay?"

"Yeah, I think it is . . . now. I need to ask you a couple of questions."

Noah waved Lee over to the table where he sat with Kaely and Erin. Lee looked a little surprised to see the women, but he smiled as he approached.

"Thanks for asking me to meet you here," he said as he sat down. "The food was so good last night, I've been hungry for pancakes ever since."

The waitress came over to the table and asked him what he

wanted to drink. Lee ordered coffee and the waitress handed him a menu. When she left, Noah leaned over and took the menu from him. "You won't be needing that," he said.

Lee frowned. "I . . . I'm sorry. I don't understand."

Noah leaned back in his seat, his arms crossed across his chest. "Here's the deal, Lee. A woman by the name of Christine Dell has threatened to sue my friend, Erin Delaney, on grounds of plagiarism. She claims that Erin stole her idea for a book titled *Dark Matters*. Of course, it's hard to prove her innocence since the claim popped up after the book was published." He shrugged. "Sometimes publishers will pay someone like Ms. Dell off just to get rid of them. Bad publicity and all that. If she'd just stopped there, she might have walked away with a decent amount of money. But she pushed it a little further in an attempt to get more money."

Lee looked confused. "I don't understand. Why are you telling me this?"

Noah's smile widened. "Let me finish, and it will become clear."

The waitress came back to the table and poured coffee from a carafe into Lee's cup. "Have you had a chance to look over the menu?" she asked.

"He won't be staying to eat," Noah said. "But thank you anyway."

She stared at Lee for a moment, shrugged, and left.

"I'm not sure what's happening," Lee said. "I thought we were friends." He stood up as if he were getting ready to leave.

"I did too," Noah responded. "Sit down. Now."

His tone was so commanding that Lee collapsed into his chair as if he'd lost the ability to stay upright.

"So anyway," Noah continued, "this Christine Dell claimed Erin's second book, the one she's getting ready to send in to her publisher, was also her idea. She says that Erin stole her concept and that the money the publisher paid her . . . her advance . . . should have gone to Miss Dell."

"Look," Lee said. "I wouldn't know anything about that."

"Oh, really?"

This time it was Erin who addressed him. Perspiration had formed on Lee's forehead, and he wiped it away with a napkin on the table.

"We did a little checking," Erin continued. "Seems you and Christine are cousins. Wasn't hard to find that information. I guess your mother died a few years ago. Christine was listed as a relative. Obituaries are easy to pull up, Lee."

"Tell him where he went wrong," Kaely said. She grinned at Lee. "You're going to enjoy this."

"Something you and your cousin must not know," Erin said, "is that the first synopsis or plot idea for a novel can change. You see, Kaely and I worked together on my new novel. We brainstormed several ideas. The notes you found in Kaely and Noah's filing cabinet? Not the plot I eventually went with. So, when your cousin told her attorney about the plot I supposedly stole?" She made a clicking sound with her tongue as she shook her head. "The wrong plot, my friend. Not even my agent knew that I'd decided to make some changes. And the only way Christine could have known about this unpublished story's plot was to get into Kaely's filing cabinet . . . or inside one of my files at home with my most recent work in progress. Your friend who raided my home in Sanctuary and shot a police officer? The police department there found his DNA. We know his name is Eddie Pilcher. Seems Eddie looked through the file with the old plot line. If he'd picked the other notebook, he would have seen the current plot. The one my publisher has for the book I already finished."

"I really have no idea what you're talking about," Lee said, standing to his feet again.

"You're the only person outside of me and Kaely who has been in our office," Noah said. "I'm sure the sheriff won't have any problem matching your fingerprints to the ones taken off the filing cabinet—the one I forgot to lock the night you stayed in there." He glared at Lee. "So, when did you hatch this thing? Was this your intention from the beginning? Or did you think of it after you knew Kaely was friends with Erin and had helped her with the book?"

Lee's fake look of confusion turned into a sneer, and he swore at them. "We cooked it up months ago. You fell right into our trap. Eddie was in charge of getting the original manuscript. I was digging up all the notes that Kaely had. If I hadn't found the wrong notes, we could have walked away with a lot of money. That publisher would have laid out a load of cash to keep their shining star clean and pure. Maybe we blew it this time, but thanks for the tips. Next time we'll make sure we have the right information. I'm going to be glad to kiss your stupid church and all the hypocritical goody-two-shoes goodbye. I'd say it's been nice knowing you, but it hasn't been."

"I'm sorry," Noah said. "Did you get the impression you were going somewhere?"

Lee laughed. "Yeah, I got that *impression*. I'll be out of town before you can call the police."

"Oh, now that's where you're wrong," Noah said. He raised his hand and waved. Lee turned around and found Nick standing behind him with a pair of handcuffs.

"Lee Johnson, you're under arrest for fraud and attempted blackmail . . . and probably lots of other charges once we find your partner who shot a police officer," Nick said. "Your cousin has already been charged. She confirmed that you were working with Eddie Pilcher. Like Noah said, we already had his identity, but we weren't certain he was in on it. Now we are. And by the way, with your record, you should get prepared for living in a cell for a long, long time." He handcuffed Lee and pushed him out of the diner, reading him the rest of his rights.

"Well, that was rather satisfying," Noah said once they were gone.

"And sad," Kaely added. "You really tried to help him, honey. Lee could have had a very different life if he'd chosen a better path."

Noah reached over and patted his wife's hand. "I know. Now we need to locate Pilcher. He has a long history of violence and theft. Not a nice guy. I'm hoping Nick can get Lee to give up his whereabouts."

"We can pray for that," Kaely said, "but for now, let's order supper. After all this excitement, I'd rather not cook."

Noah laughed. "I can understand that. I'm starved."

As the women looked over their menus, Noah thanked God silently for protecting them against Lee's scheme. He also prayed that Lee's partner in crime would be caught quickly. Pilcher was a dangerous man who needed to be captured and put away for the rest of his life.

When they finally got home, Erin went straight to bed. She was completely exhausted. She'd called Brandon to tell him that he didn't need to worry about Dell's threats anymore. He was ecstatic. As happy as she was that Lee and Christine had been caught and arrested, she was still worried about Patricia. Noah had called the command center when they got home to let them know about Lee and Christine. Erin was certain they had no connection to the Novel Killer—neither one of them was clever enough to pull off these murders—but since she'd told Noah about Christine, Noah needed to report what had happened. He also asked about Pat. She still hadn't been located. Had she left on her own? Was she safe? Or had the Novel Killer kidnapped her? If so, for what reason? None of it made any sense. Even with her concern for Pat's disappearance, and Dale's shooting, there was something running through Erin that she couldn't explain. A joy that bubbled from somewhere inside of her. And a kind of peace she'd never experienced before, even when Kaely had prayed for her the first time. This was different. *She* was different. Although she couldn't completely understand it, she knew it had nothing to do with circumstances. This peace came from something deeper. From someone who had changed her on the inside into a brand-new kind of person. Even with everything going on, Erin drifted off to sleep without worrying about the nightmares that had plagued her for so long.

I tried not to laugh as I stared down at the dirt covering the box. I could still hear her screams. She wasn't really part of my plan. I just did it because I could, and because the police and the FBI would be so distracted looking for this missing woman, they wouldn't think at all about my actual target.

I heard a noise and looked around, but the cemetery was still empty. It was getting dark and even if someone was there, they wouldn't notice me. I'd picked an old and abandoned part of the graveyard, one that was full of ancient headstones. There were no new graves here. Even if someone figured out what I'd done, which I doubted, they'd never find her in time. There was a loose end I had to take care of, but it wouldn't be a problem. I'd deal with it soon.

It really was funny. Causing pain. Making people afraid. I loved it. It had turned out to be more fun than I'd ever imagined.

Now, for the final act in my little play.

Erin Delaney had only one more day to live.

THIRTY-ONE

When Erin woke up, she rolled over on her side and looked at the clock on the nightstand. It was almost noon. How could she have slept so late? She got up, grabbed her clothes, then went into the bathroom. After a quick shower, she dressed, brushed her hair, and hurried to the kitchen. Kaely was sitting at the table and smiled when she entered.

"Sorry I slept late," she said. "I was so tired last night."

"I knew that," Kaely said. "It's why I let you sleep."

"Any news about Pat?"

Kaely sighed. "Nothing. Noah checked first thing."

"I'm sure her daughter is worried sick."

"Unless she knows where she is. Maybe she really couldn't take the pressure and went into hiding. It's possible she told her daughter the truth and asked her to cover for her."

Erin reflected on what Kaely said but then shook her head. "I guess it's possible, but she just didn't seem like someone who would pull a stunt like that. And involving her daughter? I can't see it."

"When Noah talked to the police, they told him that they went over camera footage from the hotel. Patricia is seen leaving her room about an hour after she was dropped off there. Then, she walked out the main entrance and disappeared from the camera's range. The police have no idea where she went. She never returned. They checked the cab companies and Uber. There's no record of her at all." She gestured over at the kitchen counter. "When I heard you moving around, I made a pot of coffee. I figured you'd need some."

"Thanks. You were right." Erin got up, grabbed a cup, and filled it with coffee. "She must have left with someone. I doubt she walked to wherever she was headed."

Kaely shrugged. "The police are questioning anyone who might have seen her leave the hotel, but they haven't found anyone who remembers her." She leaned over and pulled out a chair. "Sit down. Are you hungry for breakfast or lunch?"

"Have you eaten lunch yet?" Erin asked.

"No. I was getting ready to make myself a grilled cheese sandwich."

Erin smiled. "I love grilled cheese. It sounds perfect."

"Great," Kaely said as she got up from the table. "I make mine with sourdough bread. I think it's the perfect bread for grilled cheese."

"I may not be able to fit into my car to drive home if you keep feeding me like this."

"Don't be silly. You're tiny. You could probably stand to gain a little weight."

Erin laughed. "I think you need glasses, but thanks." She sat down and took a sip of her coffee. It hit the spot. "Did Noah say what time I need to go to the command center today?"

Kaely shook her head. "He said he'd call and let us know." She removed a pan from one of her cabinets, took some bread from her bread box, then grabbed some sliced cheddar cheese and butter from the refrigerator. It only took her a couple of minutes to melt the butter and place the slices of bread stuffed with cheese in the skillet. The kitchen filled with the great aroma of melted butter and cheddar.

"That smells incredible."

"It's comfort food," Kaely said. "I think we could both use some comfort."

"You're right about that. I'm so worried about Pat. I just pray she's still alive."

"I know. I'm concerned too."

A few minutes later, Kaely carried two plates to the table with the sandwiches and some chips.

"You really don't need to wait on me, you know," Erin said. "I'm capable of getting something for us. Or at least, for myself."

"Quit griping. I enjoy taking care of you. It's fun for me."

"You have a warped idea of fun, but I appreciate it." Erin picked up her sandwich and took a bite. The buttery, crusty bread was perfect, and the melted cheese dribbled down her chin. She picked up her napkin and wiped her face. "Wow. This is the perfect grilled cheese sandwich."

"Noah loves them too. I'm trying to push things that are easy to make. He doesn't know that, though, so don't tell him."

"Trust me," Erin said, grinning. "I can't risk making you mad. I don't eat this well at home."

Kaely laughed. "We ate just fine when I visited you, but most of our meals were those prepackaged dinners Steve left for us." She sighed. "Now, that's the life. If only I could get Noah to let me order them."

"Doesn't he like them?" Erin asked.

"He thinks they're great. That's not it. It's because the IVF treatments are so expensive. Since I only consult with the BAU now, we have to watch our money. Sometimes I think I might as well go back to the FBI. I was certain we'd be pregnant by now."

"It will happen, Kaely," Erin said. "I feel it so strongly."

"From your mouth to God's ear," Kaely said softly.

Erin wanted to say more, but she wasn't sure how to encourage her friend. Maybe it was time to change the subject.

"So, until Noah calls, our afternoon is free?"

Kaely took another bite of her sandwich and put the rest back on her plate. "Yeah. Why? Do you have something in mind?"

"I still want you to do your profiling . . . technique. Before we go back to the command center."

"Yeah, I think you're right," Kaely said. "I've been thinking a lot about this UNSUB. I want to help Noah and the BAU if I can."

"Great!" Erin quickly finished her lunch and got another cup of coffee. When she sat down again, she noticed Kaely staring oddly at her. "What?" she asked.

"Just remembering the first time we did this. You weren't quite this excited."

"I know," Erin said. "I found it kind of . . . spooky. But now, I know you better. Understand your relationship with God. Now it's not quite so . . ." She frowned. "I don't suppose you ever saw the movie *The Exorcist*?"

Kaely's mouth dropped open. "You were comparing me to *The Exorcist*?"

"No. Well, maybe. I mean, it seemed a little otherworldly. Especially when I felt . . . something."

"First of all, I wasn't even born when that movie came out." Kaely frowned. "And neither were you."

"Have you ever heard of movies *on demand*, Grandma?"

Kaely sighed. "Of course. To be honest, I watched it at a friend's house when I was a teenager. I think it's one of the reasons I became a Christian. Scared the pants off me."

"Unfortunately, it didn't do that for me, but I slept with the lights on for a few weeks. My Aunt Karen docked my allowance to help pay for her electric bill."

"You haven't talked about her much," Kaely said. "She treated you okay, didn't she?"

"Yeah, she did. She never married and hadn't planned to spend eight years taking care of a child. She didn't have much money. After college, I sent her a check every month until she passed away. She kept telling me she didn't want my money, but . . ." Erin shrugged. "She did her best, she really did. I missed my parents and my sister so much I didn't appreciate all she did for me until I was older. I don't know what I would have done without her. It's hard thinking about her. I wish I'd told her how much she meant to me before she died." She sighed. "Look, let's do this. We have to do everything we can to find Pat and stop this killer from hurting anyone else."

"I agree. Let me grab another cup of coffee, and we'll get started."

"Not sure what you mean by *we'll*, but I'm ready to listen."

Kaely stood up and got a cup of coffee. Then she grabbed

a notebook from her kitchen counter. After setting her coffee on the table, she brought the notebook and a pen over to the table and handed them to Erin. "Take notes for me, will you? And if you see something that I don't, tell me."

"Hold it. You think I'm going to tell *you* something? I . . . I'm not you, Kaely. I can't do what you can."

"Listen, my friend. You're not the same person you were yesterday. You have the Spirit of God living in you. Some of what I do comes from my training and experience, but most of it comes from listening to the Holy Spirit. Most people don't understand that, but now you do."

Erin could barely believe what she was hearing. "I just assumed . . . I mean, it never occurred to me that it wasn't just something special you can do."

Kaely smiled at her. "Get used to different. Things don't work the same way anymore. You need to learn to listen to your inner voice now."

Erin just stared at Kaely. "How am I going to do that?"

"First of all, you use this." Kaely opened a cabinet door and took out a wrapped gift. She handed it to Erin.

Surprised, she took it and pulled the paper off. It was a beautiful Bible with a light blue leather cover. Her name was engraved in silver at the bottom right-hand corner. "How . . . when . . . ?"

"When? I bought this not long after we started working together. How? How did I know you'd need it one day? I knew from the beginning."

"But that's impossible," Erin said. "I did everything I could to keep you from talking to me about God."

Kaely didn't say anything, just stared at her.

"You knew because God told you?" Her eyes filled with

tears. The love of God overwhelmed her. Even though she'd done everything she could to reject Him, He'd claimed her as His daughter years ago. That voice from inside her, the voice Kaely had told her about, suddenly whispered to her. The words weren't audible, but they were more powerful than any she'd ever heard. *You were always My daughter. From the foundation of the world, I loved you.* For someone who'd lost her parents when she was young, the knowledge that she'd always had a Father watching over her touched her more than words could say. For the first time in years, she felt complete. The hole in her heart had been filled with a love so strong, she wanted nothing more than to spend her life thanking God for what He'd done for her.

THIRTY-TWO

After a trip to the hospital to check on Dale, who was doing great, Adrian drove by Erin's cabin. Everything looked good. No signs that anyone had tried to access the house again. He parked and got out of the Jeep. After circling the property, he was convinced Eddie Pilcher had finally taken off. Tim had gone over all the evidence they'd collected, but there weren't any fingerprints in the house that didn't belong. Pilcher must have worn gloves. He was thankful for the blood that had allowed them to tie Pilcher to Dale's shooting.

He'd just climbed back into his Jeep when his phone rang. He didn't recognize the number. "Chief Nightengale," he said.

"Chief, this is Noah Hunter. I'm Kaely Hunter's husband?"

"Sure, I know who you are," Adrian said. "Is Erin all right?"

"She's fine. How is Officer Robinson doing?"

"He's doing well," Adrian said. "Thankfully, he'll make a full recovery."

"That's great. I just wanted to tell you about an arrest our local sheriff made last night."

Adrian listened while Noah explained the plan hatched by Lee Johnson, Christine Dell, and Eddie Pilcher.

"You're telling me that Dale almost died over some stupid scheme to make some money from Erin's publisher?" Adrian had to take a deep breath in an attempt to calm the anger that rose inside of him. What was wrong with people?

"Sad to say, it's the truth. Pilcher, the guy who broke into Erin's place and shot your officer, was looking for either her laptop or a copy of the manuscript she's working on now. He found a notebook with some outlines and story ideas from the first concept Erin had for her current novel. She changed it later. That information was in a different notebook that Pilcher never saw. He, Eddie, and Christine thought they had everything they needed to blackmail Erin and her publisher. Once he was arrested, Johnson was willing to make a deal. Lying to me and coming up with this scam isn't as serious as shooting a police officer. Don't get me wrong, Johnson's going to prison because of his previous convictions, but I felt it was more important to catch the man who shot your officer than it is to put this slimebag away."

"I agree. How did Pilcher get past Erin's alarm system?"

"He was already watching her before she left town," Noah said. "I guess she has some glass doors at the back of the cabin that lead to the patio?"

"Yeah, she does," Adrian said.

"It was simple. He saw her enter the code. He just reset it after he was done. Johnson says he might have paid someone off at the alarm company to look the other way if anything went wrong. He didn't have a name, though. Might be something you could follow up on."

"Thanks, I will."

"I'm sending you some information we have on Pilcher, including a photo. I can't explain why he doesn't have a more extensive record, but according to his ex-friend, Johnson, he's done a lot of bad things he was never convicted for. If he had been, he wouldn't be walking around as a free man now. We plan to change that. He'll be going away for good once we find him."

"I'd love to help," Adrian said.

"Johnson says he's not in your area any longer. I think law enforcement here may have a better chance of bringing him down, but I'll pass your offer along to the police. They're hoping he's on his way here because he doesn't know that his partner in crime has been arrested. They're watching for him. Whatever happens, I'll ask whoever's working the case to keep you updated."

"I'd appreciate that."

"Happy to do it," Noah said. "Call anytime if you have questions or additional information."

"I will. Thanks, Noah."

When Noah hung up, Adrian sat in the Jeep for a while. He took his phone out and called Erin. Hearing her voice made him feel better. She assured him that she was okay, but she wasn't certain when she'd come home. After hanging up, he expected to feel relieved, but instead, he felt unsettled. Concerned. After praying, he made a decision. He phoned Lisa to tell her about it, and then he went home and packed a bag.

Erin sat quietly in her chair as Kaely prepared to profile the Novel Killer. It was true that she'd been a little frightened the first time she'd watched Kaely do this, but now she was just interested. Expectant. She'd never considered that it was God helping her to create these profiles. She prayed Kaely would see something important. Something that would lead to this cold-blooded killer's capture—and to finding Pat. As time went on, the likelihood of finding her alive, if she'd been kidnapped, was getting less and less.

She looked over at Kaely, who was smiling at her. "Are you ready?" she asked.

Erin nodded. She opened the notebook Kaely had given her and picked up the pen.

Kaely closed her eyes for a moment, probably to pray. Then she opened them and looked at the chair on the other side of the table. She took a deep breath and let it out.

"You're using books as a road map for murder," she said softly. "For a while, I thought it might be because you lacked creativity. That you had to use other people's ideas to pull off your killing spree. But that's not true, is it? You're very creative. Smart. Patient. And very, very angry. You have an agenda, but what is it?"

That was the question she and Kaely had been asking for a while. The Novel Killer wasn't using plots from novels because he had to. He had a specific purpose in mind. But what was it?

"I'm not sure why you picked the novels you did, but there's a reason." She frowned at the empty chair. After a rather lengthy pause, she continued. "One of the books you chose is the most important. It wasn't the first one. Was your target always Patricia Long? I think you knew she was in Virginia, and you took her. She must be the most important author. The reason for your killing spree. You're very methodical. You haven't left any evidence behind at any of your murder scenes. And now, Patricia has disappeared without a trace. I think you picked her up yesterday, when she was out of the hotel camera's view. But why? What is it about her that's so significant? And why would she go with you . . . ?" She paused again, but this time she smiled slowly. "You took Patricia because her daughter is in Virginia. You threatened to hurt her daughter." Kaely looked at Erin. "We need to tell investigators to look for some kind of threatening message sent to Patricia. He may have made a threat against her daughter. That's the only reason Patricia would have gone willingly with him."

Erin nodded and added that to her notes. Surely the police were already checking this, but it didn't hurt to make certain. She silently chided herself for not thinking of this already. Pat was the only author with family here. That had to be connected to her disappearance.

Kaely stared at the empty chair for several seconds while Erin sat with her pen poised over the notebook. Again, Kaely frowned. Erin thought she looked a little confused.

"It still doesn't make any sense. Kidnapping Patricia doesn't follow your pattern at all." Kaely crossed her arms and leaned back in her chair. "You took several chances you didn't need to. You murdered three people before getting to your goal?" Kaely frowned at the empty chair. "You killed people in Virginia because you wanted Patricia? You killed at least two of them before Patricia even came to Virginia. You couldn't have known about that ahead of time. You also knew the state police and the FBI would probably join forces to find you. That's quite a risk. This can't possibly be about Patricia." She paused for a moment and then cleared her throat. "Okay, let's put Patricia Long on the back burner.

Let's just talk about location. Why Virigina? What is in Virginia that made you carry out your plan here? Where it was riskier?"

Erin wrote her question in the notebook. Kaely was right. Why kill people here? Near Quantico? Where the BAU . . . Something occurred to Erin. Was it the BAU that was targeted? The FBI? The state police? CIRG was here. Was the Novel Killer targeting them? Or was he trying to pit himself against them? Like a master chess player taking on a champion in an attempt to prove he was better? She wrote this down as well.

"Read me what you just wrote," Kaely said, catching Erin off guard.

She read it back.

Kaely closed her eyes and rubbed her forehead. It was obvious that she was confused. "That's a good point," she said finally. She looked back toward the chair. "Are you trying to show how smart you are?" She stared at the chair and cocked her head to the side as if she were listening to someone. A chill ran up Erin's back. "You have a reason for what you're doing," Kaely repeated. "And it's really important to you, but it's hidden among the murders you've committed. This was very well-planned and executed. Just trying to show how intelligent you are is beneath you. You'd never do that because you don't think you have to."

Erin was still concerned about Pat even if Kaely had dismissed her disappearance for now. Had the Novel Killer really threatened her daughter? Why? It didn't make sense to her. She shook her head. Again, it didn't feel right. They'd already discussed the possibility that Pat was hiding and that her daughter knew where she was, but again, that didn't feel right either.

"Let's talk about the toys," Kaely said. "There's some obvious connection to your childhood. What happened? Did Mommy ignore you? Did Daddy spank you?"

The look on Kaely's face startled Erin. It was as if someone had slapped her. It was at that moment that Erin felt something change in the room. It was as if something evil had suddenly entered.

"No!" Kaely said with force. "In the name of Jesus, you stay out of my house."

The atmosphere transformed immediately. Erin had never experienced anything like that before. She'd have to ask Kaely about it after she was finished. Did being a Christian mean she could do things like that? What was that dark presence?

Kaely took a deep breath and started again. "Those toys are at least twenty years old. The only younger person connected to the case is Pat's daughter. She's in college. Unless she collects vintage toys, they have nothing to do with her." She stopped for a moment. "Do they have something to do with Pat?" She shook her head. "Pat's around forty. She wasn't playing with toys when she was twenty. So, once again, let's move Pat out of the equation." She looked over at Erin. "What do you think?"

Erin gulped. She wasn't expecting Kaely to talk to her. "You're right about the toys. They don't fit with Pat's disappearance. So, they have to be something connected to the killer. But . . ." She hesitated, not certain she should say anything else.

"Go on, Erin. I respect your opinion. Tell me what you think."

"You talked about the UNSUB's mother or father. But

these are primarily toys for girls. Could it have something to do with a girlfriend or sister?"

Kaely rolled her eyes. "Of course. You're right. I should have thought of that. Usually, it's not a girlfriend . . . but it could be a sister. I worked a case years ago where the killer watched his sister die. It sent him over the edge." She chewed on her lip for a few seconds. "But that's not the way he killed. What is this UNSUB trying to say? I doubt he's giving the victims toys because he's trying to make something up to his sister."

She looked back toward the empty chair and sighed. "Maybe this thing with Lee has me distracted. I've said all along that this case is different." She swung her gaze toward Erin. "Let's try again later, okay? I need time to think about this for a while. I feel like I'm almost seeing it, but it's just out of my grasp. Frankly, it's Patricia's disappearance that confuses me the most. It doesn't fit anywhere. I just can't find a way to link it to the other murders. *If* he took her, it breaks his carefully constructed pattern." She leaned back in her chair. "If the Novel Killer kidnapped Patricia Long . . . maybe it's just so he can prove to the world he can."

"Or maybe she knows something that puts him in danger? She might not even realize she's a threat to him."

Kaely nodded. "You could be right, but unless we figure this out, I'm afraid she's going to be his next victim."

THIRTY-THREE

Kaely and Erin were having another cup of coffee when Kaely's phone rang.

"It's Noah," Kaely said after looking at her phone.

Erin sipped her coffee while Kaely talked to Noah. Although she could only hear one side of the conversation, it was pretty clear that she was wanted back at the command center. When she hung up, Kaely confirmed Erin's assumption. She couldn't help but look down at Chester, who was curled up on the floor by her feet.

"I know you feel bad leaving Chester behind," Kaely said, "but you know he loves being with Hoovey, right? Besides, it's important that you teach Chester that you'll always come back. I have some experience in this area. Mr. Hoover was abandoned too. For a long time, if we left the house, we'd come home to find pillows shredded and toilet paper pulled off the holders. It was the result of anxiety. But after a while, Mr. Hoover figured out that he could trust us not to abandon him. Those behaviors stopped. Now, when we leave, he barely pays any attention. Chester just needs to learn the same lesson. As hard as it is, he'll be happier in the long run."

Erin knew she was right, but it really was difficult. Even though Mr. Hoover made it much easier, Chester's expression when she left still hurt her. When they were ready to go back to the command center, Erin called Chester's name. He had two ways of handling stress when she left him alone. One was to follow her to the door. The other was to hide somewhere and refuse to look at her. Seems he'd chosen the second approach. She went looking for him, but he wasn't in the kitchen or the living room. She walked back to the guest bedroom and found Chester on the bed, Mr. Hoover curled up next to him. Although she hated to wake him up, she softly called Chester's name. He looked up.

"I'm leaving for a while, pal," she said. "I'll be back soon, okay?"

She was surprised when his tail thumped on the bed. Then he put his head down again and closed his eyes.

Could he finally be getting over the fear that had kept him in its clutches ever since he'd been dumped by . . . ? She pushed the words in her mind away. She was pretty sure that since she was a Christian now, those words were best removed from her vocabulary.

She smiled at how comfortable Chester and Mr. Hoover seemed together. "I'm not getting a cat. I'm not getting a cat," she whispered as she walked back into the living room to meet Kaely.

"Did you just say you're not getting a cat?" Kaely asked.

"Wow. You must have really good hearing."

Kaely smiled. "It's come in handy more than once. So, you want to tell me why you're not getting a cat?"

Erin laughed. "Chester is in love with Mr. Hoover. I'm not as worried now about his reaction when I leave him, I'm more concerned about what happens when we leave *here*. I think he's going to miss Mr. Hoover a lot."

"I hear you, but the truth is, even though he will miss Hoovey, you're his person. Being with you is more important than anything else."

Erin sighed. "I guess so. Having a pet is tough. It's almost like having a kid." As soon as she said it, she regretted her comment. "I'm sorry, Kaely. I didn't mean . . ."

"Don't be silly," Kaely said. "I know exactly what you mean. I'm sure it's not quite the same, but I love Mr. Hoover with all my heart. If anything happened to him . . ." Her voice broke and she cleared her throat. "Before we both start crying, let's leave."

"Good idea."

Erin had just picked up her purse when someone knocked on the door. Kaely looked through the peephole on the door. "It's Nick," she said. She opened the door and sure enough, Nick stood there, looking a little uncomfortable.

"I'm sorry," he said. "Looks like you're getting ready to leave."

"Yeah, sorry," Kaely said. "They want to talk to Erin again down at the command center. Are you here for a reason?"

Surprisingly, Nick blushed. "Just wanted to say hello. Make sure everyone's all right." He glanced over at Erin. Kaely looked at her too and winked.

"Sorry we have to leave," Kaely said. "I'm fairly sure we'll be back by suppertime. Why don't you join us? Say around seven?"

Nick nodded. "Sounds great. Can I bring anything?"

Kaely smiled at him. "How about some dessert?"

"I can do that. Well, I'd better get going. Hope everything

goes okay." He nodded again, then turned around and headed for his patrol car.

"You definitely have a fan," Kaely said.

"I think you're imagining things, but let's shelve that discussion for now."

As they got into Kaely's car, Erin wondered if she was right. Was Nick really interested in her? He was nice and very good-looking. So why was she wishing Kaely hadn't invited him to dinner? Her reaction confused her.

I watched them get into the car and leave. I needed to make my move soon. As they drove away, I began to create a beautiful strategy. Erin had to die, but it would be special. A dark design that even the great Kaely Quinn-Hunter wouldn't see coming.

The same officer who had let them into the command center last time was manning the door again. He greeted them.

"I brought my book," he said to Erin with a smile.

"Great," she said. "When you take a break, find me, and I'll be happy to sign it, Brad."

"Thanks."

As she and Kaely walked into the large command center, Erin heard someone call Kaely's name.

A man walked over to them. "So, you're back for more, huh?"

Kaely smiled at him. "Just can't stay away."

"I take it this is your famous friend, Erin Delaney?"

"Yes. Erin, this is Lucas Grant. He works for the BAU with Noah."

"Nice to meet you, Lucas," Erin said. Lucas was handsome with longish dark brown hair and green eyes that seemed to look right through her.

"How are things going?" Kaely asked.

"Not sure," Lucas said. "I just got here myself. I need to check in with Noah. We have a couple of other special agents from the BAU here today too." He smiled at Kaely. "Your friend Alex is working today. And my SAC, Todd Hunter."

Kaely returned the smile. "I haven't seen Alex for a while. She's been busy."

"I remember you telling me about her," Erin said. "I'd love to meet her."

"She, Todd, and Noah are working on the profile now. They said they could use your help." He pointed to an area on the other side of the room. Noah was there with a woman and another man. Erin assumed they were Alex and Todd. They were gathered around a desk, a dry-erase board next to them. Although she couldn't read what it said from where she stood, she hoped she'd get a chance to look at it before she left.

"Lucas, can you keep an eye on Erin for me?" Kaely asked. "Herrington will be interviewing her."

She gestured toward a serious-looking Detective Herrington coming their way—a look of determination on his face. The fear that had gripped Erin the day before tried to wrap its tentacles around her again. Before she realized what she was doing, she grabbed Lucas's arm.

"Hey," he said quietly. "I know he's intense, but he's a good guy. You can trust him. Still, if at any time you feel overwhelmed, just look for me and give me a little nod. I'll come up with an excuse so you can take a break, okay?"

"Okay," Erin said. She withdrew her hand, embarrassed by her reaction. It wasn't that she was afraid of Herrington. He simply represented the terror that had plagued her for so long. But then something happened. The voice that had spoken to her before now reminded her that life had changed. That she wasn't alone anymore. And suddenly the fear drifted away like smoke in a gentle wind. No matter what happened, she'd found Someone who would never leave her on her own again. Someone who could rescue her no matter what. Once again, peace replaced fear.

Lucas patted her on the shoulder. "You can do this," he said. "I have faith in you."

She looked up at him and smiled. "Thanks. And you're right. I know I can do this."

THIRTY-FOUR

Adrian was relieved that Lee and Christine had been caught and charged. But Eddie was still on the run. He'd just talked to Erin, and she was fine. Still working with the police and the FBI to catch a serial killer, but she was great at that. So why couldn't he get her out of his mind? He'd actually packed a bag, intending to drive to Virginia. But now, he wasn't sure he was doing the right thing. How could he leave his officers behind on . . . a whim? Even as he wrestled with himself, he realized that he couldn't back away from the decision he'd made. Doc's pills had vanquished his headache, and he was alert. Thankfully, the reaction he'd feared hadn't materialized.

"Boss? Everything okay?" He looked up to see Lonzine standing in his doorway.

"Sure. Why do you ask?"

She smiled at him. "I tried twice to get your attention. You seemed so far away."

He sighed. "Sorry. Just thinking about Erin."

Lonzine started to say something, but he held his hand up. "Don't try to read something into that. I mean . . . I don't know. I feel like something's wrong."

"You talking about your gut? Your cop's intuition?"

"Hopefully, it's not just the coffee." He frowned at her. "Lisa makes it so strong."

"I heard that," a voice called out. Lisa stuck her head in the door and grinned at Lonzine. "He used to tell me I made it too weak. Now it's too strong. I can't win."

"He just needs something to complain about," Lonzine said, rolling her eyes. "We're so perfect, it makes him feel insecure."

Adrian shook his head. "Very funny."

"He's concerned about Erin," Lonzine said. "Says his gut tells him something's wrong."

"Things are quiet here," Adrian said. "I'm going to Virginia. I feel as if . . ."

"As if Erin's in danger?" Lonzine said.

Adrian nodded.

"Then, of course you need to go."

"See, boss?" Lisa said. "Whatever you need to do, we're behind you." She took Lonzine's arm. "Let's quit taking up his time and let him get on his way."

"Good idea," Lonzine said. "We'll be praying for you, boss. And for Erin."

Adrian laughed to himself after the women left. He took a deep breath and grabbed his bag. Jake got up from his place on the floor, and they both headed outside to the Jeep. Time to get on the road.

"I know you talked to Noah," Herrington said when they were seated at his desk. "But I want to go over this with you myself. The Virginia State Police are heading up the investigation, and as you know, Noah works for the BAU. I trust him and know he did a good job of interviewing you, but I need to see if there's anything here that might help us find our UNSUB." He opened a file on his computer and began reading through Noah's interview with her. Before yesterday, the silence would have intimidated her, but this time it didn't. Erin was embracing the freedom she felt. The peace. It was nothing like the high that alcohol used to bring. This was something different. Something good.

"Coffee?"

She looked up to find Lucas standing next to her.

"I noticed that you didn't have time to get something to drink. If you'd rather have a cold drink . . ."

"No, this is great. Thanks, Lucas."

She took the cup and smiled at him. Frankly, she'd had so much coffee back at Kaely's she probably didn't need anymore. But she didn't want to offend Lucas. He really was a nice man.

"Excuse me," Herrington said, frowning at Lucas. "Maybe you'd like to get Ms. Delaney a doughnut too?"

His tone was sarcastic, but Lucas didn't miss a beat. "Would you like a doughnut, Erin?" he asked.

She gave him her biggest smile and said, "Thank you, Lucas, but I'm fine."

He nodded and winked the eye that Herrington couldn't see. "If you need anything else, let me know, okay?"

"I will. I appreciate it."

As Lucas walked away, Erin took a sip from the cup Lucas had given her and turned her attention to Herrington. If it were possible for a human being to have smoke coming out of his ears, it would be happening now. What was wrong with this guy? Did he treat everyone like this? Or just the people he interviewed?

"If you're sure you have everything you need," he growled, "maybe we can get on with this interview?"

"Certainly," Erin said as sweetly as she could. She looked at Herrington's almost empty coffee cup. "Would you like me to get you some coffee? I'm happy to do it."

Although she wanted to add *or a doughnut?* that would be sarcasm, and he would know it. This way, it would just seem like kindness—which is what she wanted. *You catch more bees with honey . . .*

Herrington stared at her with a look of confusion on his face. Finally, he said, "No, thank you. I'll get some when we're done." There was a pause before he said, "But thank you."

"You're welcome. Now what can I do to help you?" Erin asked. "I'd really like to see you catch this guy."

Herrington's tough guy persona had definitely softened some, and Erin had realized something. Sometimes the things that scare you were neutralized more with kindness and concern than they were through intimidation. Although it might not be Herrington's way of dealing with people, it needed to become hers. However, it had to be real. Not manipulation or sarcasm. Truth was, she probably was trying to manipulate him. In the past, she might not have recognized it. She sighed inwardly. *Okay, lesson learned. Thanks, God.*

After being asked to go over the details from her book once again, Erin did so.

"So, the difference is that the body was found in a private lake in Virginia. One open only to military personnel. The lake in your book was in Missouri. Private, but there's no military connection."

Erin was confused. When had she told Noah that? "Yes, that's true," she said. "Although the lake in my book doesn't really exist, I patterned it off a lake in Missouri that is owned by homeowners in a gated community. I reached out to a woman named Christine Dell who worked for the management company that owned the lake and the development."

"This is the Christine Dell who tried to blackmail your publisher?" Herrington said. "I talked to Noah this morning, and he told me about it."

"Yes, the same woman. I'm certain she and her partners in crime have nothing to do with the murders."

Herrington frowned at her. "And how do you know that?"

"Well, first of all, it's pretty clear two of the three weren't in Virginia when the murders occurred, but honestly? Your UNSUB is clever, organized, and highly intelligent. Dell, Johnson, and Pilcher are just petty crooks who could never put something like this together. They couldn't even manage a basic blackmail scheme."

Herrington raised an eyebrow and stared at her for a moment. "You got that from Noah?"

Erin shook her head. "As you know, I used to be a cop. And in writing my books, Kaely has taught me quite a bit about profiling. Of course, I'm not Kaely . . . or Noah. But realizing that those three aren't smart enough—or methodical enough—to pull off these murders is obvious even to me."

Herrington seemed to study her for a bit before saying, "I totally agree with you. The police in Tennessee and here in Virginia are looking for Eddie Pilcher. I'm sorry these people tried to use you for their own gain."

"Th . . . thank you, Detective. That means a lot to me." The phrase *you could have knocked me over with a feather* popped into her mind. She smiled at him, and surprisingly, he returned her smile.

"Detective, may I ask you a question?" Erin said.

He nodded.

"How did you know about the lake in Missouri? I mean, the details."

He looked uncomfortable and cleared his throat. "I read your book, Miss Delaney. And . . . I liked it."

Okay, here comes that feather again. "Thank you," she said. She wanted to say something more, but she couldn't think of anything that didn't sound . . . weird. So, she just waited for the interview to begin again.

"Let's get back to our interview," he said, straightening up in his chair and gazing at his screen. "I don't want to keep you too long. It looks as if Noah did a thorough job." He turned to look at her. "This must be difficult for you."

"It makes me sick to think that this guy used something I wrote to kill a human being. I'm sure all the other authors feel the same way. I know Pat Long did."

Herrington frowned. "I know you talked to her before she went missing. Are you surprised that she's disappeared?"

"My friend Kaely asked me the same thing," Erin said. "It's almost impossible for me to answer your question since our time together was so brief, but I'd have to say yes. She was upset, like I am, that the killer used her book, but she seemed to want to help." Erin met the detective's eyes. "If I had to guess, Detective, I'd say someone wanted her to disappear. I was told that her daughter doesn't believe her mother left on her own. And I'm certain Pat really loves her daughter and would never put her through something like this."

Herrington leaned back in his chair and stared at her for a moment before saying, "But who would take her? Why would our UNSUB do that? He hasn't tried to abduct any of the other authors."

"But Pat was here. In his territory. And Pat was alone."

"You're in his territory," Herrington said.

"But I'm not alone," Erin replied. "I have Noah and Kaely. And I'm an ex-cop. I'm armed, just like they are. It would be a lot harder to get to me than Patricia."

"But if our UNSUB actually does want to *get to you*, it means you could be in danger."

"We've talked about that," Erin said, "but what sense does that make? This UNSUB has to have a signature—a reason for killing that should show up in his murders. Sure, authors have critics. Some of the comments we get are a little strange, but I really don't think your UNSUB would go to all this trouble because he doesn't like our books."

For the first time since she'd met him, Herrington laughed. "I have to agree. If critics exchanged murder for nasty reviews, there would probably be a lot less books out there."

He actually made a joke. Erin smiled at him. "Look, Detective, this UNSUB is unusual. When I was a cop, I only came across a serial killer once that I know of, and the case was handed over to our detectives. I'm aware that there are thousands of serial killers out there. Most don't get caught, and most are not in the news. But in all the research I did for my books, I never stumbled across anyone like this." Erin paused, wondering if she should go any further. She didn't want to offend the man by making it look as if she was schooling him on serial killers, but since his tone had changed with her, she decided to take a chance. She told him what she and Kaely had been talking about. She took several minutes to share their thoughts. To her surprise, Herrington began to type notes while she talked. When she was done, she said, "I'm not sure if any of that was helpful. Like I said, these days I'm just a writer, not a cop. Not in law enforcement. No one, except those on the front lines, completely understand the mind of a criminal. But that's everything I've been thinking. I hope it helps, but even if it doesn't, I'm praying you catch this guy before anyone else dies."

Herrington put the pen down. "The truth, Miss Delaney?"

She nodded, waiting for the dressing down that could be coming.

"I wish I had you on my team," he said, sounding sincere. "This is more than helpful. Until we catch this guy, please be careful. And keep that gun of yours close by."

"Thank you, Detective. I will," she said. "Are you through with me?"

He nodded. "I am." He looked to his right. "I think your friend Kaely might like your help. I understand you were deputized?"

She nodded. "That's right."

"Then perhaps your insight can assist the BAU in stopping our UNSUB."

"Before I go, Detective, is anyone actively looking for Patricia Long?"

"As I'm sure you understand, most of our resources are dedicated to finding our UNSUB. But we've asked the local police department to look into her disappearance. So far, they haven't found anything. Cameras at the hotel show her walking away from the front entrance, but we have no idea what happened to her after that."

That was exactly what Noah had said, but Erin didn't tell Herrington that. Even though she'd been deputized, she wasn't certain how Herrington would feel about Noah sharing details about the search for Pat.

She stood. "Thank you, Detective. And if there's anything else I can do to help . . ."

Herrington stood as well and held out his hand, which Erin took. "I appreciate your time, Miss Delaney."

Erin smiled, shook his hand, and then headed over to where Kaely and Noah were gathered with others from the BAU. On the way, she ran into Brad, who smiled and held out his book. She gladly signed it and was gratified to see how much it meant to him.

Yesterday, she'd wanted out of this place so badly. But today, she was actually enjoying herself. Her life had certainly changed. And she knew why. It was because she wasn't the same person. She was becoming the person she was always meant to be.

THIRTY-FIVE

Adrian stopped at a convenience store near Roanoke to let Jake out, fill up his tank, and get something to eat. He bought Jake a cheeseburger, as well as one for himself. For convenience store food, it was pretty good. Then he shared his fries with the hungry dog. As they ate, he wondered once again if he was doing the right thing. What would Erin think when he showed up? He'd considered calling her, but every time he started to click on her number, he felt as if he shouldn't do it. For now, he was going on instinct, praying it was God leading him.

He'd had these feelings before. One time, he'd avoided a drunk driver, who blew through a stop sign, by just seconds when he'd felt he was supposed to pull over to the side of the road and wait. Another time, he'd drawn his gun entering a house that was supposed to be abandoned only to find a drunk man with a knife hiding behind a door. He was able to arrest him and take him out of the house without incident. And this was in Sanctuary. There were more times than he could count when he'd listened to that still, small voice in Chicago. He credited God with saving not only his life, but also the life of his partner, more than once. Today, he was following that voice again. He sensed that Erin was in danger, and he had to get there. He scarfed down the rest of his fries except for the few that he gave to an appreciative Jake. Then he got back on the road and headed toward Fredericksburg.

Erin walked up to the group gathered around the desk and the dry-erase board. Most of the things she and Kaely had talked about were written there.

"Erin," Kaely said when she walked up. "I'd like to introduce you to Alex Hart and Todd Hunter. Todd is the Special Agent in Charge of our BAU unit."

Erin said hello to the two special agents. Besides them, Lucas, Noah, and Kaely made up the rest of the group working on a profile for law enforcement.

"We're trying to finish our profile," Noah said, "but we feel as if it's incomplete. Thing is, we have to give the police and FBI something." His gaze swung over the special agents gathered there. "Anything anyone cares to add?"

"This one's tough," Alex said. "I've never been faced with an UNSUB who uses the plots of books to kill people. Even when I saw it on that TV show *Castle*, I thought it was silly. Yet here we are." She laughed. "I guess truth really is stranger than fiction."

Erin really liked Alex. She reminded her a lot of Kaely. Smart, insightful, and with a sense of humor.

"What do you think, Erin?" she asked.

"I'm not sure I'm qualified to have an opinion," Erin said. "I'm not a trained analyst like all of you are, but I think I agree. Don't all serial killers have a reason to do what they do? I'm pretty sure killing authors isn't it. He's incredibly angry. The poems show us that. And the twenty-year-old toys say something, but how does that connect to the authors? So maybe the UNSUB hates authors who have toys?" She shook her head. "Kaely and I have been over and over this. We agree that this has something to do with the killer's childhood. But for the life of me, I haven't found an explanation that feels right."

"I agree that he's definitely angry about something in his childhood," Alex said, "but what does that have to do with the authors' books he's patterned his killings after? The methods of murder are all different. There's nothing that connects them. Why did he choose these particular books?"

"I'm not sure, but we'd better figure it out soon," Lucas said. "Like Noah said, we have to deliver the profile. They should have had it by now."

"Kaely, what do you think?" Todd asked.

"I think the same way Erin does," she said. "There's a reason this guy is killing the way he is. We're just not seeing it. I feel as if there's an element missing. One aspect that would tie this all together. But like Erin said, we can't quite get hold of it."

"And maybe that's the reason," Erin said slowly.

"What do you mean, Erin?" Todd asked.

"Maybe he's just trying to confuse you. Throw you off track."

"Then he'd have to know something about our methods," Todd said, frowning. "And that begs a lot of questions."

"You mean this person could be . . . one of us?" Lucas asked.

Erin shook her head. "Not necessarily. There are a lot of books about profiling out there. It's not that difficult to learn about your methods. Maybe not everything, but enough to make it harder for us to find him."

Kaely stood up. "Look, it's late. I'm going to take Erin home. We're just running around in circles here. But if either one of us comes up with something else that could help, I'll let you know." She frowned. "His reason for killing is here. I just pray we figure it out before he strikes again."

"Thanks for sitting in, Kaely," Todd said. "It was nice to meet you, Erin."

"You too, Todd," Erin said. "And nice to meet you, Alex. Kaely has talked about you quite a bit."

Alex smiled at her. "I'd love to get together for lunch with you two before you leave, Erin. If we can find some time?"

"That would be great," Erin said. Kaely said her good-byes, and she and Kaely walked toward the exit. As they walked past Paul Jackson, she smiled at him. But he just stared at her and then went back to whatever it was he was doing. She noticed that her book was no longer on his desk. Had she offended him in some way? She would have been happy to sign his book if he'd asked. She almost went back to say something to him but dismissed the thought. She wasn't responsible for his attitude. She had too many thoughts in her mind right now. She didn't have time to worry about his ego.

When they reached the back door, the guy guarding it looked irritated. He was talking on his phone and hung up right before they reached him.

"Everything all right, officer?" Kaely asked.

"More reporters trying to get past me," he said, sounding disgusted. "We have regular media updates scheduled now. I've asked them more than once to just wait for them. This afternoon, the FBI found a woman out in the parking lot, just wandering around. When they questioned her, she admitted she was a reporter. She runs a podcast, for crying out loud. I just hope this doesn't get any worse."

"Do you have cameras watching the parking lot?" Erin asked.

"Normally, no. They're usually not necessary. But since the media found us, the FBI mounted one out there. It will be connected this evening. After that, we'll be able to monitor everything out there. Reporters will be aware that we're not only keeping an eye on them, but we're also recording their actions. Not something they'll like, but it will sure make me feel a lot better."

"Thanks for all your hard work, officer," Kaely said. "We appreciate it."

He smiled at them for the first time. "Just doing my job, but it's nice to hear you say that. You ladies have a good rest of your day."

They thanked him again and walked out the back door. Erin was surprised to find that it was already dark when they stepped outside. The day had gone by quickly.

They were both silent on the drive back to the house. Finally, Erin said, "We're both trying to figure out what's going on, aren't we?"

Kaely laughed. "We know each other so well."

"If you get any sudden inspiration, will you share it with me?"

"Of course. It goes both ways, though."

Erin nodded. "Yeah, I know."

Erin kept going over everything about the killings she could think of but felt as if she was only regurgitating the same information over and over. She sighed. "I've got a headache."

"When we get home, I'll give you some aspirin. Then we can have dinner. We could pick up something if you want."

It was at that moment that they heard a crack of thunder, and it started to rain really hard.

"Or maybe not," Kaely said, chuckling. "It was cloudy when we left, but did I put my umbrella in the car? Of course not. If we want to stay dry, our best bet is to go home and park in the garage. I've got some ground beef. How about tacos?"

"I love tacos, but only if you let me help." She frowned. "Wasn't Nick coming over for dinner?"

Kaely shook her head. "I forgot to tell you. He called while we were at the command center. He can't come. The sheriff's department figures they'll be kept busy because of the weather. We'll have him over another night." She smiled. "Now, do you really want to help?"

"Of course," Erin said. "As long as I don't have to actually cook anything. Trust me, you don't want that."

Another sudden clap of thunder made her jump. The heavy rain had turned into a torrential downpour.

"April showers bring May flowers," Kaely mumbled. She'd slowed down to a crawl so she could see the road. The other cars around them had done the same thing.

"Then there should be flowers everywhere."

Kaely sighed. "That would be nice."

It took them quite a while to get back to Kaely's house. Erin breathed a sigh of relief when they finally pulled into the garage. Kaely parked the car, lowered the garage door, and got out. "Noah said he'd be a little late, but he should be home in time to have tacos. He loves them."

Erin and Kaely went inside the house through the door that led from the garage into the kitchen.

After taking off her jacket and hanging it up, Kaely went to the refrigerator and took out some hamburger. Then she took a head of lettuce out of the crisper and brought it over to Erin.

"Get a plate out of the cabinet and shred the lettuce, okay?" Kaely said. "We should be ready to eat in about twenty minutes."

Erin got the plate, washed the lettuce, and then began to tear it into smaller pieces. It seemed like such a normal thing to do, but things weren't normal. There was a serial killer on the loose who didn't make sense to the world's best profilers—and Pat, someone she'd grown to care about, might be dead—or waiting to die.

Adrian didn't realize he was grasping the steering wheel so tightly until he felt pain in his fingers. It had started to rain, making it necessary to slow down and drive carefully. He sighed and loosened his grip. Would Erin think it was weird when he just showed up? Was this ridiculous? Should he turn around and go back? But the truth was, he couldn't. He felt a strong urge to keep driving. He had to see her. He looked at the GPS. Not much longer. He wasn't sure what he was going to say. He prayed that God would help him—give him the right words. Something that wouldn't make her feel pressured, but that would also let her know that he really cared for her. Were there any words in existence like that? He couldn't be certain, but no matter what, he wasn't going home. He would have to trust God that everything would turn out all right.

THIRTY-SIX

They'd just started eating when Kaely's phone rang. She picked it up and looked at the screen. "It's Noah." She answered and listened for a few seconds. "Are you all right?" she asked. Another pause. "Okay, just tell me where you are."

When she hung up, Erin asked, "Is something wrong?"

Kaely took a couple big bites of her taco and stood up. "Noah's car stalled. He and some guy pushed it to the side of the road, and he called a tow truck, but in this weather, they're backed up for hours. He arranged for someone to tow it to the repair shop when they can, but he doesn't want to wait. I'm going to pick him up." She shook her head. "Strange that he's having trouble with that car. We just had it checked out a couple of weeks ago."

"I know you're concerned about me, but I'd rather stay here," Erin said. "Unless you need me."

"No, it's okay. But take precautions. Set the alarm, and—"

"I know, get my gun. At least I shouldn't have to worry about that reporter. I doubt he's out in this."

"Probably not," Kaely said. "The roads are full of water."

Erin frowned. "Maybe you shouldn't be going out in this either."

Kaely smiled at her. "Part of my FBI training was driving in dangerous conditions." She shrugged. "Of course, I think that was geared more to if someone was shooting at me, but I'm still pretty good at driving in the rain."

Erin laughed. "I guess it would be worse if someone was trying to shoot you." No matter what Kaely said, Erin was still a little worried about her. But the truth was, she didn't relish going out in this weather and was happy to stay inside. "Call me when you've got him?" she said.

"I will." Kaely grabbed her purse and opened a closet in the living room, where she removed a raincoat and an umbrella. "I'll be better prepared this time. Don't eat all the tacos," she said with a smile. "I'm still hungry, and I know Noah will want some."

"No promises, but I'll do my best." Chester, who was sitting next to her, watching her eat, whined. She picked up some cheese and gave it to him.

"If you give him table food, he'll get used to it and always want some," Kaely said as she walked through the kitchen and headed toward the door that led to the garage.

"I know," Erin said with a sigh. "But I'm afraid it's too late."

Kaely laughed and left through the door. Seconds later, Erin heard the garage door open and Kaely backing out. The lights from the car lit up the living room until Kaely pulled out into the street. Then she heard the garage door close. Herrington's words drifted into her mind. *Until we catch this guy, please be careful. And keep that gun of yours close by.* Erin got up and reset the alarm.

She'd go upstairs in a minute and get her gun, but she wanted to finish eating first. She went back to the kitchen and sat down at the table again. The sound of the rain on the roof made her think of Pat. Where was she? Was she out in this? Was her body exposed to the elements? Was evidence being washed away? She so wanted Pat to be found alive, but that result was getting less and less likely.

Erin finished her taco and then cleaned up the table. She put the taco meat into a bowl, covered it with plastic wrap, and put it in the fridge. After putting the cheese, sour cream, and salsa away, she fed Chester and Mr. Hoover.

"Boy, you're going to hate going outside in this," she told Chester when he was finished. She went into the pantry and grabbed his leash from a hook. She was just getting ready to put it on him when someone knocked on the front door. It startled her. Kaely wouldn't knock. Maybe it was a delivery or something. At that moment, she wished she'd gotten her gun the way she'd planned. When she looked through the peephole, she was relieved to see Shannon standing there. She turned off the alarm and opened the door. She greeted Shannon cheerfully, but then she saw her expression. Something was wrong.

"Erin, I was on my way back from the store when I passed a bad wreck. It was Kaely's car. I tried to talk to the police on the scene, but they wouldn't speak to me. Wouldn't allow anyone near. One officer told me that the injured were on their way to the hospital. I called Noah, and he told me to pick you up and drive you to the hospital."

Erin was so shocked she couldn't speak. She just stood in the doorway.

"I . . . I need to get my purse," she said breathlessly. "Wait here."

She ran down the hall to her bedroom and grabbed her purse from the top of the dresser. She had just picked it up when she felt something sting her neck. At first, she was confused. Was there a bee in the bedroom? But as she began to lose consciousness, she realized that she'd just made a very serious mistake. One that might cost her life.

Erin was floating down a stream in a small boat. She felt incredibly relaxed until she realized that she'd lost the oars. Where the water had been calm only moments before, it suddenly began to churn. A feeling of panic set in. The boat was headed toward even choppier water, and it began to rock back and forth. She clung onto the sides, trying not to be thrown into the water. Fear clutched at her. Somehow, she knew the stream was leading to the edge of a cliff and that she would be catapulted to her death. She tried to call out for help, but she couldn't see anyone on the shore. There was no one to save her. She stared down into the water and saw dead faces staring back at her. Scott, Sarah, Pat, her parents . . . Was she responsible for all their deaths? Although her heart told her it couldn't be true, her mind condemned her.

She began to call out to God. He would save her. Right before she reached the cliff, her eyes fluttered open. She felt confused. Where was she? She'd been at Kaely's house. And then . . . She tried to get up, but she couldn't move. Her arms were tied behind her and her feet were bound together. She gazed around her. She was in a large building. It looked like some kind of large storage shed. In one corner, there was a riding mower. Next to it was a backhoe. There were also rakes, brooms . . . What was this?

"You're awake."

Erin turned her head to find Shannon standing a few feet away. "What . . . ?" Her throat was dry, and she felt dizzy. Disoriented. "Why . . . ?"

"Why what?" Shannon asked. "Why are you here? Why do you deserve to die?"

"I don't understand . . ."

Shannon pulled up a chair and sat a few feet away from her. "I left you clues. The victims' hair color. Their family status. The toys. You should have been able to figure it out, Erin. I guess you're not as smart as you think you are."

Erin fought to clear her mind, but it was difficult. Why would Kaely's friend do this? It didn't make any sense. She realized suddenly that there was something around her neck. She wanted to reach up and touch it, but she couldn't since her hands were bound behind her. As she stared at Shannon, she was suddenly struck with an awful awareness. "My neck. What's around my neck?"

Shannon's smile was so cold, her expression so full of hate that she was certain her instinct was right. But how could that be? She hadn't even turned in her manuscript to her publisher yet.

"It's *Dark Secrets*. But how . . . ?"

"Easy. You left your laptop open while I was in the house. When I said I was going to the bathroom, I downloaded your newest creation. It gave me exactly what I needed."

"You . . . you're working with Christine Dell?"

"The woman who tried to extort money from your publisher?" Shannon shook her head and laughed like Erin had just said something truly humorous. "Of course not. That woman and her little friends are buffoons. No wonder they were caught." Shannon sighed and leaned back in her chair.

"How . . . ?"

"How do I know about that?" Shannon leaned closer to her. "Nick and I are friends. Wasn't hard to get him to tell me about it."

"Do you . . . do you want money? I have some. Not as much as you might think."

"I'm not looking for money, Erin. Nor do I care about your book. Except to say that you don't deserve to make money writing. You're not a good writer. You're a hack."

Erin couldn't care less about this woman's opinion of her writing. She was in a fight for her life, and as her mind cleared, she began to strategize. How could she get out of this? Did anyone know she was here? If her phone was still in her pocket, could Kaely and Noah track her? Did they even know she was in trouble?

"Was it . . . was it you? Did you kill all those women?"

Shannon's self-satisfied expression answered Erin's question. Everyone had assumed the Novel Killer was a man. How could they have been so wrong?

She focused on clearing her head. *Focus.* Of one thing she was certain. Erin had to keep Shannon talking. The longer Erin could distract her, the more time someone had to find her. If Shannon was a psychopath, she was very narcissistic. She'd want to hear how smart she was.

"How were you able to pull this off?" Erin asked, trying to ignore the pressure of what she now knew was a garrote around her neck. "Kaely is an extremely talented profiler. Why didn't she see through you?" She tried to clear her throat, but the garrote made it difficult. The cord cut into her neck. "We . . . we were sure you were a man."

Erin's assessment of Shannon proved correct. She looked proud. Haughty. She fell silent so Shannon would talk about herself. She couldn't help it. Her narcissism was the one thing she couldn't control.

"I've been planning this for a long time," she said softly, her eyes shining with her own madness. "In fact, I knew who I was when I was only nine years old."

This told Erin that Shannon truly was not only psychotic, she was very organized, something she and Kaely had both believed. She had the ability to plan. Her actions were measured and well thought out. Unfortunately, that meant Erin was in real trouble, but it also meant that Shannon could be manipulated. Erin just needed to ask the right questions. She had to appeal to Shannon's ego.

"You planned all of this when you were a child?" Erin repeated, trying to sound incredulous and impressed.

"No, of course not." Shannon laughed. "Not all of it, but I certainly knew this day would come."

"Why befriend Kaely?" Erin asked, trying to lead Shannon away from their present situation. She needed her to concentrate on the past. Make her want to prove how brilliant she was.

"It was a great plan. I saw the dedication in your book. That's when I knew it was fate. I was already living in Virginia. So, I began to hatch my plan. Of course, finding Kaely wasn't difficult. You can find anyone if you look hard enough. I moved to Fredericksburg, got a job, and rented a house. I followed her, learned her patterns, and then introduced myself. Becoming friends was easy. Knowing that she used to profile—what do you call them— UNSUBs? That made it exciting. A game I knew I could win. I learned a lot about profiling. It's not hard. You laid out the pattern in your book. Then I worked on a story of my own, so Kaely would introduce you to me. Again, not difficult. You both think you're so smart, but you're not as clever as I am."

Shannon's insanity seemed to twist her features into something frightful. Evil. A chill ran down Erin's back. This woman was not only deranged, she was extremely dangerous. Erin needed to keep a cool head and try to stay one step ahead of her.

"Then you . . ." Erin let her voice trail off so Shannon would keep talking.

"Then I manipulated Kaely until she was right where I wanted her. When everything was in place, I started to kill. Step-by-step, each one brought me closer to you." She shrugged. "I have to admit that I was going to stop after I used your ridiculous book, but then, Patricia Long showed up in Virginia. Her daughter posted something on social media about her mother visiting. It was fate. I had to kill again. I just had to." She shook her head and sighed. "Everything I planned. Everything I've done, fate was with me. Even tonight. I was out in the parking lot at the . . . what do you call it . . . the command center? I cut the fuel line on Noah's car, so he'd have car trouble. No one saw me do it, but some muscle-bound Neanderthal noticed me in the parking lot. I told him I was a reporter. Then it started to rain. That made him run for cover. Fate on my side once again." Her wide smile reminded Erin of a child at Christmas. Shannon was enjoying this. Reveling in it. She met Erin's gaze. "Finally, tonight, the opportunity I've been waiting for presented itself. The piece de resistance, as they say. Of course, I know the alarm code, so I could get inside if you didn't let me in. I've been in Kaely's house quite a few times. Watched her enter the numbers. And if you'd gone with Kaely to pick up Noah, I had a backup plan. But I was pretty sure you wouldn't leave. Tonight, everything worked out just the way I'd planned it. It's so clear to me that this was meant to be. You can see that, can't you?"

"But why didn't you come up with your own methods to murder those women?" Erin asked, frowning at her. "I mean, someone like you, creative, intelligent, why copy the ideas of others?"

Shannon's expression quickly changed. "You're missing the point," she replied, her voice tight and angry. "All of this was my idea. Every single killing led me to you."

"I don't understand. Why me? I don't even know you."

Shannon jumped to her feet. "You haven't figured it out yet? Really?" She took off her glasses and flung them a few feet away from her. Then she put her fingers up to her eyes and removed her contact lenses. Once she had them out, she stared at Erin for a moment. Her eyes were green. Why had she hidden them?

Suddenly, the toys left behind at the crime scene made sense. All items she had when she was young. Things her sister had either taken from her, or something she wanted but didn't get. All the victims having blonde hair. Why hadn't she seen it? If Shannon had auburn hair . . .

"You . . . you're . . ."

"You finally figured it out? Man, how dense are you?" She got a few inches from Erin's face and grinned maniacally. "Hello, little sister. Tonight I'm finally going to achieve my life's goal. Killing you."

THIRTY-SEVEN

By the time Kaely and Noah got back to the house, Kaely was a little concerned. She'd tried calling Erin several times, but her phone had gone straight to voicemail. She assumed it was the storm that was causing the problem. Still, she'd feel better once she could check on her.

"I still don't understand what happened to the car," Noah said as they pulled into the garage. "We just got it back from the shop. I guess the mechanic missed something. He's usually so good. It's weird."

His concern over the car added to Kaely's unease. "It will be in the shop again by tomorrow," Kaely said. "We'll find out what's wrong." She shrugged. "Sometimes car engines mess up. Maybe it flooded?"

"Initially the water on the road wasn't deep enough to flood the engine." He shook his head. "Like you said, we'll know more tomorrow."

They headed into the house, and Kaely called Erin's name. Chester sat in the kitchen and got up when they came in. Mr. Hoover was a few feet away, watching them. As soon as he saw them, Chester started to whine.

"Where's Erin, boy?" Kaely asked.

He whined again and began to pace back and forth. Kaely noticed his leash on the floor. "Noah, I think he needs to go out. Why don't you take care of him? I'm going to check Erin's room. Maybe she's lying down. It's late, and I know she was exhausted after spending so long at the command center." Even as Kaely voiced the possibility, she knew that couldn't be right. If Erin was in bed, Chester would be with her. And she would never forget to take Chester out. Her heart began to beat faster, and she gulped in air.

"Sure." Noah grabbed the leash and attached it to Chester's collar. The dog pulled on the leash as if he didn't want to go out. "Must be the rain," Noah said. Chester had never had any problems with weather when Kaely stayed with Erin a few months ago. Something was wrong.

Kaely turned and hurried toward the guest room while Noah urged the reluctant dog to go outside. When she opened the door, Kaely found Erin's purse on the floor; the contents, including her phone, lay scattered nearby. No wonder she hadn't been able to get through to her. Kaely ran upstairs to check, even though she knew in her heart that Erin was gone, and she hadn't left under her own steam.

"He did his duty," Noah said as Kaely came back into the living room. They were both wet. "But he didn't want to. Whatever's bothering him has nothing to do with needing to go to outside." He frowned when he saw Kaely. "What's wrong?" he asked. "Didn't you find her?"

"No," Kaely said, her voice shaking. "She's not here, Noah. The alarm wasn't on when we came into the house. Someone took her. Erin's in trouble."

Noah pulled out his phone. "I'm calling Nick. We need his help."

Kaely hurried over to the front door and checked out the alarm again. If someone had come into the house who didn't belong, the alarm company should have been notified. They would have sent help. She stood there, staring at the keypad for several seconds. She'd told Erin to turn it on before she left. Had she just forgotten?

"Nick's on the way over," Noah said. "He happened to be close by."

"Oh, Noah, what are we going to do?" Kaely said, fighting to remain calm. "I'm afraid she's in danger. I think the UNSUB has her."

Before Noah could respond, the doorbell rang. While Noah answered the door, Kaely went back to the bedroom. She looked around, hoping to find some kind of clue that would show her where Erin was. She couldn't find anything helpful. "She's just found You," Kaely prayed, softly, unable to keep tears from dripping down her face. "Show her who You are. That You're her protector. Her defender. Please, Heavenly Father, keep her safe, and show us how to find her."

She searched the room one more time, mostly because she couldn't think of anything else to do. Was it true? Had the UNSUB abducted her the way he'd taken Patricia Long? They still hadn't found her or her body. Was Erin going to disappear too?

"Kaely."

She turned around and found Noah and Nick standing in the doorway. "We need to check our outside cameras," Noah said. "That will tell us who took her."

Kaely felt stupid. She should have thought of that right away. The fact was, they rarely looked at them. There just wasn't much of a reason to do so—until now. "My phone's in my purse. I need to get it."

Noah could have pulled up the images on his phone, but Kaely felt she needed to do it. She had to do something that would make her feel she was helping to find her friend.

Noah and Nick followed her into the living room, where she grabbed her purse. It only took her a moment to pull up the images. The first one was from the doorbell camera. But what she saw left her speechless.

"I can't . . . Wait a minute," she finally said. She advanced the images until she saw the person who was holding onto Erin, supporting her since she was clearly impaired. She could barely walk and the look on her face showed confusion. Was she drugged? She watched as Erin was loaded into a car and driven away from the house. She switched to the camera that was mounted on the house. Before the car drove out of sight, she paused the image.

"You can make out the license plate," she said to Nick. "Can you put out a BOLO?"

"Yes," Nick said, "but I also want to see if we can track the car. There are traffic cameras around town. Let's see if we can figure out where they went." He shook his head. "I know Shannon. I . . . thought we were friends. We just had coffee this morning." He suddenly went pale. "She asked questions about . . . about Erin. I thought . . . I thought it was because she was famous. I hope I didn't say the wrong thing."

"There's nothing you could have said to make this happen," Noah said. "Unless you gave her our alarm code or told her when Erin would be alone."

Nick shook his head. "Of course not." He ran his hand across his jaw. "I just don't understand . . ."

"*You* don't understand," Kaely said. "Shannon's been my friend ever since she moved here. Why would she do this? It doesn't make any sense."

"Didn't she move here not long before the murders started?" Noah asked.

"A few months before the first one." Kaely suddenly felt dizzy and sat down on the couch. They'd been looking for a man. There weren't many women serial killers, although it had happened. One of the most famous was Aileen Wuornos, but her victims were all men. A woman who killed women? It was so rare that it had never occurred to her that Shannon could be the perpetrator. If only she hadn't been so focused on men. She looked at Noah. "How could I have missed this?"

"Honey, I've been working on a profile with others from the BAU. We didn't seriously consider that the UNSUB might be a woman. The murders weren't . . ." He paused for a moment. "She really was using those novels as a guide. She never developed her own MO. That's how she was able to hide. Shannon is young and strong. And if she's drugging her victims . . ." He frowned. "Nothing ever showed up in the tox screens, but I'm certain only the basic tests were done. As you know, there are drugs that don't show up unless more in-depth tox screens are done."

"But why? Why would she do this? And why Erin?"

Noah shook his head. "I don't know."

"Listen," Nick said. "She might think she's a step ahead of us, but I know something she doesn't. We've been installing a new security system in Virginia. It looks for certain license plates." He quickly wrote down the license plate number showing on the image from the camera.

"You can track her car with it?" Kaely asked.

"I've heard about this," Noah said, "but it's only in spots, right?"

Nick nodded. "That's true, but I can also pull up traffic light cameras. Between those two, we may be able to track the car close to its final destination."

"How long will it take?" Kaely asked.

"Let me grab my laptop from my car," Nick said.

He hurried toward the front door. Once he went outside, Kaely turned to Noah. "Do you really think this will work?"

"Yeah, I do. If the traffic light cameras don't give us the information we need, this new system can. Those cameras are set up in various places. Like Nick said, they look for the license plate as well as the car. It's not hard to use. In fact, I think almost anyone can do it."

Nick came back inside and put his laptop on the coffee table. He sat down and opened it. Then he brought up a website and entered the license plate number. Kaely waited, holding her breath and praying this would work. She couldn't think of any other way to find Erin in time. Kaely had to believe that she was still alive.

"I found them," Nick said suddenly. He clicked some keys and then said, "After she left here, they traveled west toward the highway." Kaely could see the images Nick was able to pull from the various cameras. He paused for a moment and then clicked the keys again. "Then they drove a few more miles." He shook his head. "I lost them. Just a moment." He stared at the screen for several seconds. "The car doesn't show up again, and there aren't any traffic lights in that area.

That means Shannon must have turned off." He frowned. "They may be in an area with a few houses and a couple of warehouses. If I remember right, they might be abandoned. The only other thing near the spot where we lost them is an old cemetery. My money's on one of those warehouses."

Kaely looked at the area he was referring to. "That's still a rather large area. We need to find her before it's too late."

"Shannon would have turned off onto one of these three streets." He pointed them out. "She would want to reach her destination quickly because she knows that by now, you've contacted the authorities. She'll want to hide her car so we can't find her. I'm calling the police and some of my deputies. I'll send them over there right away. Hopefully, we can locate them quickly." He sighed. "This rain certainly doesn't help anything."

As Kaely waited for Nick to make his phone calls, she prayed once again that God would keep Erin safe. She glanced at the clock on the wall. How much time did they have? Would it be enough?

THIRTY-EIGHT

"Courtney?" How could it be true? Erin had given up hope of ever seeing her sister again. But even if she had shown up, this certainly wasn't the scenario Erin had expected. She couldn't believe this was happening. She realized that she'd tried to forget Courtney. She'd had to deal with the death of her parents. Thinking about Courtney was too much. Now, memories came rushing back. Courtney had been jealous, even mean sometimes, when they were children. But how could she despise Erin enough to do something like this? Planning her death for years?

"I don't understand," Erin said. "How could you hate me this much? You're my sister."

"Your sister? Your *sister*? Our parents always loved you. Babied you." Courtney's face was a mask of loathing. "They gave you everything I wanted. The Barbie, the Beanie Baby, the bracelet . . . even the stickers."

Erin had no memory of Courtney being upset over what their parents had given her. "That's . . . that's not true," she said. "They gave you the toys you asked for. They never preferred me over you." She frowned. "And I never got the Barbie."

"Oh, they bought you your precious Barbie. It was hidden in their closet. After they died, I found it and took it. You had no right to that doll. I asked them for a Barbie when I was younger than you, and I didn't get it."

"Courtney, I remember your Barbie."

"Are you calling me a liar?"

"No," Erin said, "but you did have a Barbie."

Courtney laughed. Erin had never heard a laugh that sounded so angry before. It was chilling. "But not a special edition like the one they bought you. Mine was a plain old Barbie. Cheap. I hated it. I pulled its head off and burned the body in the backyard."

What could she say to calm Courtney down? The shock of realizing who the UNSUB was and that Courtney had killed innocent people only because of her hatred for her own sister made it hard to think. She had to come up with a way of escape. She needed to think. And to stall Courtney while she came up with a plan.

"I'm . . . I'm sorry, Court. I wish I'd stood up for you. I was just too young. I didn't understand how you felt. Please forgive me."

For just a moment, Courtney's expression shifted. But as quickly as it had transformed, it reverted back to the rage that had clearly consumed her sister. Reasoning with her wasn't going to work. *Help me, God. Show me what to do. Please.*

"Where did you go after the accident?" Erin asked. "We looked for you. Aunt Karen and I. But we couldn't find you anywhere."

Courtney shrugged. "Bought a Social Security number from some guy I bought drugs from. Used it to get a driver's license. From there it was easy." She glared at Erin. "I don't believe either one of you really looked for me. Our dear Aunt Karen made it clear that she blamed me for our parents' deaths."

This was news to Erin. Karen hadn't told her that she'd said anything like that to Courtney.

"She said you both blamed me," Courtney said in a low voice.

It was clear to Erin that Courtney was unraveling, right in front of her. Her hands were shaking, and she was blinking excessively.

"I never said that, and I never heard Aunt Karen say it either," Erin said, trying to stay calm. It was true that Aunt Karen had partially blamed Courtney because her brother and his wife had to drive to the hospital that night when the roads were icy and dangerous, but in the end, the road conditions were to blame, not Courtney. Aunt Karen had cared about Courtney and so did Erin. *If* she said something like that to her sister, it was probably in a state of grief. Karen and their father were very close.

Again, Courtney looked startled by Erin's statement. But as before, hatred won any kind of a battle her emotions might be waging. Even psychopaths could feel rage. What they lacked was empathy. Love. This war wouldn't be won by appealing to Courtney's love of family. She had none.

"In the end it doesn't matter, little sis," Courtney said. "Today, I'll finally have the last laugh. You're going to die. And it will happen according to your own imagination."

"If you wanted me dead, why didn't you just kill *me*?" Erin asked. "Why kill four other innocent women?"

"No one's really innocent, little sister," Courtney snapped. "Besides, where would have been the fun in that? This was perfectly planned. I gave you every chance to stop me. To figure it out. I even left a bit of a clue in that dumb manuscript I wrote and Kaely read. It was about a sister killing another sister. But she didn't get it. If she had, we might not be having this conversation right now."

Of course, Courtney hadn't mentioned that when she told Erin about her story. She wasn't certain it would have changed anything. She still wouldn't have figured out who Shannon really was. "Why here?" Erin asked. "Why in Virginia?" She knew the answer, but she was still trying to keep Courtney talking.

Courtney sighed. "I told you, I already lived here. That makes it . . . what is it you call that? A comfort zone? *This* is my comfort zone. Besides, I wanted to pit my intellect against the police and the FBI. And most of all, against the great Kaely Quinn-Hunter. The profiler's profiler. And I beat her." Again, Courtney's eye's blazed with insanity. "Up until the moment you take your last breath, you'll know that this time *I* win. Maybe our parents loved you more than me. Maybe you got everything you wanted, and I got nothing, but this time . . . this time, I win. I win!"

"What happened to Patricia Long?" Erin had to calm Courtney down. If she didn't, Erin was afraid Courtney would lose control and decide it was time to kill her. Besides, in case Erin was able to find a way out of this, she needed to know if Pat was still alive. And where she was. Erin couldn't give up hope that Kaely and Noah were trying to find her. Although she was afraid Pat was dead, this would give Courtney a chance to gloat about abducting her. Would it work?

Courtney stared at her for a moment, her green eyes dead. Then she laughed. But again, it was cold. Chilling.

"I told her that I had a partner. Someone who would kill her daughter if she didn't come with me. She willingly got into my car." She grinned at Erin. It reminded Erin of the Cheshire cat from *Alice in Wonderland*. She remembered Courtney as being selfish and sometimes mean, but this? She never would have believed that her sister would become the crazed woman sitting only inches away from her. Suddenly, a deep wave of sadness washed over her. This was her *sister*. The only family she had left. And the most important goal in Courtney's life was to kill her?

"But where is she now?" Erin asked, trying to ignore her emotions.

"You need to think back to the book she wrote before *Grin*," Courtney said.

Erin's mind fought to remember Patricia's books. It had been quite a while. What was the book before *Grin*? Suddenly, an image of the cover flashed in her head. The title was *Cry*. There were blank eyes with bloody tears on the cover. But what was Courtney referring to? Her mind clicked through the plot. Suddenly, she remembered something.

"You . . . you buried her alive?"

Another round of maniacal laughter.

"When? Is she dead?"

Courtney made a big show of looking at her watch. "Probably not yet, although I doubt she has much time left."

Cry featured a killer who buried his victims alive, putting them in a box with a hole in the top, a long thin tube sticking out of the ground. The killer did it to draw out the victim's death, making it more torturous before they went mad with fear. How long had Patricia been under the ground? And with the rain, could she possibly still be alive? Erin had to survive this encounter with Courtney. It was the only way she could save Pat. She'd do whatever she had to. No matter what.

THIRTY-NINE

Kaely, Noah, and Nick sat in the kitchen, waiting to hear something from the police or the sheriff's department. The minutes felt like hours. Finally, Nick's phone rang. He answered and then listened for a while. Then he said, "Okay, good. What's the plan?"

Kaely listened intently, praying silently. She realized suddenly that she'd stood to her feet. She didn't remember doing it. She loved Erin and felt partially to blame for what had happened. She was supposed to be a talented profiler. How had Shannon been able to fool her so completely? Maybe someone had pressured her to take Erin from the house? The more she asked herself that question, the more convinced she became that Shannon was the only person behind Erin's abduction. She'd only been here for six months. Not long before the first murder. She could see now that the first meeting at the coffee shop was manipulated, not coincidental. She went back to the profiling session she'd had with Erin, and suddenly one of her comments about the items found at the crime scenes played in her head as if she'd never heard it before. Then she remembered the novel Shannon had written. How could she have been so stupid? She grabbed Noah's arm.

"I know who Shannon is," she said, "and why she kidnapped Erin."

"Hold on," Nick said. "This could be important. I'm going to put you on speakerphone." He nodded at Kaely. "I've got Detective Munoz from the police department on the line. He's overseeing the search for Erin."

Kaely stepped a little closer to the phone. "Detective, it's clear to me now that Shannon Burke is really Courtney Delaney, Erin's sister. She left the family when Erin was ten. Erin said her sister didn't like her, but I never realized until now, just how much she actually hated her. I believe Erin's success as an author drew Courtney out. This woman is a psychopath and a narcissist, Detective. Her only goal is to kill her sister. She murdered all the other women simply as a way to disguise her true intent. She was playing a game. She's incredibly dangerous. If you confront her, reason won't work. She has no compassion, no remorse."

"I understand," the detective said. "Do you think Ms. Delaney is still alive?"

"I think it's possible. Erin understands how the mind of a psychopath works. She'll do everything she can to stall her. She'll appeal to her ego and try to buy enough time for you to find her."

"We know approximately where they are," he said. "We have a BOLO out for the car. Hopefully, we'll find it soon."

"Listen, Detective," Kaely said. "This is really important. When you figure out where Erin's being held, no lights and sirens. If Courtney hears anything suspicious, she won't hesitate to kill Erin. Remember that's her ultimate goal. Nothing is more important to her than that."

"Okay. I understand." He sighed. "I just hope we have enough time."

Nick picked up the phone again. "If you could keep us updated, we'd appreciate it," he said. "We'd like to be there for Erin once this is over." He glanced at Kaely. She was aware that he'd asked to be contacted when everything was over because if it went wrong, he didn't want Kaely to be there. But she couldn't let that possible outcome into her mind. God would protect her. Erin had just gotten saved. She had a new life and should be able to live it.

When Nick disconnected the call, Kaely sat down and held out her hands toward Noah. "We need to pray, Noah. We need to pray hard for Erin."

As he sat down next to his wife, Kaely took his hands and began to appeal to heaven for her dearest friend.

"I hope you're not trying to stall, sis," Courtney said. "No one's coming to your rescue. Your phone's back at the house, so no GPS help for you there. And there's no GPS in my car. I read your books. I made sure there's no way for anyone to track us."

Erin's eyes had started to adjust to the dark room. She tried to look it over without Courtney realizing what she was doing. The mower, the backhoe. There were chairs. Lots of chairs. And a couple of large wooden boxes at the back of the large shed. Next to them were large metal containers. They reminded her of something. What was it? It was then that a memory from her parents' funerals popped into her mind.

283

"This is . . . This is a—"

"Are you trying to say 'this is a cemetery,' little sister?" Courtney said. "Good job. You finally figured it out. The perfect place for you to die, huh? I mean, it's so, so convenient."

"Pat is buried here? But how . . . ?"

"How did I pull it off?" Courtney took a flashlight out of her pocket and shone it at a corner of the shed.

Erin gasped. There was a body propped up against the wall, covered with plastic.

"Meet my friend Oscar. He dug the hole for your friend Patricia. People will do almost anything for money. I offered him a lot of it to help me. But in the end, once he'd stopped being useful, I decided not to pay him. He was unhappy about it, but it is what it is."

"But . . . what did you bury her in?"

Courtney sighed loudly. "So many questions. Okay, but this is the last one. We really need to get on with the reason you're here, little sister. Your friend Pat's inside what they call a *burial vault*. Most are made of metal or concrete. They keep the ground from collapsing onto the casket. They used to be made of wood, but they don't hold up as well. Thankfully, this place still had a few of them."

If Courtney had buried Pat in a vault, and used a tube for air, Pat could still be alive. Erin was determined to save her. She had to believe that help was on the way. By now, Kaely and Noah knew it was Courtney—or Shannon—who took her. Their cameras would have recorded it. And the police would have checked traffic cameras. They knew the area. If Kaely could just put it all together . . . The problem was that no one knew Courtney had used the plot from *Cry* to kill Patricia. Only she could tell them that.

"Before I die, I want to apologize to you, Courtney," Erin said. She needed to keep saying her sister's name. Hopefully, it made this situation more personal. She prayed it would make it harder for her sister to kill her. She was certain it wouldn't ultimately change her mind, but it might give Erin enough time. Although she was trying to postpone her own demise as well as Patricia's, she was telling the truth. She really did feel the need to apologize. Once she'd realized what Christ had actually done for her—how much He'd suffered for her freedom—she felt true compassion for her sister. How could she hold hate in her heart when He had died for Courtney too?

Courtney chortled. "How dumb do you think I am? I'm not falling for that."

"Listen, Courtney. I'm serious about this. If I'm going to die, I need you to know something. I . . . I did blame you for Mom and Dad's deaths. Not directly, really. But I believed it was your drug use that led them to try to reach you at the hospital that night. But it wasn't that, Court. I know that now. It was love. They got out on those icy roads because they loved you. And you . . . you were sick. You needed help and understanding, not judgment. If I made you feel as if it was your fault they died, I'm sorry. I was wrong. It's true that I was only ten years old, and I was mourning my mother and my father, but if I did anything to make you think you were responsible for their deaths . . . It's just not true. You didn't want that to happen."

"You know what Karen said to me after the funeral? She said she wished I'd never been born." Courtney shrugged. "So I obliged her. Courtney Delaney disappeared, and Shannon Burke was born." She looked away and for just an instant, Erin thought she saw a glimpse of anguish on her face.

"I truly had no idea Aunt Karen said that to you." Karen had never told her about that. They were awful words to say to a teenager who was grieving. "I'm so sorry, Court," Erin said. "I know she didn't mean it. She loved her brother, and she was grieving. But it was a cruel thing to say. You didn't deserve that."

"Doesn't matter anymore. Everyone loved you. And hated me."

"You know that's not true. Mom and Dad loved you, Court. There wasn't any difference in how they cared for us." Erin was seeing small signs that Courtney still had feelings. She could still be touched emotionally. But how did that make sense with all the cold-blooded murders she'd committed? It was a deviation from the normal profile of a psychopath. It gave her a spark of hope.

Courtney shook her head. "No. You were their little princess, and I was nothing more than their responsibility. Their messed-up, druggie daughter."

"Courtney, you're wrong," Erin said. "They loved you so much. That's why they spent so much time trying to help you. Taking you to doctors, attempting to get you the support you needed. You were so angry. So out of control. But they never gave up. Why do you think they went out that night? Why they drove to the hospital when the roads were so bad? They could have easily stayed home."

Courtney sneered at her. "Because they were so perfect. They couldn't be seen as not caring about me. It would have messed with their perfect image."

"No, Court. They didn't care about what people thought. They would have done anything for you."

Her face twisted with fury, Courtney got up and slapped

Erin across the face, almost knocking her chair over. "You don't get to tell me I'm wrong. Never, you hear me?" She pointed down. "I saw your lovely tattoo, by the way. *Mom and Dad*. After I kill you, I'm going to carve my name above theirs. Because the day they died, I died too. You'll go to your grave with *my* name carved on your body. How do you like that?"

Erin could taste blood in her mouth, but she didn't care. "I got that tattoo after I moved out of Aunt Karen's. I didn't add your name because I always hoped you were still alive. That I'd see you again someday." She tried to take a deep breath, but it was difficult. "If I have to die today, I'm okay with it. But first I have to tell you something. This is more important than anything I could ever say to you." Her voice caught in her throat. "Kaely. Kaely told me about God, Court. I . . . I never believed in Him, even though Mom and Dad did."

"Are you talking about how they *found religion* a few months before they died?" She made a noise that almost sounded like a growl. "It was ridiculous. Are you trying to tell me that you've fallen for that nonsense?" Again, she got up in Erin's face. She was so close, Erin could feel her breath on her face. "If you think trying to *save* me so I won't kill you is gonna work, you're nuttier than I think you are. Donna Penrod took me to her church when I was nine. I didn't fall for it then, and I didn't fall for it when our mother and father tried to manipulate me with religion. You can forget it, little sister."

Erin thought she heard something from outside. It wasn't loud. Could be anything, but just in case time was running out, she had to try to save her sister.

"Listen Court. God's real. I know that now. I've wasted

so many years rejecting the idea . . . If only I'd listened. If you'd listened. I know who Jesus is now. I know that He suffered unimaginable pain and rejection so He could pay the price for everything we've done wrong. *Everything*, Court. Listen, when I die, I know where I'm going. And believe it or not, I'm not afraid now. I want to live, believe me, but if I don't . . . You have to know this. All you have to do is tell Him . . . tell Jesus . . . that you're willing to accept the sacrifice He made for you. That you'll let Him pay the price for everything you've done, Court."

"You're saying that God thinks so little of His creation that I can just walk away free and clear after all the people I've killed?" She glared at Erin. "Your God doesn't sound like someone who cares very much about the human beings He supposedly created. In fact, I don't think He cares enough about you to save you either, sis. Too bad."

Once again, Erin was certain she'd heard something. Had Courtney noticed? She was so intent on her target, it seemed as if she'd blocked everything else out.

"Please, Courtney. Just remember what I said. What Mom and Dad said. No matter what happens . . ."

Courtney suddenly drew back as if she was the one who'd been slapped. Her expression was one of incredulity. "You think this God of yours is going to save you, don't you?" She stared into Erin's eyes. "I'll make you a deal. If this great God of yours, who cares so little for the lives I've taken, magically saves you, I'll call out for this Jesus who loves me so much. But if God lets you die, then I'll gladly spend an eternity in hell. It will be worth it to watch you get what you deserve." She stepped around behind Erin and put her hands on the garrote that had been tied behind her back. "Hey, God! If you love my sister, then do something to save her. If you don't, she dies now!"

As Courtney tightened the garrote, Erin gasped, trying to suck in air, but finally she couldn't breathe at all. Just before her world turned dark, she heard an odd sound, but it was too late.

She couldn't save herself, and now she couldn't save Patricia.

FORTY

As the pain faded, Erin struggled to take a breath. She found that not only could she breathe, she could see . . . light. Where was she? Had she survived? She tried to call out. She had to save Pat. It was odd, though. It was as if she could hear her thoughts even before the words left her mouth. The light was so bright, it should have been blinding, but it wasn't. And it didn't hurt her eyes. It was then that she saw Someone standing in the middle of the light. She couldn't make Him out clearly, but she had to tell him about Patricia. Before she could find a way to express herself, she heard a voice.

"I know about Patricia. She'll be all right. Don't worry," He said.

"But You don't understand. You have to find her . . ."

"When you wake up, you'll know where she is. I have a work for you to do. I want you to tell people about Me. Use your stories to let them know how much I love them."

"I don't understand . . ."

She suddenly felt something wash over her. Peace and . . . joy. It was so powerful.

"You will."

Erin could see people standing near the Being of light. It was hard to make them out, but she sensed that her parents were there. And someone else. Someone stood next to her parents, and there was a feeling of overwhelming elation emanating from . . . her. But who . . . ?

Suddenly, she was being pushed away from the light. She tried to cry out, beg to be allowed to stay, but the light faded away. She realized her eyes were closed and she forced them open. Now there was searing pain. She remembered the garrote and grasped at her neck.

"Stay still," a man said. "We need to put a tube down your throat to help you breathe."

She looked up into the face of a woman who was obviously concerned about her. "No," she tried to say. Her voice was so hoarse she was afraid the woman wouldn't be able to understand her. "Patricia . . . Patricia Long. You've got to save her."

The woman looked past her and called someone's name. She moved back, and a man with a short beard and a mustache flecked with gray looked down at her.

"I'm Detective Munoz," he said. "Did you say you know where Patricia Long is?"

Erin forced herself to nod. Her throat hurt so much it was painful to even swallow, but she had to get the words out.

"Cry," she choked out.

"You want to cry?"

"No. *Cry*, the book. She's buried. Here. Nearby. Check the cemetery."

The man came back into view. "I'm sorry, Detective, but she's delirious. We've got to get her to the hospital."

"No . . . no . . ."

"She's not delirious," another voice said. He leaned down close to her face. "I understand, Erin. I read the book. We'll find her."

Adrian? Erin felt the tears in her eyes. How could Adrian be here? Somehow, she knew he would save Patricia. God had sent Adrian, a man who'd read and remembered a book that had been out of print for years. It was truly a miracle. The woman, who Erin realized was an EMT, came back into view.

"I've got to put this tube down your throat," she said gently. "It's going to hurt, but your throat is swelling. If I don't do it, you won't be able to breathe. Do you understand?"

Erin nodded. She didn't care if it hurt. She now had hope that Patricia would be saved.

"After we insert the tube," the EMT continued, "we're going to lift you up and put you on a gurney. Then we'll get you to the hospital, okay?"

She nodded again. It was then that she looked to her left. Courtney lay near her, staring into her eyes. Erin began to cry. She was alive. All Erin wanted to do was to find a way to save her sister. She looked back at the EMT, who now had the tube in her hand.

"Please," she croaked out, "help her first."

The woman's expression changed, and she looked over at the other EMT who had rolled the gurney up next to them. Then she turned her attention back to Erin.

"We'll take care of her in just a minute," she said gently. "Let's get you on your way first."

Erin wanted to argue with her, but before she could say anything, she felt the tube slide down her tender throat. It hurt so badly, but she was more worried about Courtney than she was herself. Once the tube was secured, they lifted her onto the gurney and then adjusted it so she was off the ground. She was able to turn her head and look over at Courtney once again. Her eyes were still open, but this time Erin noticed that she was lying in a large pool of blood. Why wouldn't they help her? Why was she lying there all alone? Someone took her hand, and she turned her face. Adrian. There were tears in his eyes. It was then that she realized the truth. There would be no salvation. No chance for forgiveness. Her sister was gone.

"I'm going to make some coffee," Noah said to Kaely. "You need to eat something, honey. Staring at the phone won't make it ring."

"Can't you call Detective Munoz?" Kaely asked with tears in her eyes. "I have to know that she's all right."

"No, I can't. I have no idea what he's dealing with right now. He said he'd call when he knew something, and he will."

"Why didn't I see it? It was in Shannon . . . I mean, Courtney's book. A sister killing her sister. I'm supposed to notice things like that."

"Kaely, that's ridiculous," Noah said. "You had no idea Shannon was Courtney. And there's no way you could have known. Don't do this to yourself."

Before Kaely could respond, the phone rang. Even though she'd been waiting for it to ring, she jumped at the sound. Noah picked up the phone.

"Yeah?" he said, his voice tight.

Kaely watched his face, hoping to see relief, something

that would tell her Erin was okay. He closed his eyes and sighed deeply. Her heart sank.

"Thanks, Detective." He listened a little longer, then said, "We'll be there soon. Let her know." He disconnected the phone and turned to Kaely. "She's alive, honey. On her way to the hospital. A little beat-up, but okay. Let's get to the hospital so we can see her." He took Kaely's hands. "You won't believe this. Adrian's with her. He stopped Courtney before she could kill Erin. It was almost too late."

"Adrian? How did he know where to find her?"

Noah shrugged. "I have no idea. When we get to the hospital, we'll ask him, okay?"

"What about Courtney?"

"She died, honey," Noah said. "I'm sure Adrian had no choice. If he hadn't killed her, I'm pretty sure Erin wouldn't have survived."

Kaely wanted to feel compassion for Courtney Delaney, but she couldn't. God forgive her, but at that moment, she was glad Courtney was dead.

Erin was tired and sore. She wanted to sleep, but she couldn't. At least the tube was out of her throat. She could barely talk. Her right arm hurt, but thankfully, it wasn't broken. She was bruised, and her lip was cut. A nurse had given her a cup of ice. That helped to ease her dry, painful throat. The same nurse told her that Kaely and Noah were on their way. For some reason, the news made her cry. She wasn't sad. She was relieved and couldn't wait to see them. She kept running the images she'd seen before she was rescued through her mind. Was it a dream? It was so strange. What did it mean?

Earlier, a doctor had stopped by to see her. According to him, Courtney had injected her with GHB. It had been enough to make her pass out, but thankfully, she hadn't died. The doctor had explained that injecting GHB was very dangerous. "It's a miracle you're alive," he'd said. "GHB isn't something to fool around with. We were lucky to find it in your tox screen. The good news is, there won't be any lasting effects."

She realized Adrian was still here. He'd been beside her ever since she got to the hospital. He was holding her hand.

"Why are you here?" she whispered to him.

"Would you believe me if I told you that God told me to come?"

Tears ran down Erin's face as she nodded. "I would now." She tried to take a deep breath, but it was difficult. She needed to ask a question. One she wasn't sure she really wanted to ask, but she had to. "Did . . . did you kill my sister?"

Adrian squeezed her hand. "I'm sorry," he said softly. "If I could have found another way, I would have taken it. I told her to stop, but she just started pulling the garotte harder. You almost didn't make it."

She squeezed his hand back. Erin had wanted her sister to survive, but she believed Adrian. He did what he had to do. What God had sent him to do.

"What about the police?" she asked.

"They were close, but they weren't sure just where you were. I called Kaely when I got to town and found out what was going on. Then I contacted the local police, and they let me join the search. We'd split up, everyone trying to locate you. I just happened to find you first. I called them once I knew you were safe."

"Pat?"

"I don't know, Erin, I'm sorry. I told them what to look for. But I left with you while the police were searching the cemetery. The detective—Munoz, he said he'd come to the hospital to let you know if they found her."

Erin didn't respond, she just nodded. She continued to hold his hand. It made her feel better.

"Is it okay if I come in?"

Erin turned her head to see a woman in an EMT's uniform standing in the doorway.

"Weren't you . . . ?"

"At the cemetery?" the woman said. "Yes, I was."

Erin struggled to respond.

"I know your throat hurts," the woman said. "You don't need to say anything. I just need to tell you something."

Erin nodded and waved her closer. Adrian stepped back so the woman could stand next to Erin's bed.

"My name is Jane," she said. "I tended to the woman who died . . . at the cemetery? Before I worked on you. Someone told me she was your sister?" She looked closer at Adrian. "Wasn't it you?" she asked.

He nodded. "You asked me if I knew who she was." He looked back at Erin. "Kaely told me that Shannon was actually Courtney."

"Yes, that's right," Jane said. She met Erin's eyes. "You probably know that your sister was trying to kill you with a garrote. Before she could accomplish her goal, she was shot."

Although she could have told Jane that it was Adrian who ended Courtney's life, she stayed silent. There wasn't any reason to bring it up.

Jane cleared her throat and took another step closer to

the bed. "She didn't die right away. Even though we tried to save her, the bullet hit her carotid artery. We couldn't stop the bleeding. But before she passed away, she grabbed my arm and . . . Well, she asked me to pray for her. She said she wanted to go to heaven. I have no idea what you believe, but I feel like I'm supposed to tell you this. She accepted Jesus right before she died. The last thing she said was your name. I believe she wanted you to know."

Erin couldn't stop the tears of elation that ran down the sides of her face. She smiled at Jane and nodded again. Even though it hurt, she croaked out, "Thank you."

Jane smiled. "I'll be praying for your quick recovery. For a while, we thought we'd lost you too. I'm glad you're okay." Then she turned around and walked out of the room.

Erin wasn't certain, but she had to believe that what she'd seen had been real and the person with her parents was Courtney. Maybe it had been the last moment of her life, but she'd accepted the forgiveness that Christ had died to give her. Someday she and Courtney would be together again. But this time, they would have the kind of relationship they were robbed of. They would be real sisters. Was this God? Someone who fixed what was wrong, even if people didn't deserve it? Kaely's words whispered in her mind. *Jesus was perfect, yet He became sin. He didn't just pay the price for all of humanity, He actually became sin itself. The agony of that moment is beyond our comprehension, yet He did it for all of us. He did it for you, Erin.* Kaely was right, she couldn't comprehend that kind of love. But she'd just seen an example of it. The last time she'd felt love like that was from her parents. This is why God called Himself Father.

"I'm so happy for you," Adrian said. "You've been given a great gift."

"I know," she whispered. Erin wanted to tell Adrian about her dream, but her throat hurt too much. There would be time later.

"There you are," a voice said.

Erin smiled at Kaely and Noah as they stepped into the room. Kaely hurried over to the other side of her bed and put her hands on the rail.

"Are you okay?" she asked. "You look awful."

"Thanks," she whispered. "Quit appealing to my ego."

"You know what I mean," Kaely said. "Did Shannon . . . I mean, Courtney, hit you?"

Erin nodded.

"Anything broken?" Noah asked.

She shook her head. Erin wiggled around in the bed, trying to get into a more comfortable position.

"The doctor said she can go home sometime later today," Adrian said. "First they just want to make sure she doesn't have any internal injuries."

"I assume you're Adrian," Noah said. He stuck out his hand. "I'm very happy to meet you. And very thankful you got to that cemetery just in the nick of time. Detective Munoz tells me that if you hadn't arrived when you did, our girl probably wouldn't be here."

Adrian shook his hand. "Glad to meet you. Believe me, no one is more happy than I am for the timing."

"We're so grateful you found her," Kaely said. "God is so good." She leaned over the railing, a little closer to Erin. "I . . . I'm so sorry. I should have realized something was wrong with Shannon, but nothing she did made me suspicious. Not even her book. I think she was trying to leave clues. The book, the toys, all the victims being blonde... For someone who used to be a behavioral analyst, I really messed up. I let you down and put you in grave danger."

"No," Erin whispered. She was glad Kaely was close to her because her voice was almost gone. "Courtney hid from us both. She was my sister, and I didn't see it. How could you?"

"Maybe, but I'm still disappointed I didn't realize what was going on." Kaely took her other hand. "I'm just glad you're okay. And I'm sorry about your sister."

A man walked into the room. "Good to see you, Detective Munoz," Adrian said. "I hope you have good news for us?"

"We found Patricia Long," he said. "Your sister told one of the EMTs where she was. At first, they didn't understand what she was trying to say. But when they repeated it, I realized the message was for me. Your sister told us what section of the cemetery to search. It wasn't hard. There was only one place where dirt had been turned over. The tube sticking out of the ground was confirmation."

"Is she... alive?" Kaely asked.

The detective smiled. "Yes. She's down the hall in another room. The doctor said she'll be okay. But it was close. If it wasn't for you... and your sister... she wouldn't have made it."

"If it wasn't for my sister, she wouldn't have been in that situation," Erin whispered. She placed her hand on her throat as if it would help her. It didn't.

Kaely squeezed her hand. "But in the end, she also saved her. You influenced her to do the right thing, Erin. I'm so proud of you."

Erin shook her head. Pat was alive because God gave her

the chance to tell Courtney about Him. In that cemetery, three people had been saved, even though sadly, the groundskeeper had died. Erin and Pat were alive. And Courtney was in heaven with their parents.

Erin wanted to tell Kaely what she'd experienced before Adrian arrived to save her life, but it would have to wait. Not just because of her voice. She wanted to keep it in her heart for a while. She was still trying to understand it. One thing for certain, she was no longer afraid of the future because she'd learned that God truly held her life in the palm of His hand.

FORTY-ONE

Erin was glad to be out of the hospital. It had taken longer to check out than she'd anticipated, but she had to see Pat. She was so glad to find that she was doing better. She'd been through a lot, but her daughter was with her, and Erin was confident she'd make a complete recovery. She and Pat exchanged numbers and promised to stay in touch. Now, Erin wanted nothing more than to try to get back to her normal life. She was still uncomfortable, but thankfully, Kaely's guest bed was soft. Perfect for her bruised body. Erin was just grateful that hitting the cement floor while tied to that chair hadn't caused serious damage. Chester had gotten up on the bed so he could be near her. He seemed to know something was wrong. He stayed as close as he could without actually touching her. It was as if he knew it might hurt her. Every time she looked at him, she found him staring at her, his deep brown eyes peering into hers. She'd missed him so much.

Kaely had insisted that she go to bed as soon as she got home from the hospital. "The doctor said you need to rest. We're doing what he says. No arguments."

"Yes, ma'am," she said with a smile. She was happy to

be ordered to bed. She didn't want to be a wimp, but after taking one of the pain pills the doctor had prescribed, she didn't want to do anything but lie down and let the medicine do its work. Thankfully, her voice was getting stronger. She still sounded a little froggy, but it was much better than it had been in the hospital. She'd just nodded off when she heard the bedroom door open. She opened her eyes and saw Kaely holding a tray. When she saw what was on the tray, she grinned.

"Hot chocolate and Mallomars? Now *that's* what the doctor ordered."

"I thought it might do the trick."

While Erin gingerly pulled herself into a sitting position, Kaely put the tray over her lap.

"I know you ate something at the hospital, but I noticed you left most of it on the plate. Not that I blame you."

"What is it about hospital food?" Erin said, unwrapping one of the Mallomars. "It's like they all get together and try to figure out how to remove taste from everything they serve."

Kaely grinned. "Actually, I think they're trying to make sure they keep the food rather bland so as not to cause stomach upset or interfere with medications."

"Well, that makes sense. And actually, there was a cinnamon roll this morning that was really, really good."

"Did it taste like a Mallomar?"

Erin laughed. "No, but if it was in a restaurant, I'd order it. Started my day off right."

"Well, you need to rest. Enjoy your Mallomars and hot chocolate," Kaely said. "I'll be back."

Erin frowned at her. "Could you . . . just wait a bit? There's something I want to tell you."

"Sure," Kaely said. She sat down on the chair near the door. "I'm happy to listen to you anytime, Erin."

Erin took a deep breath and told Kaely about what she'd experienced after the attack. Kaely listened without interruption. When she finished, she waited for Kaely to say something. Did she think Erin was imagining what she'd seen?

At first Kaely didn't say anything. Finally, she cleared her throat and met Erin's eyes. "I had a similar experience," she said. "Some people didn't believe me when I told them, but I know what happened. God is so good. He wanted you to know that Courtney is okay. That she's safe with Him."

"It . . . It's hard for me to understand how He could love someone like Courtney. That He could allow her into heaven after she killed all those people. That kind of love is beyond my comprehension. But I'm so grateful. I . . ." Erin stopped when she heard a noise from downstairs. "Is Noah home? I thought he was going to work?"

Kaely frowned. "He did. And Adrian's not supposed to be here until dinner."

Erin looked at the clock on the nightstand next to her. It was only a little after four. "That's what I thought. I . . ."

A man stepped into the bedroom. He held a gun in his hand. Kaely stood up.

"Who are you, and what do you want?" she asked.

Erin saw her pat her right side. It was instinct, but of course Kaely wasn't armed. There wasn't anything she could do.

The man came closer, his gun still pointed at Kaely, who had stepped between the man and Erin. She was clearly trying to shield her. Erin couldn't let her risk her life like that. Chester began to growl and tried to get off the bed. She was certain he sensed danger and wanted to protect them. She was afraid the man might shoot Chester, and she couldn't let that happen. She grabbed his collar and told him to stay. Although he still continued to growl softly, he obeyed.

"If you don't hold onto that mutt, I'll kill him," the man said.

"Who are you?" Kaely asked again.

"I'm Eddie Pilcher." He glared at them. "Your friend Lee Johnson and his cousin promised me a big payday. I'm here to collect it."

"He's not my friend," Erin said. "He's yours."

"Nah, he's not," Eddie snarled. "He ratted me out. I'll take care of that weasel, trust me. I've got friends in prison. They don't like snitches either."

"But why are you here?" Kaely asked. "Your plan to get money from Erin's publisher is dead. Surely you realize we don't keep large amounts of cash in our house."

"I bet your husband will pay a pretty penny if I offer to keep you both alive," he said. "I need enough to get out of town. Start a new life." He waved his gun around. "You call him. Tell him to empty out your bank account. Bring the cash here now."

Eddie Pilcher was delusional. It was after four. Most banks closed at four. Noah could get some money from an ATM, but not enough to give Pilcher the *new life* he wanted. Erin prayed Kaely wouldn't tell him that his plan wasn't going to work. That knowledge could push him over the edge. He might shoot them both if he thought they were no longer any use to him.

"All right," Kaely said. "I'll call him. Just quit pointing that gun at me."

"No way, lady," Pilcher said. His mannerisms and the wild look in his eyes made Erin think he was on drugs. That would only make him more dangerous. He stepped closer to Kaely. "You dial the number. I'll talk to him. I want him to know that I'm serious."

Kaely nodded. "Okay, but my phone's downstairs. If you let me go get it . . ."

"You must think I'm really stupid." He pointed the gun at Erin. "Give her your phone. She can use it to call her husband."

Her phone was on the nightstand next to the bed. And Erin's gun was in the top drawer. She usually kept it unloaded, but with everything that had been going on before she was abducted by Courtney, she'd loaded it. She'd forgotten about it until that moment. If she could just open the drawer . . .

"You," he said to Kaely, "get her phone. Now."

Kaely walked over to the bed and picked up Erin's phone. Erin gazed down at the drawer for just a second, hoping Kaely would pick up what she was trying to tell her. Her almost imperceptible nod told her she understood. She turned around quickly, handing the phone to Eddie while blocking Erin from his line of sight. Erin quickly pulled the drawer open and took out her gun, but before she could fire, she heard a shot and Kaely fell.

Before she could stop him, Chester leaped off the bed and grabbed Pilcher's wrist. Erin aimed her gun at him and pressed the trigger.

FORTY-TWO

"I almost had a heart attack when you went down," Erin said. She was downstairs, sitting at the kitchen table drinking a new cup of hot chocolate and munching on another Mallomar.

"I couldn't tell you I was just trying to get out of the way," Kaely said after taking a sip of her own hot cocoa.

"I'm just grateful it turned out okay," Noah said. "I never thought for a moment that Eddie Pilcher would come after you, Erin. I figured a crook like him, with his record, would take off after his pal was arrested." He shook his head. "I'm grateful to God that you were able to get that gun, Erin."

"And I'm thankful that Pilcher missed when he fired." Erin smiled. "I think it startled him when Kaely went down."

"Well," Kaely said, "*I'm* thankful that you kept your cool and shot that jerk. If you'd missed, we probably wouldn't be here. Seems that cop in you is still there."

"There's someone else to thank here," Erin said. She looked down at the floor where Chester sat between them.

She patted the border collie's head. "Chester latched onto Pilcher before I had the chance to do anything. He grabbed Pilcher's wrist in his mouth so he couldn't fire his gun again. How he knew to do that is beyond me, but he's one smart dog. That made it possible for me to shoot Pilcher." She shook her head. "Chester gave me time to think. I wanted to put a bullet through his head, but in that moment, I felt . . ." She looked at Kaely. "Compassion? I wanted him to live. My sister was changed through God's love. Who knows? Maybe someday, Eddie will make the same decision." She paused for a moment, trying to explain a reaction that went against what was drilled into her by her instructors at the police academy. "I was trained to shoot to kill. Neutralize the threat. But for the first time in my life, something else was more important than my training. That's why I shot him in the shoulder. It brought him down, but he'll live."

"That's what God does when He's invited to live in you," Adrian said. "He changes you—as long as you let Him."

Erin nodded. She was different now. She didn't feel alone anymore. And there was something else. The guilt she'd been carrying had lessened. She would always regret accidentally killing Sarah Foster. But now she had a certainty that Sarah was in a wonderful place where there was light and love. She'd seen it. Death wasn't a tragedy for a Christian or an innocent child. It was a promotion. Salvation. An eternity of being loved and sheltered from fear, pain, sickness, and death. With that in her future, she no longer felt the need to protect herself from life. It was time to live it.

"Another cup of hot chocolate anyone?" Kaely asked. She laughed when everyone nodded.

Adrian picked up a wrapped Mallomar, opened it up, and

took a bite. His eyebrows arched. "Hey, these are really good. I think I could get addicted to them too."

Kaely got up and collected everyone's cup so she could fill them with the hot chocolate that was in a pan on the stove. "Oh no," she said, sighing deeply. "Not another one."

"Hey," Noah said. "Maybe I'll try one."

Kaely turned around and shook her head. "Don't you dare. One friend who's hooked on those things is enough."

"I think I noticed some empty wrappers in the trash can in our bedroom," Noah replied, grinning. "Seems maybe you've developed a slight craving?"

Erin laughed. Her body was still sore, but she was feeling much better. She would always be grateful to God for saving her life and Pat. Now, Lee was in jail, and Pilcher would be there after he got out of the hospital. Christine Dell was facing fraud charges, which might land her in prison as well.

"Still hard to believe Pilcher would come here to threaten you," Adrian said. "He could have gone into hiding and might have gotten away with his attack on me and his scheme to blackmail Erin's publisher."

"He's the kind of man who doesn't take failure well," Erin said. "His anger led him here to try to get what he's convinced he was owed. I truly believe that if Noah had given him money, he would have gladly killed us all."

"Well, he might have finished us before that," Noah said. "We don't have that kind of money. He should have realized that."

"Maybe I was his backup," Erin said. "He knew I was a well-known author and probably assumed I could get him what he needed if you couldn't." Erin chuckled. "The reality is that most authors don't make anywhere near what people think they do. Unless you're someone like Stephen King. Of course, I would have gladly given him everything I have if it would have saved our lives, but I think he would have been pretty disappointed." She waved her finger at Adrian. "I still wish you'd told me the truth about his attack on you. I realize you were trying to protect me, but I want to know when someone I care about has been hurt. I can decide whether or not I need to come home or stay where I am. Please don't hide anything like that from me again."

"Sorry," Adrian said. "I thought I was doing the right thing, but in retrospect, I guess I made a mistake. You're a lot stronger than I realized."

Erin noticed an odd look on his face. She'd said he was someone she cared about. Had that made him uncomfortable? She wasn't certain, but she wasn't going to worry about it. Maybe it was time for her to admit that she had feelings for Adrian. Of course, maybe he didn't feel the same way.

She looked into his eyes and was pretty sure that what she saw there wasn't embarrassment or rejection. Instead, his slow smile made her feel as if something wonderful might be happening. Had she finally met a man she could trust with her heart? For the first time since Scott died, she believed it was possible.

"How long are you going to stay here?" he asked her.

Erin sighed. "I'd like to rest a couple of days until I'm not quite so sore. Unless Kaely tosses me out before then. You know what they say about houseguests and fish. After a few days, they both stink."

Kaely carried two cups to the table and handed them to Erin and Adrian. "Well, you don't smell even a little. You can move in for good as far as I'm concerned, but I hope you'll at least stay until you're truly ready to go home." She smiled at Erin. "I still have plenty of Mallomars."

"Well, in that case, I'm good."

"I'm heading back tomorrow," Adrian said. "I checked into a hotel close to here, so I might swing by in the morning if that's all right with you," he said, looking back and forth between Kaely and Noah. "I'll bring doughnuts."

"Well, okay," Noah said with a smile. "As long as you bring some chocolate long johns."

"I'll do my best."

Erin grinned at him and gazed around the table at these friends who had become more like family. When she'd left the police department, she'd felt as if her life was over. Now, she had true friends, and a relationship with a God she hadn't known existed. She'd also learned that no matter how dark things look, with God, life can become beautiful. Although a few months ago she wouldn't have believed it, now, she was actually looking forward to her future.

NOTE FROM THE AUTHOR

Dear Reader,

I hope you've enjoyed this book. I try hard to write stories that will entertain you, but even more importantly, I pray that something I've written will touch your heart. If you find yourself relating to my characters who struggle with fear, loneliness, and sorrow, just like the rest of us, I want to give you some good news. God has the answer to every problem you face, and He loves you with a love that is deep, eternal, and boundless. If you've never asked him into your life, you can take care of that today. John 3:16 NIV says: "For God so loved the world that He gave His one and only Son, that whoever believes in Him shall not perish but have eternal life." Below is a prayer you can use to change your life forever.

> "Lord Jesus, I turn to You in my time of need. I believe that You are the Son of God and that You died on the cross to pay the price for my sins. Lord, I receive You as my Savior, and I want You to be my Lord. Wash me

clean with Your blood and fill me with Your Holy Spirit. Help me to follow You the rest of my life. Amen."

If you've prayed this prayer, will you let me know? You can contact me through my website: NancyMehl.com. Please find a good local church where you can become part of a family that will help you on your journey. May God bless you abundantly.

DISCUSSION QUESTIONS

1. When Kaely asks Erin to stay at their house in Fredericksburg, Erin feels insecure about the invitation. She's not sure Kaely really wants her there. Do you struggle with insecurity toward other people—even when they claim to be your friend? If so, why do you think that is? What does the Bible say about this?
2. Kaely is very careful about witnessing to Erin. She doesn't want to turn her off. She believes it's ultimately the Holy Spirit's job to lead someone to faith in Christ. Have you ever been in Kaely's situation? How did you handle it?
3. Adrian Nightengale is a Christian, but Erin isn't. Yet he has feelings for her. How do you feel about this? The Bible tells us to not be unequally yoked. What advice would you give a friend in Adrian's situation?
4. At one point, Kaely advises Erin to not worry about the woman who is claiming that Erin stole her book. Matthew 6:34 says, "Therefore do not worry about tomorrow, for tomorrow will worry about its own

things. Sufficient for the day is its own trouble." Do you have problems concentrating on today only and not worrying about what might happen? Why do you think we struggle with this teaching sometimes? Is there a difference between planning and worrying?

5. Before going into the command center, Kaely prays for Erin. For the first time, Erin feels the peace of God. She feels His presence and realizes that God is real. Have you felt the presence of God? How important is that experience to you?

6. After finding out that a serial killer committed murders based on the plots of books—including her own novel—Erin wonders if she should ever write again. Is this a reasonable reaction? How do you think you would have reacted?

7. When Jesus paid the price for our sins, He not only bought our forgiveness with His blood and His death, He "became sin." How does that knowledge impact you personally?

8. When Erin accepts Christ, she is full of joy. Do you believe that you're the righteousness of God through Christ? Or do you struggle with being "good enough"? Do you find yourself trying to earn God's love and acceptance?

9. After accepting Christ, Erin struggles with how to change her writing. Did you have any kind of similar experience after becoming a Christian? What adjustments did you have to make in your life?

10. At one point in the story, Erin sees the difference between heartfelt kindness and manipulation. Can you

share an example of how that might happen in your own life? How do you make certain your motives are pure when you want someone to do something for you?
11. The killer in *Dark Design* rejects Christ as a child and kills innocent people. But in their last moments, they ask Jesus to save them. How do you feel about that? Is this Scriptural?

ACKNOWLEDGMENTS

My heartfelt thanks to my editors: Jessica Sharpe, Susan Downs, and Kate Jameson. Thank you for pointing out when I've said the same thing ten times! LOL! Also, thank you for the great ideas you share, which make my stories so much better. I'm so blessed to work with every single one of you.

My thanks to retired police officer Darin Hickey. Your help is invaluable to me.

To my wonderful assistant Zac Weikal, thank you for creating my incredible website, running my street teams, and all the other things you do, which are too numerous to mention. You're not only my assistant, you're my dear, dear friend. I couldn't do this without you.

My thanks to my incredible family: Norman, Danny, Aidan, and Bennett. You are the most important people in my world. I would lay down my life for you. Thank you for loving me and each other, even when we don't deserve it.

Last, but most importantly, I want to thank God for allowing me to write. Thank You for Your inspiration and

Your incredible love, which fills me with peace and hope. I pray that I'm one of the servants who used their talents to honor You and give You back more than You gave me. This is the desire of my heart.

READ ON FOR A *SNEAK PEEK* AT THE FINAL BOOK IN

THE
ERIN DELANEY MYSTERIES
SERIES.

AVAILABLE MAY 2026.

THREE

Erin tried Kaely's phone again. She should be off the plane by now. Maybe she'd forgotten to charge her phone.

Erin wasn't certain why she was worried. She just felt . . . unsettled. She shook her head. It must be because she was in law enforcement again. When Adrian had asked her if she wanted to join the Sanctuary police department, she'd balked at the idea. But the more she thought about it, the more she wanted it. It was just part-time, and Sanctuary certainly wasn't St. Louis. Sure, they'd once had a serial killer living among them. But now, things had settled down. The calls were all minor. No one had been murdered since she'd joined. The wall those in law enforcement created to protect themselves was almost nonexistent.

So, why did she feel . . . something dark? When the phone rang, she grabbed it, hoping it was Kaely. She didn't recognize the number, but it might be because Kaely was using a different phone.

"Hello?" she answered. "Kaely, is that you?"

"You should get a pen and a piece of paper," a man's voice said. "I'll count to six."

"What? Who is this?" Erin asked.

"One," he said.

"I asked who this is. If you can't tell me, I'm going to hang up."

"That's up to you," he answered, "but if you do, you'll never see your friend again. Two."

Erin felt her body stiffen. What was happening? With trembling fingers, she grabbed a notebook from the coffee table and moved it closer.

"Three."

She picked up a nearby pen, intending to write down the time in case it might be important later. The feeling she'd had earlier intensified, and she knew she had to take this seriously. She tried to write, but the pen was out of ink. It wouldn't work.

"Four."

"Just a minute," she said, her voice shaking. "I need to get another pen."

"Five."

Erin got up and ran into the kitchen, grabbing a pen off the counter. She almost stumbled over the slippers she'd left on the floor earlier.

"I've got a pen," she said as she picked up her phone again. Nothing. No sound. Had he hung up? Was he going to hurt Kaely . . . or even worse?

"I'll only say this once," he said. "From now on, when I call, I won't wait. You need to be prepared. Do you understand?"

"Yes."

The man took a deep breath. "First, you have to travel from riches to rags. Here's hoping your answer won't tarry or lag. Unless you hurry, you'll never get the chance to say good-bye, because your failure will cause your good friend to die."

Erin wrote furiously, getting it all down. "Is Kaely alive? What have you done with her?"

"You have six days to save her. I won't change my mind. No police or she dies. No FBI or she dies. Do you understand?"

"No. No, I don't. Why are you doing this? Where is Kaely?"

There was a brief moment of silence. And then he said, "Six."

NANCY MEHL is the author of more than fifty books, a Parable and ECPA bestseller, and the winner of an ACFW Book of the Year Award, a Carol Award, and the Daphne du Maurier Award. She has also been a finalist for the Christy Award. Nancy writes from her home in Missouri, where she lives with her husband. To learn more, visit NancyMehl.com.

Sign Up for Nancy's Newsletter

Keep up to date with Nancy's latest news on book releases and events by signing up for her email list at the website below.

NancyMehl.com

FOLLOW NANCY ON SOCIAL MEDIA

Nancy Mehl Author Page   @NancyMehl1

Be the first to hear about new books from Bethany House!

Stay up to date with our authors and books by signing up for our newsletters at

BethanyHouse.com/SignUp

FOLLOW US ON SOCIAL MEDIA

@BethanyHouseFiction